MR. BONES I

FROM OUT OF THE DARKNESS

JEFF WRIGHT

To my late grandmother, Mildred Waters. Born in 1901, she personally witnessed our great nation come of age; from radio, to silent movies, television - seeing the first automobile roll off the assembly line - watching the Wright Brothers fly their contraption across a field and then to witness man walking on the moon. Her story alone was a novel; however, she was the greatest storyteller I ever knew. She was a diehard New York Yankee fan. She sat right behind home plate and watched Babe Ruth point his bat before smacking that baseball right out of the park.

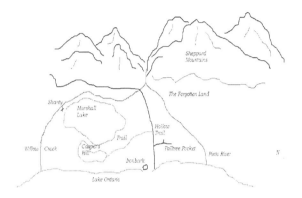

Ironbark
1910

Chapter 1

As a full moon rose above New York's worst recorded heat wave in a century, David Bradshaw's phone rang in Harrison, New York. He rolled over and looked at the clock; 12:00 a.m. He knew who the caller was and why they were calling. He sighed, picking up the phone. "David here, what-cha got?"

"Sorry boss," Detective Dan Jackson replied. "We just received some more information on that drive-by shooting this morning. We have a kid holed up inside an abandoned warehouse on Willow Street who fits the description of the shooter. I just thought you might want to be in on this one."

"The scene covered?"

"Yes."

"Good. I'll see you when I get in," David replied, and then hung up.

He rolled over, sat up, and rubbed his face thinking of Dan's report; *Kid holed up inside a warehouse. How young could he be?* he thought, opening his eyes.

As he stood up, the fumes of freshly painted walls, wood varnishes, glues and that old, musky smell of dirt and dust swept up his nose. *My God, why did I start this renovation project now?* he thought, walking over to the window. The night breeze felt good. He turned and walked into the bathroom.

Because of his size, the bathroom looked like a grade school lavatory. The sink and toilet were better suited for children. He reached over, turned on the light, and glanced at himself in the mirror. He looked like death warmed over with the dark circles under his eyes. He frowned, feeling like a washed-out Bronx boxer. *Not even a mud bath treatment would cover up how I feel right now,* he thought, running his fingers through his black, floppy hair.

After a long shower, he stepped out and gazed into the mirror once again. His eyes still looked as if he swam through a pool of bleach. He splashed on some shaving cream and ran a razor across his face. With a towel wrapped around him, he walked out of the bedroom and into the kitchen.

The kitchen looked like a paint store with all the cans, brushes, rollers, and tools strewn across the counters and table. He cleared a spot next to the blender. From the fridge, he took out four eggs, a can of tomato juice and then tossed them inside the blender. After a few minutes of blending, he poured the mixture into a glass and downed the whole glass while surveying his home improvements.

Three weeks working into the late hours seemed to be getting him nowhere. *Maybe, I've over done it a tad. One room at a time would have been much better than tearing the whole place apart,* he thought, walking back into his bedroom and getting dressed. Stepping outside, he looked up and noticed the full moon already hovering over New York like a giant ball. *If somehow I could just arrest that,* he thought, *our problems would be solved.*

He did not know how or why a full moon affected people, but it did, especially the criminally minded. *It seemed that every time it drifted over New York, the criminals would come out of their holes in droves,* he thought, opening his car door and getting in. His destination, the One Hundred and Tenth Precinct on the north side of town.

That same afternoon, David's cousin, Bill Glenmore, a ten year seasoned police officer from the same Precinct walked out of his house in New Rochelle, New York, ready to go back on the beat. He instantly felt the humidity clinging to him like cellophane. Nothing got to him more than having to deal with the inner city problems on nights like this. He'd rather have stayed inside like the rest of the population during these last few weeks, but another night shift was about to start.

With his arms full, holding his police bag and dinner inside a Tupperware container; he walked over to his truck and got in. Slipping on his sunglasses, he started his truck, and then turned on the air conditioner to full blast. *Thirty minutes of cool, relaxing air is just what the doctor ordered*, he thought, rolling off the curb.

As he drove down the long, narrow street, he looked through the trees seeing the moon drifting over the eastern seaboard in the late afternoon sky. He watched it for a few seconds, as it seemed to shimmer helplessly. Even the pavement down the street looked as if it were about to buckle and melt like snow. He thought of the moon, and the heat and the problems both gave to the officers in having to deal with it. *The Big Apple wasn't a place that you'd want to be in during a full moon,* he thought. If the place did not have enough nut cases already – the prospect of a full moon seemed to lure them out like dumped-over garbage cans.

With the sun pelting his windshield he took the service ramp onto the freeway. *This damn weather has got to break soon*, he thought. *Weeks now, without any sign of falling off is sure to make the population start to get a little cranky - if they weren't there already.* He glanced out his window looking up at the moon following him along the freeway. He watched it for a moment and then focused back on the road up ahead. *Music, maestro,* he thought, turning on the radio. When the song stopped playing, the

DJ came over the radio. "It's another scorcher out there in the Big Bad Apple this afternoon. I know a band that suits the conditions. Here's... Johnny Glass and the Rabbits with - *Heat Wave.*"

"Oh, great, just what we needed," Bill grumbled under his breath.

As the song started, the DJ continued his weather report. "Not even the mild winds pushing off the Atlantic and rolling across that beautiful harbor of ours is going to give us any relief from this radiation shower. And it seems we'll be dipping our heads into our refrigerators for another week as the main weather service predicts another week or so of this fine stuff."

Bill clicked off the radio and sat back. *Another week, hell one more minute and I'll explode.*

As the city loomed larger, and he gained some distance on the traffic going into the city, he noticed the sky changing - the sun was about to give up the ghost and depart with a bang. Through his scorched windshield, the sun flashed its last remaining light as if a painter were splashing watercolors across the vast sky. Oranges, reds, purples and even light pinks fanned across the sky - like whispering streamers drifting on the winds of time and rippling off the clouds that were drifting on by. Even the moon could not escape the painter's brush; as the clouds drifted across in a haze of colors. It looked like heaven itself descending down on the poor souls trying to get home and out of the blistering city.

He looked down just in time to see the beginning of the mad hour as he called it. Traffic began backing up in both directions; those wanting to leave the city after a hard day's work - and those trying to get into the city for their nightshift.

Bill sat there listening to horns, shouts, and a few screams from the poor souls stranded in their cars while inching along. *People,* he thought, *what kind of mentality does it take to see that everyone has to do the same thing at this time every night?*

He looked down at the floorboard and noticed his magnetic, police emergency roof light sitting there. *Even if I put it on the roof and lit it up, I'd be no better off parking my truck along the freeway and walking in - than trying to bluff my way through this shit,* he thought. "Oh yeah, the gridlock crawl," he fumed, waiting to inch up a few more feet. *Not even New York's finest can push their way through this crap!*

The day shift was ending, and the One Hundred and Tenth's patrol units stationed on the north side were slowly rolling into the station after being relieved from the kid holed up inside the warehouse. After a day's patrol in the sobering heat, every officer just wanted to go home to his or her air-conditioned homes.

The oncoming nightshift personnel felt as if they had already completed a week on the job just trying to get to work - as one after another rolled into the back parking lot. As they pulled in one by one, some liked to sit around to hear the latest gossip from the day shift while the day shift personnel cleaned and refueled the patrol cars. The others completed the daunting task of finishing their paperwork - prior to the next shift taking over.

Mary Anne Cannon, who had been a police officer for three years, sat in her car watching her team pour in like melted chocolate bars. She too could not wait to finish the shift, and it hadn't even started. She watched the last car roll into the parking lot. The officer was her new partner, Bill Glenmore. She called him *the tree.* To her, he was the best cop, pound for pound, at the station. He had been a police officer for ten years with a family tree of retired cops dating as far back as the dinosaurs. She looked into the rearview mirror, fixed her hair, took out her cap, and then waited for Bill to get out of his car.

As much as the gossip at the station was more about them, being teamed up together by Captain Clark, than what was happening out on the street - she didn't feel bitter or even nervous about being assigned with Bill.

Other officers had warned, "You'll fall like a knight on your own sword if you agree to team up with him." *Knight? The guy wasn't that special to make you want to bow to him*, she thought, watching Bill gather his things. However, she did like the one piece of gossip that seemed to get a good laugh throughout the corridors, "The tree now has a pet monkey to climb all over him."

Being only five foot six, might make her look like his pet monkey, but she knew she had all of his guts and all of his wits, and could keep up with him leg for leg. She had her family tree, as well. It had its own exceptional qualities too. Maybe it could not stand toe to toe with Officer Glenmore's family of cops, but her father, Dan Cannon, her uncle, Hank Cannon, and her grandfather, Peter Cannon, were all highly decorated officers. It was her grandfather, who shined the best. He was one of New York's finest Police Commissioners and still wielded some weight in the city of blue. She watched Bill open his door. They got out together, and faced each other across the parking lot. He smiled at her.

"Hi partner," she said, walking over to him. He looked more like a basketball player than a cop with his large framed body, long slender arms and giant hands. *He'd of probably made a good basketball player at that*, she thought, looking up at him.

"Good evening, Officer Cannon," he greeted her.

11

"It's not a good evening, it's a hot evening, Officer Glenmore," she replied with a smirk.

"Hot isn't the right word. More like desperate, don't you think?" he replied, placing his bag over his shoulder and walking toward the blue metal door at the back of the station.

"Desperate?" she questioned, walking alongside him. *It sounded good*, she thought. *They were desperate – desperate to get the hell out of the heat.*

He glanced over at her and noticed she was carrying her bag over her shoulder too. She looked like a hunter carrying a carcass. She was small, but had the arms of a fighter, and the guts and the brains of a good cop. He tossed a glance at her curly blonde hair streaming down from underneath her cap. She looked more like a school kid than a cop; you would not know she was one if it weren't for that uniform. However get her on the street and you'd see real quick that she was one-hundred pounds of pure cop. "So what do you think the latest will be from the funny man?" Bill asked, walking in.

"Are you talking about Jack Coffee? I couldn't even guess what he'd be shooting his mouth off about – he seems always to be in the thick of things out there though."

Bill looked at her and then moved aside when two plain clothed officers walked by.
The sounds coming from the training room meant that Jack was already on a roll.

"Well, shall we?" she asked, pointing up the corridor toward the training room.

They walked up past the large wall plaque containing pictures of those retired and those who'd lost their lives in the line of duty. A crowd of officers, those going off duty and those coming on duty, had gathered in the room listening to Jack describing his day.

Jack Coffee was a short, stocky, little man with a bulldog face. He had large cheeks, a pug nose and round beady eyes that looked like two black buttons. Bill stood just inside the door watching Jack playing all the parts; victims and suspects - and wondered why he always got the calls to respond to all the crazy shit that went down in the city. He guessed that if he had Bulldog on his team, he'd probably send him out on those calls too. What better way to solve a situation involving a nut case then by sending another nut case like Bulldog out to handle it. He looked at Mary Anne. She was leaning into the room trying to listen to Jack's latest story. The small crowd around Jack looked like people in church listening to their priest.

He nudged her and pointed to two empty seats. They walked in and sat down on the outskirts of the crowd.

"Bill, you old sly dog," Jack barked, seeing them entering the room. "Listen to this one."

"Yeah, you have to hear this, Bill," Jim Manson spat.

Bill and Mary Anne sat there listening to some of New York's finest, Jim Manson, Steve Kindle, and Barbara Sharp, from the day shift, gas bagging about the bank robbery on 12th and Main that went awry when the getaway driver left before his partner came out with the money.

Jack went on to explain, in finer detail, about what happened to the man when he finally did get out of the bank and started running down the street. The people on the street said he jumped about a mile in the air when the cloth moneybag exploded all over him - dousing him in red dye. Jack called him "the red man" and everyone laughed. He went on to explain how he apprehended the suspect. The bag exploded. Jack distorted his face so they could see what the guys face had looked like. The red man ran into an alley, slipped into a garbage can, and then waited for all the patrol cars to leave the area. Jack parked just inside the alley and was about to start up his unit when all of a sudden the red man poked his head out of the garbage can. "You should have seen it," Jack said, laughing and slapping his leg. "He looked like the grouch that lives in the garbage can on Sesame Street coming out of that can!"

When everyone settled down to listen to the next one, Jim started in, but this time it wasn't funny. He told them about the drive by shooting that Detective David Bradshaw had covered that day. The room became quiet when Jim said that the shooting occurred on Williams and Pine and the victim, a teenage boy was shot in the back while riding his bike. The bullet killed him instantly.

Barbara lightened the atmosphere when she told them all about how she and her partner had gotten a doctor's degree in medicine when they rescued a pregnant woman, by helping her give birth in the back seat of her car on the freeway. Everyone laughed when Barbara told them about the father who had passed out when he stuck his head in the window and saw all the blood. "He passed out on the grass and didn't come to until the ambulance arrived," she said. The whole room was laughing. Barbara then froze when she saw Captain Clark standing in the doorway. Everyone instantly turned and stood up, as if they'd all been caught stealing from the corner candy store.

"Well, no wonder I didn't see a cop car on the street when I drove in," Clark said, eying up everyone in the room. "There must be a lot of criminal activity right here for so many cops still to be standing around," he bluntly stated.

Bill smiled seeing all the embarrassment spreading across the faces as the officers walked out past the Captain.

"Bill, can I see you in my office, please?" Clark asked, seeing him and Mary Ann stand up.

"Sure thing, Captain," he replied, waiting for the officers to file out.

Mary Anne walked down the corridor with Barbara. Barbara gave her a tug on the arm and motioned for her to go into the women's changing room. Mary Anne thought that Barbara wanted to hear how she was faring with Bill. As the door closed, Barbara checked to see if anyone was still in the dressing room. No one was there. She walked back around to Mary Anne. "Tell me about, Sergeant O'Neal. How the hell did he get demoted to desk duty for a month?"

Mary Anne sighed. *Thank God*, she thought. She did not want to explain her situation with Bill. Even though he'd taught her a lot in the last few weeks, she wanted everyone to think she was pulling her own weight as his partner. However, the news about O'Neal's demotion was the best internal gossip the division had had in a while - and her squad had it in the bag as far as giving up the dead on the good old sergeant. The news about Sergeant O'Neal, Squad 4 nightshift watch commander having his balloon popped was quietly hushed up, but by the end of the week, everyone knew what had happened, except Barbara. Mary Anne sat there on the wooden bench watching her getting undressed.

"So what happened?" she asked again.

Maryanne looked at Barbara's extremely white face, light green eyes, and red hair - and then gazed down at her ghostly white skin. If it weren't for her strawberry freckles splashed across her face and arms, you would have thought she was dead.

"Are you going to tell me - or just sit there looking at this gorgeous body of mine?" she asked, placing her hands on her hips and rolling her head back like a model.

"Sure, I just think you need a little sun, that's all."

"Sun hell, you know what the sun does to redheads. We don't tan like normal people, we fry. Now, go on - tell me, before I burst," she scolded.

"Alright, already. You know about Captain Clark putting Springfield Park off limits to all patrol units while the drug task force was setting it up for a sting."

"Yeah."

"Sergeant O'Neal thought he was above Captain Clark's orders and hauled in the main drug runners."

"You're kidding?!" she gasped. "What a damn fool!"

"Yeah, he's more than a fool. So Captain Clark demoted O'Neal for overstepping his boundaries. I can't believe he'd get in the way of the agency's drug task force. Wasn't that stupid?" Mary Anne whispered as if saying something about your superior officer would get you in trouble.

"That's more than stupid. I'd hate to have him as *our* watch commander," Barbara whispered back, standing up and getting dressed into her civilian clothes. "If the big guy can't take orders, then how can he give them?" she continued.

"He can't," Mary Anne whispered, crossing her legs. "I'm just glad Clark demoted him and has allowed Bill to try his hand at running the streets for awhile. Who knows, O'Neal may come back and have to take orders from Bill."

"Well, in my opinion, Glenmore is a better cop out there," Barbara agreed.

"He sure is. The only problem he has is Jenson and Steward. If he can keep them in line, he'll do alright," Mary Anne replied.

"Yeah, those two clowns couldn't find an exit out of a grocery store if their lives depended on it."

Mary Anne laughed.

"Roll call. Let's get moving everyone," O'Neal's voice came over the loud speaker. "I gotta run, Barbara. You take care."

"Sure will. Just want to get home and sit my butt on the couch for the night."

Mary Anne hurried out, ran down the corridor back to the training room and sat next to Bill. He looked at her with a beaming smile. "Good news?" she asked, raising her brow.

He leaned over and whispered, "Yeah, but I think I'll let the sergeant tell ya."

Matt Banner, off-going watch commander, had nothing to turn over to the nightshift except the usual problems; burglaries in the business district, keeping out of the park while their drug squad was there, and the violent domestic that went down on the north side. He wished the shift well, and then departed.

O'Neal, who was standing there looking like he'd rather be home, shuffled back and forth on his feet and spoke of his new assignment. Sighs and moans went out from the team. Some covered up their delight, but Steward made it quite clear about his dismay at the news. "Listen up everyone. Officer Glenmore is you're new watch commander for the month."

Laughter and shouting erupted. O'Neal raised his hands to get everyone's attention.

"Hold up. That's from the top, guys. So, get out there and support him. Bill you have anything to say?"

Bill looked at him and then glanced at the other officers. "No. I'll start my presentation tomorrow. See ya all out there," he replied, getting up and walking out with Mary Anne.

Chapter 2

After the teams pulled out and began their patrols, Sergeant O'Neal sat quietly at the dispatcher's desk, reading a Sherlock Holmes novel. He figured, after Captain Clark removed him from the streets for making a bad call, he might as well read a good detective novel and see if he could try to solve the crime before the brilliant crime wizard did.

Before he opened the book, he sighed sitting there at the dispatcher's desk. *Of all the places to pull duty for one month,* he thought, *just because I squeezed 'Sam the Needle' a little before letting him go?* Hell, the greasy shit was just a small fish in the slimy drug pond. You'd think the Drug Task Force would have been pleased that we hauled him up and questioned him a little, but they weren't. They wanted Sambruno, the drug kingpin of the lower eastside, and were outraged when they learned that the local's as they called the street cops down here in the mud pits of New York stopped the greasy shit and questioned him.

He remembered Captain Clark's sly remark inside his office; "That's all we need, O'Neal, the Drug Task Force breathing down our necks! It's like accepting a handshake from a guy while he's urinating on your leg and smiling at you!" Clark didn't trust any police branch that wasn't in a vehicle patrolling the streets.

O'Neal thought of his troublemaker, Officer Steward. *If Bill can't control him out there, his whole squad could be in the shits,* he thought. He only hoped that Bill could keep Steward tied up until he got back on the street. So, until Captain Clark gave him the word to get back out there, he was going to be glued to the desk like flies on flypaper, typing blotters, writing out the vehicle log and taking calls.

He sighed, sitting back in his black swivel chair, and opened his book. As soon as he began to read, the dispatcher's phone rang. He looked up from his book to see the emergency line flashing. "Can you believe it? I can't even get in a few lines and the phone rings."

He set the book down and slid a pad of paper in front of him. *Now remember Sherlock, use a good, solid but calming voice when you answer the phone during a 911 emergency call as if you're the person's mother, father, etcetera,* he thought. "Like I can't remember my own dispatching days," he grumbled, picking up the phone.

"Good evening, Hundred and Tenth Precinct, Sergeant O'Neal here. May I help you?"

"My neighbor's lying on the floor inside her house. There is blood everywhere. I think she's been murdered!" Kathy screamed over the phone.

"Please, ma'am, settle down and tell me what happened," O'Neal asked, steadying his pen.

"God, I don't know! She's next door lying on the floor in a pool of blood!"

"Did you check if she was alright?"

"I tried, but the smell drove me back. I'm worried. She has a child!"

From Kathy's description of the woman lying on the floor and the smell, O'Neal knew he had a homicide on his hands. You only have to smell that once, and it lives with you for the rest of your life. Now she was screaming about a child. That hit him in the chest like a hollow, point bullet!

"She has a child?" he quickly repeated, writing down the information.

"Yes, a boy, he has to be there."

20

"What's the woman's name?"

"Susanne Day."

"Did you check to see if the kid was inside?"

"No, damn it - I told you - I almost lost it opening the door," Kathy fumed.

"Where are you now?" O'Neal asked.

"I live at ten Plankton Street."

"What's your full name?"

'Kathy Shrine.'

"Where did this happen?"

"I just told you that!"

"No. I mean the house number of the woman, Kathy?"

"She lives right next door - house number eight."

"Alright, Kathy, I'll dispatch a unit right away. Please stay inside your house, and don't open the door for anyone until the officers arrive!"

"Open the door? You must be crazy if you think I'm going to open this door after seeing that!" Kathy countered, hanging up. The phone went dead in his ear.

Great job, Sherlock. What happened to keeping the person on the line? He quickly scribbled her name, address on the pad and then grumbled, "Damn, another homicide! I hope the kid's alive." He checked the vehicle log to find the nearest unit to respond. His eyes raced down the page until he spotted 23rd / 28th street patrol - Unit 54; officers Glenmore/Cannon.

He put his mouth up to the microphone and hit the button, "Unit Fifty Four – Control."

"Go, Control," Bill replied.

"Please respond to eight Plankton Street on a fifty one -ten. Proceed code one."

"Roger, Control. We're on our way," Bill replied.

"The reporting person (RP) resides at ten Plankton. Also be advised, child involved. Ambulance will be responding," O'Neal relayed back, typing the details in the blotter.

"Ten-four," Mary Anne replied. She reached over and switched on the siren.

Bill dug the wheels into the concrete, spun the vehicle around and then raced up the street toward Plankton. It only took the words "child involved" to make them both panic.

"Get your ass there as fast as possible, Bill!" Mary Anne yelled, hanging on to her door handle.

"It looks as if we got another one. I hope the kid's safe," Bill said, glancing in his rearview mirror.

"You know with a kid involved, Bill, we may be dealing with a domestic," Mary Anne sighed.

"Maybe. You can never tell these days," he replied, taking a corner too fast. "Hang on!" he yelled, swerving and racing down the street.

"This might sound stupid, but I was hoping we'd make it through the shift without one."

"Here in New York?" he replied, looking over at her. "Come on, how long have you been on the force?"

"Three years," she said, switching the siren's frequency to "wail" as they approached an intersection.

"Have you ever not had a homicide during any of those shifts?" he asked.

"No, I can't say that I have," she replied, "it's pretty sad – huh?"

"Yeah," he agreed, slowing at the intersection and then racing through after the traffic had stopped for them.

Mary Anne reached over, switched the siren back to normal pitch as the unit sailed up the street. Bill glanced over at her and knew she could handle this. She was a street-smart cop. She knew the ropes and knew how to deal with people. Gifted with quick instincts and quick with her words, she had all the makings of following her grandfather to the top. He wished he could bring it on as she did. Gun or tongue, she always chided him; use one or the other. Her nickname was Goldie Locks. He smiled thinking of that. The name was given to her because of her curly, blonde hair. Short as it was, it still looked good hugging that soft dimpled face.

Up ahead, the street was congested with cars and people crossing. "Take this one slow, Joe," she warned, switching the siren again. Bill pulled up right behind a couple with a baby and saw panic on the man's face in his rearview mirror. The man swerved his car in between two parked cars, but in his panic, he gunned it too hard and rammed the parked vehicle in front of him. Mary Anne looked over at the couple as they rolled by. The woman was yelling at the man. "Gee – you caused another one. Looks like they're all okay," she said smiling back at Bill.

Bill quickly looked over as they passed and saw the fight going on inside the car. It made him cringe. "Sorry," he said, grabbing the wheel with both hands while looking ahead and seeing what was in front of them. He saw that no one was going to move or break the light. "We can't push 'em, maybe best we swing around," he yelled, turning out of traffic. "Hang on! I'll try the other side."

Mary Anne tried to brace herself and then screamed, "Look-out!" seeing headlights coming down on them. She quickly felt the sideways force of the unit swerving back.

"Damn! That was close!" Bill gasped.

After the car passed, Bill slightly swerved out of his lane and looked down the street, all clear. He swerved back and raced down the opposite side toward the red light. Mary Anne hit the wailing siren. Bill's head jerked right then left to check the traffic coming from the other street. Clear, he swept under the light on the wrong side of the road and punched it. On-coming traffic started breaking and fishtailing as they saw the red and blue lights screaming down on them.

"Hook it now!" she screamed, seeing an opening to get back on the right side. Bill swerved again then righted the car and continued racing towards 24th Street. "Holy Cow – I hate driving through this God awful traffic!" he screamed.

Mary Anne looked over at him and noticed sweat pouring off his forehead. "Hell, Bill, for a moment there I thought you'd try the curb."

He rolled his eyes to the side and glanced over at her. She smiled and looked on.

Even though, he drove like a maniac, she felt safe with him on the street. Bill was a veteran cop who knew the streets like the back of his hand. Tall, well built with muscular shoulders and a set of biceps to match; he never had much trouble with offenders trying to weasel their way out when Bill opened the door and introduced them to the backseat of the patrol car. He also had the prettiest white teeth she had ever seen on a man, and those eyes of his, heck, he could look at you and you'd think for sure he knew what you were thinking before you could spit it out.

All the times she watched him interviewing suspects - she honestly thought he was incredible. He'd stand there as if he hadn't a care in the world, except to wait for a line of bullshit and the criminals could see it. Not many dared to toss a line of innocence at him when they knew that he knew they were about to try and lie their way out of the trouble they were in. If it weren't his size that intimidated them, it had to be those eyes. It was like having your father's eyes staring down at you while being

asked, "Where were you tonight, Miss Fancy Pants?"
Christ - try side-stepping your father's stare and getting
away with it. If you were able to, heck, you'd find a whole
world of youngsters falling around your feet wanting to
know how you did it.

She came out of her thoughts when she spotted the
black and white whipping around the corner up ahead.
"Look," she said, pointing at the patrol unit. "Isn't that
Jenson's unit?"

"Sure as hell is," Bill spat. "He's running code two.
It looks as if he's trying to take back-up before being
assigned!"

Officer Jenson was driving as Steward spotted
Officer Glenmore racing up the street.

"Damn! We beat 'em again. You better request the
assignment or Bill will be up your ass quicker than a
snake," Steward said, looking back at the unit.
Jenson quickly picked up the microphone and called
control. "Control this is Unit Twenty. We'll be pulling
backup for Unit Fifty Four."

"Roger, Unit Twenty," O'Neal replied, looking for
more units to fall in to assist.

"You hear that crap?" Bill said. "That boy is
running hot!"

"He's after O'Neal's job," Mary Anne replied from
the side of her mouth as if gossiping.

"You think so?" Bill asked, tightening his grip on
the wheel.

"Know so. I heard him talking to Danny-Boy
before shift. Thinks he's a shoe-in and that he's got the
Captain's blessings to strut his stuff out here."

"Well, he isn't spreading his wings on this
assignment," Bill replied, tightening his jaw. "I'll have him

take the back. He can enter that way then sit out there until we're finished roping this place off for homicide."

"You've got a big enough chain in the trunk?" she asked, pointing at 24th Street.

"Hook it, Bill!" she then yelled

Bill swerved on cue and then raced up 24th to Plankton. "Which way?" he barked, coming to the intersection.

"Left," she yelled, grabbing the door handle and hanging on. He spun the wheel hard left and headed up Plankton. Jenson and Steward were out of their vehicle, guns drawn when they pulled up.

"Take the back!" Bill barked at the pair, getting out of his unit. Jenson looked at him and saw that cold steel look in Bill's eyes. He nodded to Steward to move out without an argument. "Mary Anne, go see the RP. Get all the details and the layout of the interior." Bill ordered, drawing his weapon.

"Roger," she replied, taking off toward the house.

He stood on the far side of his unit watching Jenson and Steward spilt up and proceed down each side of the house. The place was dark, and nothing seemed to be moving inside. He glanced down the street surveying the trees, bushes, and anywhere else a suspect could be hiding and watching them. Some criminals liked to watch the police after committing a crime - instead of heading for the hills. *Could we be that lucky?* he thought, looking back at the house, scanning the steps and porch. Could they still be inside? He wasn't going to chance it knowing the suspect might be still there.

Jenson and Steward slowly made their way around the back. As they spotted one another, Steward pointed his gun toward the back gate; Jenson nodded and crept cautiously toward it. Steward watched him as he kept his gun drawn on the back door. Once Jenson was at the gate, he slowly walked back keeping his gun trained on the house. They opened it to check the alley; all clear.

Back out in front, Bill stayed behind his unit and waited for Mary Anne to return with the details. More units arrived and began blocking off the two intersecting streets. The ambulance pulled up and stopped next to the patrol unit barricades. The driver was ordered to wait for the "all clear" from the officer in charge before proceeding to the scene. Mary Anne reappeared at the door and raced down the steps.

"Two, a mother and son," she said half running toward the back of the unit. "The main floor is split like a horseshoe into four adjoining rooms. The stairs lead up left from the door. Mother's in the kitchen on the floor."

"What about the boy? Does the RP have any idea where he might be inside?"

"Don't know," she replied, gasping - looking up at the house. "She said the place smells to high heaven."

Bill looked at her and twisted his chin. If it smelled that bad, the scene was cold, and the woman inside had been dead for some time. *Then again, maybe the smell of fresh blood made her sick*, he thought. "Alright, let's take the door," he whispered, creeping around to the front of the unit. Mary Anne slowly followed. They hunkered down at the front of the unit. Bill slowly unfastened his radio and called Jenson stationed around the back of the house. "Is the back clear?"

"Yeah, no sign of forced entry," Jenson whispered back.

"Is there any way out the back end?" Bill asked.

"Yeah - there's a gate back here leading to an alley."

"Have your partner check it out and then you two hightail it back to the door," Bill ordered, kneeling by the front bumper.

"We've checked – it's all clear," Jenson whispered.

Bill turned and looked at Mary Anne. She was scanning the front porch then caught his eye. He twisted his face and whispered, "Shit!" She looked at him; he looked as if he'd forgotten something. She watched him placed his radio up to his mouth.
"Hey you two," he whispered into his radio. "Watch your step back there - I don't need you walking over any evidence."

Jenson and Steward stopped in their tracks and looked down at their shoes. "Roger," Jenson replied.

"OK – you ready?" Bill asked. "Yeah," Mary Anne replied, holstering her sidearm and then reaching into the unit for the shotgun. She pulled it out, chambered a round, and then said, "I've got your back."

He looked at her, glanced down at the barrel of the shotgun, and then slowly stood up. She stood up firm with the shotgun slung over her arm. It looked too bulky for her, but he knew she could use it. "OK, you take the left side of the door and I'll take the right," he whispered. She nodded then quickly crossed the street.

Creeping up the steps, they stayed clear of the windows and slid up against the wall on either side of the door. Their eyes locked, reading each other's thoughts. His face was a mass of tension - his eyes were like hollow point rounds, ready to explode on impact. She felt her knees buckle under the weight of extreme fright, knowing they could be under fire as soon as they opened the door.

Bill raised his hand. She wrinkled her brow and then watched him reach up into his pocket, and take out a Vick's lip cream. He quickly smeared it under his nose and handed it to her. "The smell," he whispered.
The smell – the RP stated that the place stunk to high heaven. *Death*, she thought. It was the worst smell you could come across.

"Thanks," she replied, smearing the cream under her nose. The vapor hit her senses the moment she inhaled - freezing her nose instantly. Her eyes watered. "Damn!" she gasped. "I can't smell anything now. My nose is numb."

"Good," he replied, looking at the door. The grip of fear re-entered his thoughts. It made his muscles twitch. He hated having to gain entrance into a building; not knowing if the suspects were still inside. To him, entering and clearing a scene was just too damn dangerous! He knew too many friends that had died a quick death, after entering a scene, believing the suspect had already fled. The one that hit him the hardest was John Burns.

After responding to a house robbery and stabbing on Manhattan's west side, the place had been cleared, but the police were still crawling all over it like termites. John thought he'd give it one more shake down before turning it over to forensics.

As he started to check the upstairs rooms again, he opened a bedroom closet door and was stunned to see and feel the cold, dark steel of a sawed-off double-barreled shotgun sticking into his ribs - as one of the suspects was kneeling behind some boxes. It happened so fast that he probably never even placed a bead on the man's forehead with his own weapon, or never had the time to even blink an eye before it was all over. He took both barrels at mid-section. The blast tore him completely in half. Flesh, bones and blood went everywhere as his remains splattered across the room. The image stayed with Bill as he fixed his eyes on the door handle. *I'm not about to play Johnny tonight,* he thought, pressing his body up against the wall and reaching for the handle. "Ready?" he asked, tossing his dark, cold eyes upon her.

"Yep," she whispered, lifting up the barrel, still sniffling, and then pointing the shotgun at the door.

He reached up, grabbed the handle and turned it slowly. The door opened. He pushed it hard to get a clear view inside. "Going in," he whispered into his radio to Jenson.

Jenson and Steward stepped up to the back door. Steward slid his hand around the doorknob and turned it; locked. He turned his back to the door and back slammed the glass window, busting it all over inside.

Mary Anne slipped in and suddenly froze when she spotted a figure standing in the corner next to the stairs! Her heart leaped out of her chest, and then she realized that it was only a hat and coat hanging on a coat rack.

"Clear," she whispered to Bill. She swallowed hard, scanning the room with her eyes while pointing her weapon out in front of her.

Bill quickly stepped in. He crouched down by the sofa that divided the front room from the doorway. His hands gripped his weapon in a tight fist with his finger pressed slightly down on the trigger. "Clear," he whispered back to her.

Mary Anne stepped away from the wall, raced to the stairs, and pointed her weapon up the staircase. "Clear."

As Bill's eyes adjusted to the darkness, he saw what the RP was trying to describe the interior. The rooms all connected with openings that made the main floor look like a horseshoe. He had to decide on which way to go. *There are only two ways, old chap*, he thought. One, race to the hallway slip around and check the dining area out, or two, head straight into the kitchen. He tightened his jaw muscle, made a mad dash through the room and held up at the wall next to the hallway. "Clear," he whispered.

Mary Anne, not taking her eyes off the stairs, rushed to his side and then pointed her weapon toward the front room and dining area. Bill looked in the kitchen and saw Jenson and Steward standing there with their guns drawn; holding their noses from the stench. Bill reached for his flashlight, turned it on, and scanned the kitchen. The RP was right. The body of the female lay sprawled across the floor, face down.

Steward looked at Bill and said, "We're clear."

"Check the dining area," he ordered, pointing his weapon at the entrance to the room.

Jenson kept his fingers wrapped tightly around his nose and moaned, "I don't think I can do this. I think I'm going to toss it right here."

"Move damn it!" Bill grunted. Jenson, while covering his nose and mouth, slipped through the kitchen and then holed up at the wall to the dining room.

"Clear," he whispered to Steward.

Steward was half doubled over from the stench too, but he wasn't going to be seen as a pussy to anyone, especially Mary Anne. He hated female cops with a passion and nothing was going to make his backside buckle while she was watching. Steward wanted nothing to do with Officer Glenmore either. Bill was built like a brick shithouse and was meaner then a pack of lions on a kill - and that, Steward thought, was enough for him to stand down when he came across Bill on the street. He knew first hand that Raging Bull, Bill's nickname on the streets, could punch you quicker than a strike from a rattlesnake.

He'd seen him in action once in the locker room. That was enough to send shivers down his spine. Bill was arguing with Tim Roberts over something that happened on the street that day. Sitting there, he could see that Tim was biting off more than he could chew. Tim knew he couldn't take Bill physically, so he thought he'd outwit him with words. That was a big mistake. As the words flew back and forth, it simply got out of hand, and Tim said something smart to Bill about his father, retired Detective Larry Glenmore. Tim mentioned something about Bills father's inability to track down criminals and compared him to a blind, crippled man with one leg. Raging Bull said nothing, and Tim never saw it coming. Bill just came around the corner and squared him off right under the jaw. Tim landed a few feet back against the wall, out cold. He woke up a few moments later spitting teeth and blood from his mouth. Steward smiled remembering Tim Roberts mumbling toothless for a month afterward.

He tossed a sharp glance at Bill, trying not to look the man dead in the eyes, and then sidestepped the dead female and fell in behind Jenson. Crouching down, he spun past Steward's leg and pointed his weapon into the room. Mary Anne slipped through the front room and came in on the other side. The room was clear. The three came back into the kitchen and gathered around the dead female.

"You two clear the upstairs and find that boy. Make damn sure you check the closets together - you hear me?" Bill barked at Jenson and Steward, without looking up from lifeless female on the floor.

After they left the room, he pointed his flashlight around searching for a light switch.

"There -over the stove," Mary Anne said, pointing.

He turned on the lights and walked back of to the female. She was lying face down in a large pool of dark red blood. She had two large, dark red spots on the back of her clothing that looked like puncture wounds. He reached into his pocket, pulled out his surgical gloves and stretched them over his hands. Kneeling down, he slowly pulled the woman's bloody hair back and then turned the woman's face toward him to check for a pulse.

"Shit!" he gasped, looking down at the large knife wound that had gone in deep, slicing the woman's neck from ear to ear. He grabbed his radio and called the other unit.

"Unit Five," he said, kneeling. "Send in the ambulance and inform them that we'll need a black bag."

"Roger – Fifty Four," the officer replied.

"Check on Jenson and his sidekick," he ordered Mary Anne in a rough tone, still kneeling there and attending to the dead female.

Mary Anne looked down at him and could tell by the way his hands were shaking that he was overwhelmed with the find. She knew he hated dead bodies and hated even more having to touch one. She slipped out quietly and slowly made her way up the stairs.

As she reached the first landing, she saw Jenson wallowing out of one of the bedrooms. He leaned against the wall. His face looked as pale as a dead fish, and the smell coming from inside the room was worse than the smell downstairs. He looked at her and then vomited all over the carpet floor. "Don't go in there," he gasped between heaves - vomiting again.

"Get the hell out of here, now!" Mary Anne yelled, holding a hand over her face and rubbing the Vicks cream farther up her nose. "You'll destroy the crime scene with that foul crap," she barked.

Jenson staggered past her and made his way to the stairs. He stumbled going down, raced for the door, and then stumbled down the porch; gulping air like a fish out of water.

Mary Anne wondered where Steward was. She swallowed hard and stepped toward the door. She felt queasy and light-headed from the stench that was filling the hallway.

Standing at the open door, she peered in and saw Steward sitting on the bed holding his head in his hands. She swallowed hard and stepped in. Steward looked up from the bed. His face was whiter than a ghost. The look in his eyes told her not to look. He pointed to the corner where the boy's crib was and then he placed his head back into his hands.

She turned slowly to see what he was pointing at and saw the wooden crib sitting silently in the stench.

She spotted a large, red smeared, handprint on the back headboard and two red palm prints on the crib's guardrail. The body was covered in a blue blanket that looked purple from the blood soaking through it.

As she stepped toward the crib, she didn't realize that her upper teeth were sinking into her bottom lip so hard that her lip went numb. She leaned over the crib, looked down and then slowly pulled the covers off the small child's head. The face looked fine except for the star that was carved on the poor boy's forehead. She pulled the covers back exposing the child's body – the entire chest cavity had been ripped open and part of the child's insides were strewed out and spread over his poor little chest.

Her eyes tried to relay the scene to her brain, but nothing was registering. Nothing was adding up. Humans do not do this to other humans, especially to a child. Her mind began waging war against the insanity that was stealing her thoughts. Nothing was registering – nothing was filtering in that made any sense. All she felt was numbness while standing there frozen like a statue and shaking uncontrollably. Everything started to run in slow motion as she stood there frozen looking down at the lifeless body – no movement – only stillness – and the blood, the God awful blood that was dripping down the bars and onto the floor.

I need to get out of her, I need to get the hell out of here! her thoughts screamed. "Steward," his name spilled over her lips. He looked up and said nothing. He didn't have to - his eyes said it all. They were like dark pins that sat on the edge of sanity getting ready to leap off into the abyss of emptiness. "Steward!" she barked again.

He released his head and looked up at her. "Go, go get some fresh air."

Still looking white, he said nothing. He got up and staggered out and down the stairs.

She turned and looked down at the lifeless body. It made her stomach fluids lurched up into her throat. She quickly walked down the hallway toward the bathroom. Inside, she turned on the faucet, splashed water on her face and looked into the mirror. She suddenly felt faint, cold - and then it came rushing up. She held her hand to her mouth and quickly leaned over the tub and puked.

"Christ," she moaned, kneeling down and clamping her hands on the top of the tub. She heaved again.

"Damn – I..." she started to say, feeling her stomach wrenched again, and then she heaved. As she reached up, turned on the tub faucet and began washing her mouth out, she heard a voice from behind her.

"Officer Cannon, are you Alright?"

It wasn't Bill's voice or Jenson's or Steward's. She turned her head and looked up to see Detective Bradshaw, Bill's cousin, standing there looking down at her.

"When did your team arrive?" she asked, wiping her mouth and tossing more water on her face.

"A few minutes ago," he replied, looking at her with all the compassion that he could muster. "Bill's downstairs relaying the scene to my partner now. I've seen the child. Don't worry, we'll get the bastard that did this!"

She deeply sighed, hoping he'd have more to say, but he didn't.

"Here, let me help you up," he said, reaching down for her hand.

"Please, give me a minute, Detective. I can't believe I just did that. I've never puked before."

"Well, we all go through it at some stage in our career," he replied. "I've seen it happen, especially when it's a child. Don't be ashamed," he continued, holding out his hand to her.

"I'm not. I just thought after kicking Jenson out for blowing his cookies, and then tossing Steward out for looking as if he was slipping over the edge - that I was the one who could handle it."

David looked down at her kneeling there like a helpless child herself. "You did. You handled it great. Go ahead - clean yourself off and I'll meet you downstairs with the others. I won't tell anyone," he said, turning and leaving.

"Thanks, Detective."

After he departed, she fumed. "How embarrassing," she whispered, splashing more water on her face. *Of all the cops that could have walked in, it had to be him*, she thought with a sigh. She stood up feeling her knees still weak. She leaned her body against the sink and looked back into the mirror. David *Bradshaw, AKA- 'The Handsome Detective,' as all the women on the force referred to him,* she thought.

She stood there looking in the mirror remembering when she first laid eyes on David. It was at O'Malley's Irish Tavern. The One Hundred and Tenth Precinct was there celebrating the trial of Sam Knots, better known as Sammy De'Bone, underworld hit man for the Labino Crime Family. He was given that nickname after he flayed one of their runners for dipping his fingers into the till. When they tortured him, Sammy slowly flayed the man's chest skin off and de-boned his ribs while he was still alive.

When the cops finally found the runner – all that was left of him were bones - the rest, they believed, went into the river as fish food.

Sammy was finally arrested, after murdering his own cousin in cold blood in the back of a van. One shot to the back of the head and then they tossed his body underneath the Manhattan Bridge. Upon his arrest, Sammy spilled his guts to the cops hoping to get a lighter sentence. Sammy De'Bone quickly became *Sammy the Rat* to the entire underworld. Every New York mob boss and all the under bosses took a hit that day when Sammy testified. After the trial, they whisked Sammy away and tossed his ass into the federal witness protection program. Captain Clark picked up the tab that night at O'Malley's and everyone showed up.

She remembered walking through the big wooden door with its green shamrock window at the top. The place was always dark and smelled of cigars, cigarettes, and Irish beer that seemed to blend nicely with the scent of dark oak timber. The bar itself was made from the finest maple which had a large shamrock and two four leaf clovers carved into the front. The top had a leather-padded armrest for customers to lean on. The bar stools were covered in black padded leather, as well.

The group, six in all, strolled around one of the large timber stanchions and took up a table in the back. Like all cops, everyone tried to sit with his or her back against the wall so they could see everything in front of them. Only three could sit with their backs against the wall and Bill, Jenson and O'Neal grumbled when the women took up the back seats first. Captain Clark didn't care where he sat, the place was crawling with cops that night, and he knew that his back was being covered from every angle. She remembered watching him gas bagging to some officers up at the bar.

After they tossed a few back - toasting Sammy the Rat for singing sweetly on the witness stand, this lumbering oak tree of a man stepped in, walked right up behind Bill, and then wrapped his big limbs around his neck. Then the guy says to him -"Your money, or your life."

The bar went dead quiet. Who was this thug? Everyone on the planet – that is, on the New York planet, knew that O'Malley's was "The Boys in Blue" hang out, and this giant tree just walked in and tried to take over by ribbing one of the biggest cops on the force.

Bill grabbed the man's arm, wrapped around his neck like a boa constrictor, with his own giant paws, and then pulled the lug into him and said, "How about your money, or your wife?"

Everyone started going for his or her gun, except Captain Clark, who just walked up and smiled at the whole scene in front of him. The lumbering oak tree smiled at him and then looked over at her and winked. "I never seen such fine baby blues before in my life, Miss," she remembered him saying from across the table, still holding Bill in a coiled up, snake grip.

Mary Anne splashed some more water on her face and looked into the mirror thinking; Bill then slapped David's arm and they began to laugh.

"Hey – what gives?" the big lug said, standing there looking them over as if they were a bunch of schoolchildren.

"Sorry, Cuz," Bill replied. "If I knew you were going to come down off your high perch, I would've invited you," he continued turning around. "Everyone, listen up. I'd like you to meet the finest New York homicide detective the world has ever seen, my cousin, David Bradshaw. Detective David Bradshaw, that is."

The tree sidestepped Bill and pulled up a seat next to him. She remembered kicking Sue Jones' shin, and Sue in return, kicked Barbara's shin.

Mary Anne smiled to herself in the mirror as she thought about the three of them sitting there drooling over David. *Thank God there were no other females inside the bar that day*, she thought. *If there had been, they'd of been the only ones who would have noticed how silly the three of us looked, sitting there with our tongues hanging out and drooling all over the barroom floor over David.* He was tall, dark, and handsome. Yes, the likely description most women gave when describing the hunk of their dreams; when telling their friends of the one they met, took home and devoured.

However, there was something else about David that made you want to just grab him when he looked at you. He had the softest, teddy bear eyes, and a smile that warmed your heart. You couldn't help but want to crawl right up his shoulder like a kitten, and purr in his ear when he smiled, and played with that little curl of hair at the top of his forehead. *And, if that weren't enough to send them all into a spin,* she thought, *David made them all drool even more with another great talent of his.*

Bill began chiding him to go over and play the piano. When they all heard he could play, they started in on him, and you know how it goes - while under the influence - and you discover that someone can play an instrument that's sitting there beckoning to be played. She remembered tearing into David along with the rest of them to see if he'd stand up and make a real ass out of himself.

David got up, after a few minutes of chiding. He walked over and asked the bartender if he could play. The barman nodded as if to say – "give it your best shot, sonny." David lumbered over, sat down on the bench, and slowly opened the top. He looked at everyone, cocked his head back like a concert pianist and then stretched his fingers across the ivory.

His head went down, which made you visualize that he was out in front of an orchestra with his black tails dangling off the back of the bench. Then, he began to play. From one end of the keys to the other, his fingers waltzed down the black and white ivory as the notes followed his fingers. It was Mozart or Beethoven, she couldn't remember which, but it sounded wonderful. After the clapping subsided, he played one of her favorite Elton John songs, "Candle in the Wind," and then he sprang into John Lennon's "Imagine". She was gone, along with Sue and Barbara.

They all got up with the excuse to freshen up after he played and ran into the bathroom. She laughed remembering how they all stood there splashing water on their faces and cooing in the mirror.
"My God he's so delicious," she remembered Barbara saying to herself in the mirror.

"Delicious, hell girl, you're telling me. The man's a dream – a wild dream," Sue gushed, applying another coat of lipstick. She looked at the two of them and said, "To me, he's like a fine porcelain dish."

"Porcelain dish?" Sue laughed. "What were you looking at girl?"

"His eyes. Those teddy bear eyes of his. They remind me of a beautiful, golden colored porcelain dish I saw one time."

"Oh, now you're on to something girl, but I think he's the," Barbara started to say.

"The Handsome Detective," she quickly said, interrupting her.

"Yeah, the Handsome Detective, Mary Anne. You tagged him right, girl."

Mary Anne splashed another handful of cold water on her face and looked at herself in the mirror again. Her face looked as white as a bed sheet. She pinched her cheeks, wiped her face, and walked out of the bathroom -

hoping Detective Bradshaw had kept his word and hadn't made any comments about her throwing up in the tub.

Detective Bradshaw watched Officer Cannon slowly swagger down the stairs. Her face looked ash white, and her shoulders drooped as if she now carried the whole world on them. His eyes drifted down to the barrel of her shotgun swinging back and forth. He sighed knowing that this case was going to drain most of the officers who had been called to the scene.

Detective William Hall, David's partner watched David intently looking at Cannon. He could see that David was moved by the sunken figure descending the stairs. When she finally hit the floor and headed for the door, David try to grab her back to reality.
"Officer Cannon, thanks for staying up there and preserving the scene. I don't think many would have volunteered."

She looked at him, nodded tight-lipped, and walked past him without saying a word. David turned and watched her take the steps down. He wondered if she knew that he'd kept his promise.

"So, what do you think?" William said, placing a hand on David's shoulders. David kept his eyes on Cannon as she made her way out the door. "We've got a maniac on our hands, and we better act quickly before we start finding more bodies," he replied, taking his eyes off Cannon and looking at him. "Start with the RP next door. We'll need to take her in for questioning tonight."

"Anyone locate the husband?" William asked.

"No, but control is searching for him," he replied, walking back into the kitchen and looking down at the body.
William stepped up to him and looked down over his shoulder. "This could also be a break-in gone bad," he remarked from the corner of his mouth.

"It's possible, but don't count on it. Go and see the RP. We need to find out what she knows."

"Right," he replied, turning and walking out.

David stood there as still as a snail thinking of William's thoughts, "a possible break-in gone bad?" He slowly lifted his eyes off the body and began scanning the room. If it were a random hit, the place should be a mess, everything opened and scattered about as if the person was in a hurry. If it were systematic, the perpetrator knew his subject and the layout of the place. The hit would be clean with nothing disturbed.

He kept searching, walking the entire downstairs looking for anything that might give him a clue as to who was responsible. He stood near the mantle in the front room and glanced at all the framed photos lined up in a row. One was a picture of an old man, but no other men were in any of them. The rest of the pictures in the room were of a baby boy and his mother. His eyes zeroed in on the mantle - it was covered in a light film of dust. He reached over, picked up a picture, and tried to figure the last time the dead woman might have cleaned the place. *Two, maybe three days at the most*, he thought. The place was too clean to be a random hit. No kitchen cupboards were open, nothing tossed about; as if someone was searching for something. The bedrooms upstairs looked as clean and undisturbed, as well, except for the boy's room, and the only thing out of place - was the boy being dead. This was a systematic hit – the perpetrator knew the victim. He'd left his signature all over the house. David knew the perpetrator had been there before and had known every inch of the place.

He walked back into the kitchen and placed his arm around his good friend, Terry Rye, New York's forensic squad leader.

"You got a time of death yet?" he asked him.

Terry looked at him, tossed his chin to the side, and began rubbing his fingers through his beard. "Two, maybe three days, at the most. We're still waiting on Kim's results upstairs."

"Are you sure about that?" David asked, watching Terry playing with his beard, as though it somehow stimulated his brain when thinking.

"As sure as I can be, Detective," Terry replied - half in thought, bending down over the body.

"See this?" he said, lifting the woman's head. "The neck wound isn't bleeding. The blood has hardened. She was sliced days ago. The blood around her body is large enough to be every pint she had in her."

David's eyes followed Terry's hands as he gestured to the victim's throat wound and the circle of blood.

"Terry?" Kim O'Malley yelled from the top of the stairs. Terry and David quickly walked out and looked up at her standing there on the stairs. David noticed the haunting look in her eyes as if she had discovered something.

"It's the boy – come, take a look," she said, turning and heading back up.

They both ran up hoping she had, in fact, discovered something - something more than David's presumptions about the perpetrator. As they walked in, they noticed Kim had been analyzing the child's chest wound. She looked up at them, smiled, and then picked up a part of the child's internal organs in her gloved hand. "You know what this is?" she asked.

"My God, Kim, what the hell do you think you're doing? It looks like the child's liver," Terry replied alarmed.

"Yes, it's a liver, alright - but it's not this child's liver."

"What?" David gasped, stepping up and taking a look.

"It's a pig's liver, and so is the rest of this stuff," Kim said, removing the remains off the boy's chest. "It's the guts of a pig. The boy wasn't cut open - he was smothered to death and then covered in all this shit."

"Why?" David asked in horror.

Kim looked at him and smiled. "Now, Detective," she started to say. "Isn't that your job? My job is to inform you of the findings."

"Right – right," David replied, stepping back and reaching into his pocket. He pulled out his Vicks nose cream and inhaled it. "So that's why it smells to high heaven up here," he coughed.

Terry and Kim looked at him in amusement. Kim reached into her pocket, pulled out a surgical mask, and handed it to him.

"It's been scented, and it's a lot better than rubbing that God awful stuff up your nose, Detective"

"Thanks, but no thanks," David whispered, stepping up to the boy and examining him closely.

Except for the blue tint in the child's color, the boy looked as if he was sleeping peacefully. *Why the pig guts?* he thought. He hadn't come across a case like this before, and the only thing that came to mind that made any sense was a religious one; a religious fanatic, or a twisted cult that performs sacrifices. *But why kill a child and his mother?* He had no answer.

"You better find this bastard, Detective," Kim said, bringing him out of his thoughts.
David deeply sighed; her words hit him like an arrow. She was dead on. He did not have to ask why she was worrying. This type of maniac will strike again, and again, and again - until they're caught.

Chapter 3

Bill heard O'Neal on his unit radio. He reached in and picked it up.

"Go, Control."

"Bill, we got another one. It looks like the same MO as the one you're now on."

"What? You've got to be kidding! Where?"

"On the tracks at the abandoned railroad station. Also be advised, this time we have a witness who saw the person drop the child and run."

"Roger, Control, we're on our way," Bill replied, dropping his microphone and racing inside. "David!" he yelled from the door. David heard his cousin yelling his name downstairs. He rushed out of the room and flew down the stairs. The look on Bill's face was utter horror! "What? What is it?" he asked, taking him by the shoulders.

"Dave," he replied, gasping. "We got another one! This time we have a witness who saw the person drop the child on the railroad tracks near the old abandoned train station."

"Son-of-a- bitch!" he barked. "Let's move people!" David continued, running over to William who was conducting an interview with the RP next door. The look in David's eyes indicated something bad had happened! David looked at the woman and then bent down and whispered, "We got to go now. I've got a uniform outside to take you downtown for a statement."

William looked up at him and then tossed his attention on the woman. "Sorry, ma'am," he said, standing up. "If you'll go with the officer outside, he'll take you to the station so you can complete a written statement."

"OK, that would be fine," Kathy replied, getting up. She could tell the detectives were in a hurry to go somewhere.

When they got into their unit, David sped off down the street. William sat there staring at him waiting for David to spill his guts. He watched David grab the microphone, ordered Bill to follow as back up, and then look over at him.

"We got another one," David spat, turning the corner.

"What?!" William yelled.

"The officer on scene states it looks like the same MO. The child has a star carved on his forehead."

"Son-of-a-bitch, we got a child serial killer on our hands," he replied, feeling the tension running down his body.

David looked over at him again. William's face looked so pale as if just the thought of a child serial killer on the loose had drained him of all color. However, it was within William's eyes that David saw the horror of the thought. His eyes were sharp pinpoints staring blindly out of their sockets. He felt his own heart skip a beat with that hair-raising thought.

They rolled up and entered the old station through the service gate. He noticed the two small buildings on either side of the eight lanes of track where they repaired and cabled the boxcars together. Looking up and down the tracks he counted fifteen boxcars parked there looking like old, rusted dinosaurs with their sides wide open. There were coned shape lights lined up on both sides of the railroad tracks that threw off some light, but the rest of the place was as dark as black velvet. He shivered seeing a lot of hiding places where someone could step out of the shadows and start blasting away.

From the old buildings and open boxcars, his eyes scanned the premises searching for any other nook or cranny that someone could hole up. He drove down the tracks past the boxcars, buildings, the fenced-in generators, and headed slowly for the patrol car with its emergency lights flashing.

Two officers were standing there waving their arms underneath one of the cone shaped lights. David picked up his microphone. "Bill, have your men light this place up like a ballpark, I want the entire area searched."

"Roger," Bill replied, rolling up on one of the buildings as patrol units were pulling in. All the officers got out with weapons and flashlights drawn and then fanned out across the area - searching the old buildings and rusting boxcars.

William looked over at David; his face looked a mess with worry. He watched him put the microphone down and slowly roll up the tracks toward the two officers who were first on the scene.

"What cha think?" William whispered, looking out into the darkness and feeling the nape of his neck go cold.

"This place gives me the creeps. It's like walking into a cave and not being able to see the slimy creatures that you're stepping on."

As they pulled up alongside the officers, David spotted the witness sitting down next to the officer's front tire with his head in his hands. He looked as old as the rust buckets sitting back on the tracks. And his face - that too looked as dirty as the old Vietnam army jacket he was wearing. He put the unit in park and stepped out.

Officer Wayne Picket stood there looking like a sunken ship that had been on the bottom too long. "I found the child after this one waved us down on Nova Street near the gate," he said.

David watched Picket's hand point to the homeless man sitting near the front wheel of his unit and then looked down the tracks where they had roped off the area. "William," David said, walking toward the small bundle lying under the one of the track lights. William looked down at the homeless man as he walked past him following David.

David lifted the yellow tape and knelt down next to the child. The kid had to be two, maybe three years old with short blonde hair. He opened the blue blanket that the child was wrapped up in. There were no sign of pig guts. However, the star carved into his forehead made his blood curdle.

"Whatcha make of it, David?" William asked, kneeling down next to him.

"Looks like our guy, but no pig guts this time," he replied, turning the boys head and noticing the blue coloring that Kim had found on the first child.

"Suffocated, probably with his own blanket," William remarked, standing up. He looked around and notice shoe prints leading up to and away from the scene. "Check this out," he said, turning to see David still looking down at the lifeless child.

"What?" David asked, looking up.

"Shoe prints," William replied, pointing toward the ground.

David stood up and shone his flashlight on the print.

"Shoe prints," William said again.

David took a closer look. "They don't look like shoe prints, Will. They look more like bootprints to me."

William bent down and looked at the indentations in the dirt. "Boots all right, maybe snow boots at that."

"Really?" David said, looking closer at the prints. "Unbelievable," he whispered.

"Whatcha think?" William replied, waiting to hear his thoughts.

"I've seen that print before."

"What?" he gasped confused. "Where on earth would you have seen that before?"

David stood up, closed his eyes thinking.

"Well," William pushed.

"Shut up for a minute. Let me think."

William watched him roll his eyes toward the night sky and think back.

"I can't remember, but for God sake, I've seen that print before!" he finally said, looking back down at the print again. "I know I've seen it somewhere."

"Well, forget about it for now. It may come to you later. Let's go see what the hobo has to say," William replied, turning and heading back toward the patrol car.

Before they walked up to the vehicle, William asked, "You think the dip shit did it and is trying to blame it on someone else?"

David smiled for the first time that night. His partner was steering blind.

"Observation, dear boy, is he wearing boots? I think you've forgot the first thing you learn on this job."

William wrinkled his brow.

"Oh, come on now, Will, maybe if the bum has two sets of shoes and a police scanner underneath his jacket, he might have done it, but I don't think so."

As they walked along, David could not help but to slip in one more jab. "You think the bum put that star on the child's forehead too?"

William stopped dead in his tracks. It was worse than being hit in the back of the head with a sledgehammer. *Duh - stupid*, William thought. David turned his head without losing his stride, smiled at him from the corner of his mouth, and then let him off easy. "Forget it."

They walked up to the officers who were looking down at the bum as if to say, "he's all yours, gentlemen."

Out of a population of close to eighteen million, New York could boast to having the most street people in the world. Some lost everything and found themselves out there, others however, just walked away from life. As a detective, David could never solve that one, why people just gave up. He hated seeing the human spirit so trampled. It haunted him having to wade through the grime of the city and mixing with these people to catch the criminally minded.

"OK, sir, it's your turn. What did you see?" William asked, walking up to the bum. David watched the man stand up and lean his butt against the patrol car.

"You can call off your dogs, gentlemen, there's no one here but me and those rust buckets," the man said, taking out a cigarette. David looked down the tracks at the officers searching the buildings and boxcars, and then looked back at the man in the filthy army jacket.

"You mind?" the bum asked, lighting it.

David looked at William, shrugged his shoulders. "No, go ahead. I think you were going to anyway."

The man took a long drag, blew out the match, and tossed it on the ground. He looked at the cop in the suit next to him. "I can assure you that we're alone. I re-conned this area five years ago after the city pulled stakes on this graveyard of rust buckets and constructed that new station down on the other side of town. Since moving in, I haven't seen anyone down here except a few stray dogs and a couple of alley cats that live off the rats that run around here."

David stepped up to the man to take a better look at him. He then stepped back when his body odor hit him full-force. *He was certainly white, but could easily pass for a Mexican with all that dirt ground into his face,* he thought. *The ripped up, green jacket was his trophy.*

Nobody wore one these days unless they were there.
"Nam?" he asked.

"Yeah," the man replied, looking away as if he did not want to talk about it.

"What was your rank?" David asked.

"Corporal, Corporal Carter, I ran point for Charlie Company."

David glanced over at William. They both flashed that look to one another knowing all about Charlie Company. If you knew anything about that war, you would have known all about the unit called Charlie Company. They were a highly trained, special ops unit, trained in the art of killing deep behind the enemy lines. Both detectives knew they weren't dealing with a bum after all. He'd been a soldier – a damn good soldier at that.

"So you haven't seen anyone down here until tonight – is that right?" William asked, breaking the spell Corporal Carter had just placed on them.

"That's right."

"So what happened?" David asked.

"Not much," Carter replied, looking at William. He figured he was going to fire off another shot. William kept silent.

"I was sitting under that light over there, when I saw this guy walking up the tracks toward me, carrying a bundle in his arms. I thought maybe the guy was doing a little bit of re-conning himself for a place to lay his head. But when he spotted me, he stopped over there by that light, put the bundle down, and ran off."

"He didn't say anything?" William asked.

"No. He just turned and ran."

"Can you describe him for us," David asked.

"Black."

"He was a black man?" David asked.

"No. He was wearing all black; long black poncho with a hood, black gloves, black pants and black boots."

"Can you think of anything else about his appearance?" William asked.

"Yeah, he was wearing a black scarf around his poncho. I thought it was odd. He looked like he just stepped out of a blizzard."

"Meaning what?" William asked.

"Meaning the man looked like he just stepped right out of winter, or maybe he's a Ninja. Does that brighten up your picture?" Carter flipped off, scanning both men to see who'd fire off the next question.

William wasn't going to touch that last line. He respected Carter. David stood there deciphering Carter's description, especially about the boots. He'd seen those prints before, but couldn't remember when. *It had to be a winter boot*, he thought. The tread was too large and appeared to look like a tire tread instead of a shoe print, which would leave small inlaid ripples across the dirt. He looked back at Carter and noticed a small silver pin hiding underneath his jacket lapel. Carter caught David's eyes staring at his upper jacket.

"It's the Silver Medal if that's what you're looking at, Detective," Carter said, lifting up his lapel.

"Is it yours?" William asked. He quickly shut his mouth when Carter's eyes beaded on him like a rifle's sight. If looks could kill, William figured he'd be dead.

"Listen up, asshole! You can't buy one of these. You have to earn it," Carter spat, puffing up his shoulders to appear bigger than he was. He didn't have to. He was small, but so were scorpions. Either one could put you down quicker than shit.

Carter stood up and finally relayed a little reality on the officers standing in front of him.

"I took two bullets in the back carrying an injured soldier over a small bluff after we got the shit kicked out of us in an ambush. Charlie spotted me carrying my buddy and figured he'd get two for the price of one."

William looked at him. "Sorry. Sometimes the lips move before the brain kicks in."

Carter released his bead on the smart-ass detective and glanced over at his partner. The detective just smiled at him and said nothing. David glanced over at William. After taking a slap like that, he figured William had no more questions to ask.

"Alright, Corporal, we'll need your statement in writing. In the meantime, just hang around and wait until we're ready to go back," David said.

"Sure thing, Detective. Do you think I could get a hot cup of coffee out of this?"

"Done deal," William replied, turning with David who was already heading toward the rest of the officers standing watch over the place.

"Oh, one more thing, Detectives," Carter shouted after them, leaning his hands back on the patrol car.

David turned around and looked at him. "Yeah?"

"There's something else I remember about the guy's clothing that was weird."

"What about them?" David asked.

"They hung on him like you hang clothes on a hanger."

David looked at Carter, his eyes showed the same puzzlement as his statement. Carter caught the confusion in his expression and rephrased his thought.

"You know - as if they were too big for him."

"Maybe he stole them off a clothes line, and they didn't fit," William shot back.

"Maybe, but I've never seen anything like it before."

"Are you saying the man was that thin?" David questioned.

"Yes," Carter replied. "Dead thin. I came across gooks like that in the jungle. They were dead maybe two or three days. Nothing left, but a little flesh clinging to their bones."

Carter stopped talking and peered out toward the fence line near the small woody area adjacent to the tracks. "This might also interest you. It sure frightened me."

David and William glanced over at the dark, stand of trees on the other side of the fence and then at each other. They both headed back toward Carter. Sometimes people block out certain events when witnessing a crime. It usually takes a few days, even weeks before the picture comes back to them. Carter was seeing these pictures now. They stepped up to him and waited. Carter looked down at the ground placing his hands in his pockets, "He was fast," he said, looking up at them. They gave no reply to the statement and let him finish. Then, Carter's memory kicked in. "When the man put the kid down, he turned and ran across the tracks toward the fence. It looked like he hesitated in full stride when he saw it. His head went left then right as if he was looking for an opening in the fence to run through. There are no gates, but the service gate over there," he continued, pointing to where the patrol cars were sitting. "Without skipping a beat in his stride, he ran toward the fence and jumped it in a single bound like a buck chasing a doe in heat."

David, William, and the two officers turned around and looked over at the fence. The calculations were easy to security-minded men like them. It was a standard security fence, seven-feet high with a one-foot barbed wire top guard - making it eight feet in total. *No way. Not even an Olympic sprinter on a flat run could leap that fence without a pole,* David thought. He turned toward William to see if his thoughts were the same. His facial expression said, "yes" without him having to move his lips.

Carter watched the detectives calculating his story and began nodding his head like one of those puppies in the back window of a car.

"I'm not bullshittin', I saw him do it with my own eyes," he replied to their dead stares. "The man literally jumped over that fence and was gone in a flash."

David looked over and eyed the fence up one more time. "Impossible, you find me the man who can jump that on a flat run, and we'll all be rich," David remarked, rubbing his foot across the ground in front of him.

Carter rolled his eyes looking at the four. "I sure wish we had someone like that in that God - forbidden jungle back in Nam. A man with the ability to run and jump like that, hell, I can't even imagine what he'd of done with a weapon in his hands. He probably would have taken many lives – and saved many too," Carter said, arching his back as if his bullet wounds were causing him trouble.

David just stood there with gaping mouth. The nape of his neck felt cold. He had a gut feeling on this one. Carter was no fool. If he witnessed it, then he had to believe him. The man had stepped on, crawled over, and swam through more shit than what most people could even imagine, in that God - forsaken place called Nam. "Will, give me your flashlight," he said, stepping out of his thoughts.

William dropped the flashlight in his hand and watched David turn and walk back over to the dead boy. He followed David without saying a word. When they reached the boy, David knelt down, put the light on the bootprint next to the child, and then scanned the area. The prints led over the tracks. He got up and slowly made his way across the tracks, but they stopped where the ground was covered in stones. He continued in the same direction until he picked up the prints again. One print was sitting clearly in a muddy patch and then the stride got longer.

He's running now, David thought, scanning the ground and following the prints toward the fence line.

The last print he picked up was a right print. It went deep into the ground as if the person placed all his weight on that foot. David looked up. He was approximately five-feet from the fence. No prints left and no prints right. The suspect did not run along the fence either. David sighed, walking up to the fence, and then shone the light through to the other side. Back and forth, he scanned the area on the other side of the fence. Then he saw them. There were two large, deep impressions where the person had landed. "Son-of-a- bitch!" he whispered.

William stepped up to him. He looked across where David's light was shinning. "Unbelievable!" he gasped, turning toward David.

David's eyes were glued to the prints. "Call in the dog teams. Let's see if they can track this bastard down," he said, staring through the fence.

William pulled out his radio and requested the dog teams ASAP.

They stood there for a few seconds without saying a word. Both grappling with - who the hell were they chasing? David believed whoever the suspect was; he was a freak of nature. A super human freak, or worse - someone that was so high on drugs that he was able to leap an eight-foot fence in a single bound.

He turned and looked over at Carter and the police officers standing there.

Carter's description about the man tapped at the back of his head. Tall, thin, wearing all black. He could imagine such a person carrying a bowie knife and slicing the throats of high- ranking officers behind enemy lines. He turned back and looked at the fence. However, this asshole wasn't behind enemy lines. He was here in New York slicing the throats of his own people. David stepped out of his thoughts, tapped William's arm, and started walking back.

As they walked along, William's thoughts were clicking over too. Could they be on the heels of a drug addict, maybe an escaped sick-o from the nut house? He had heard stories where average people had committed acts beyond what the average human could do; lifting cars, or objects that even an elephant would have a hard time lifting up. He tried to think of something that could lead them in the direction of this sick-o. He played Carter's words and descriptions of the man back in his head; black on black, thin – so thin that his clothes hung on him like a clothes hanger, and the ability to run like a deer and leap over fences. *Maybe,* he thought, *maybe we have a drug-induced freak, killing children.* He looked over at David. His head was down; he was still in deep thought.

"Is there something on your mind, David?" William asked, hoping he could use his thoughts to try and fit some of the pieces of the puzzle that were now spinning around inside his own head.

"Yeah, those bootprints," David replied. "Carter said the Ninja looked like he'd just stepped out of a blizzard. The print has to be a snow boot."

"I'm sure forensics will tell you soon enough," William replied, pointing up the tracks toward the forensic van rolling in.

As David looked at the van, he spotted Bill running up the tracks toward them. He was carrying his radio, and had a look of horror on his face.

"David!" Bill yelled. Bill stopped in front of him gasping for air. "We got a report that a child is missing on Conner Street – that's three blocks away!"

"Here, give me that radio!" David barked, ripping the radio out of Bill's hand.

"Control, this is Detective Bradshaw. What the hell is going on?"

"Detective Bradshaw, we just received word from a babysitter on Conner Street that the boy she was babysitting is missing," O'Neal relayed back.

"What is the color of his hair?"

"Blonde, three years old."

"Shit! It looks like we found this kid's home," David said, handing Bill his radio.
"Get over there right now and don't let anyone near that house until we get there, you got that?"

"Yes, but…" Bill replied.

"Look, Bill," David interrupted. "I don't want any other foot prints on that property that aren't already there."

"I understand. What the hell is going on?" he asked, looking at William. William shrugged his shoulders. "We're in trouble - now go."

"Right," Bill replied, turning and running back to his car.

Chapter 4

Two patrol units spun out of the gate heading for the scene. William watched them leave then turned around. "I'll inform forensics on our way out," he said.

David nodded, walked over to Carter and thanked him. He informed him that he'd be spending a little time downtown. Carter tilted his head, smiled and asked, "They got any donuts?"

"Sure."

David did not wait for a reply; he turned and ran for their unmarked unit.

The babysitter was frantic when they arrived. She was sitting on the sofa, holding the child's picture in her hands. William took the picture and then passed it to David. David frowned; it was the same child.

"Alright now, just take your time and tell us what happened," David requested.

The poor girl looked up with tears in her eyes and told them everything she knew. "I just put him down an hour ago. I checked on him once and then checked on him just before I laid here on the couch. A few minutes later, I went upstairs to go to the bathroom - he was gone, and the window was wide open. I went to the window and saw the ladder leaning against his window," she said, sniffling and blowing her nose.

William looked at David and shook his head. They were not going to inform the girl what had happened to the boy just yet. "Let's get you outside for some fresh air," he said, helping the girl up and wrapping his arm around her. He escorted her outside to Mary Anne.

David began canvassing the house looking for any signs of his suspect. He found nothing downstairs. He went upstairs and checked the boy's room. Nothing looked out of place. *He must have just slipped in and slipped out through the window with the child,* he thought, looking down at the ladder still clinging to the side of the house. *How utterly brazen!* he thought. *You'd need a set of balls to do this! The average person doesn't think like a cop. Leaving a ladder outside your home is like leaving the key in the door.* That pissed him off. He headed downstairs, went out the side door, and rounded the back of the house. He stood there on the driveway scanning the ground with his flashlight near the ladder looking for that bootprint. Being careful, he approached the ladder and knelt down. His eyes landed on a partial shoe print next to the ladder. It wasn't the same print he was looking for. "Damn!" he whispered.

It looked like a tennis shoe. He looked up the ladder and saw mud on the rungs. He closed his eyes and sighed; *we've got two suspects.* He stood up and started to scan the ground hoping the bootprint was there, it wasn't. He looked up the ladder again wading over his thoughts. One came in alone and took the child while the other waited out front as lookout. Now that was possible. Any criminally minded person would come up with that analysis. However, things don't always pan out the way you want; real life is not like they show it on TV. Cops on TV must solve a case in an hour.

He knew the suspects were connected, but he could not quite tie them together to both crimes. *Were they together during both crimes?* David drifted over Corporal Carter's statement. Carter said he only saw one person on the tracks. *Where the hell was the other suspect when this was happening?* One suspect could have dropped him off at the tracks and waited until he got rid of the child's body. *However, Carter never mentioned that he saw a car.* If his hunch was right, the suspects had to park along the tracks somewhere. That didn't make sense either. There's only one entrance into the abandon train station.

So, the two drove down the outside of the tracks; one guy gets out of the car, climbs the fence with the child. He walks down the tracks, dumps the body when he sees Carter, and then runs and jumps the fence in a single bound to escape. "Right," David whispered. "Why not just toss the kid along the outside fence line and take off?"

The dots were not connecting. Something was wrong with the picture. One set of shoe prints at the scene and another set of prints at the tracks. Before he tied his mind into knots, he thought he should concentrate on one at a time and then try to tie it together.

Snowman – he dubbed the first one. *But, why was he wearing snow boots and all that clothing; unless he was wearing it to hide his identity?* He mused over that thought. A Halloween mask would have worked just as well. *Who the hell are you?* The thought twirled around his head like a dozen butterflies that would not land long enough for him to gather any answers.

For the first time in his career, David felt stumped. The whole crime was a freak show; two murders, two suspects possibly working together, but nothing to tie them together except the stars carved on the foreheads. It was going to take all his knowledge and then some to figure out this one.

He checked his watch. Hopefully, they could get through the rest of the night and start putting it together before they struck again. He stood up, walked out of the backyard, and rounded the front.

The papers will have a field day with this, he thought. *The whole city will go into panic mode, and the Captain will be on my back like a swarm of jellyfish stinging me every step of the way.* When the fire is lit underneath the Captain's chair by the mayor, it always seems to get hotter, as it burns down the line.

"Find the parents yet?" he asked Mary Anne, walking up and looking inside the patrol car at the girl. Mary Anne followed his eyes to the girl in the back seat. The girl was sitting there with her head in her hands with her little pigtails - tied in yellow ribbons, drooping over her shoulders. She was just a child herself. "Yes, they're on their way," she replied.

"Good. I think we better call the Chaplin. I'm sure he'll be needed."

"Right," Mary Anne replied, pulling out her radio.

Chapter 5

The sun came up before David and William were completely finished interviewing Kathy, Corporal Carter, and the babysitter, Jill. As tired as they were, David and William had to endure the interview with the parents of the second child found on the tracks. Because of the circumstances, they met with Mr. and Mrs. Dunbar at their home. The Dunbar's sat on their sofa in total despair as David and William, along with Chaplin John Cleary, informed them of what had happened to their son. Mrs. Dunbar went into complete shock and was taken to the hospital. Cleary stayed with Mr. Dunbar in the waiting room. His baby boy was laid out downstairs in the morgue and his wife was under observation in 'Ward B.'
David reported the situation to Captain Clark when he arrived at the hospital, and then he, William, and Clark drove back to the station.

At the police station, David and William sat there while Captain Clark read their report. The phone suddenly rang. It was the department's canine team. He put down the phone disgusted. "Nothing, they found nothing."

"What? They had to have found something," William questioned.
"They found nothing. They followed the prints but only with the help of the handlers. Once they walked the woody area out to the road, the dogs fumbled and floundered and then just sat there next to the curb."

David went flush. That information just added more garbage to the can that was already full inside his head. Clark got up, waved his hand toward the door and said, "Go home, both of you, and get some sleep. We got some long days and nights ahead of us."

David sat in his kitchen, opened a six-pack of beer, and began to drink each can as if it were his last. Sedatives would be the last resort if the beer failed to put him to sleep. He rubbed his bloodshot eyes; they felt like they were bleeding down his cheeks. He knew they were no closer to discovering who the perpetrators were, much less the motive for committing such a horrid act of violence on such innocence. The only thing that kept circling his thoughts were those bootprints. He knew he'd seen those prints before, and that part tormented him the most. *Where the hell did I see them?*

He waded back, way back in his memory and began tearing up everything in his past to try and figure out where he had seen those prints, but nothing came to him. He left his brain at the table, placed the empty cans in the overflowing trash bin, and went to bed. Maybe there, his brain would bring it to the surface.

When he woke up, he felt as tired as he was when he first went to bed. The beer put him to sleep, but he felt that his brain remained in overdrive the whole time, trying desperately to place those prints. He got up, showered, dressed and headed to his office.

His first line of business would be to call forensics. He needed to know if Terry or Kim had picked up anything on either crime scene. With his luck, it would be a *no,* but they needed that information before they could start tracking the suspects.

The office was sectioned off into cubicles; it gave the eight-man investigative squad privacy - two partners to each cubical with their desks facing each other. He found William sitting inside their cubical.

"Anything?" he asked without a formal greeting.

"Nope, I was waiting for you to get here."

David picked up the phone and called Terry. Kim answered. William sat there looking into David's eyes for any sign of luck.

"We didn't find anything groundbreaking that would be of any help," Kim said. When David's eyes fell to the floor, William knew they were going to have to go it alone. David sat and listened to Kim explain the cause of death and each crime scene's findings.

"The coroner's report this afternoon gave some insight, but nothing that you don't already know. Susanne Day was murdered by a single cut to her throat. The autopsy report states that the blade went in from the left along to the right, sinking deep, severing the jugular, and ending at her windpipe. She also sustained a slight scratch to the top of the left side of her forehead, might be where the suspect grabbed her from behind, pulled her head up and made the slice. That's why there was no sign of a struggle. She never saw it coming and was dead before she hit the floor. The two stab wounds in the back were done after he cut her throat. The boy was suffocated with his own pillow while he slept. The carving on his forehead showed two blood types – his and his mother's - so you can add up who was killed first. The guts and other internal matter that were found on the boy's chest were from a pig. We found one smudge mark of blood on the back door and believe the suspect entered and exited using that door. Nothing in the house was touched other than that."

"Do you have anything else that might lead me somewhere besides a bathroom to vomit?" David asked, frustrated.

"No."

"Can you give me any identity traits about the suspect – like, how big was he?"

"Well, my guess is he must have been big enough to pull Susanne back hard enough because she wasn't a small thing herself. I put the suspect at six-foot, weighing approximately one hundred and ninety to two hundred pounds.

"What sort of knife?" David asked.

"The coroner believes it was a hunting knife with a serrated edge, a bowie knife maybe. The skin was sliced clean - the flesh was ripped on the inside which was caused by the end of the blade."

"What about the second scene?"

"That one was baffling," she replied. "Great set of shoe prints. Size ten – we're checking the treads, but it's a running shoe. We believe the suspect had pegged the house days in advance. He probably slipped around back when the parents left, and then placed the ladder against the house. The suspect climbed in, lifted the sleeping child out of his crib and carried him down the ladder. That's our guess, due to the fact that no one in the adjacent houses heard anything; no crying from the child, no footsteps or the ladder being put against the house, nothing."

"Maybe he used something to knock the kid out before he took him."

"Sorry, Detective, but we thought of that. The child was smothered with his own blanket. We found some blanket fibers inside the mouth and throat. The boy must have woken up when he couldn't breathe and inhaled the fibers."

David sat for a second with the phone in his ear watching William writing something down on a piece of paper and then passed it to him. The slip of paper simply said, "K9s." David shook his head. They already had that information. William mouthed the words, "Ask anyway."

"What about the canine unit?"

"I'm completely stumped on that one, Detective. First of all, the bootprint is a snow boot that hasn't been manufactured in some time."

"Do they know approximately when they were made?" he asked.

"Possibly as late as nineteen hundred and fifty, or earlier," she replied.

David scribbled; snow boot / manufactured 1950 or earlier. He slid the note across the desk. William shook his head in disbelief.

"Secondly, we believe that the suspect should have left a scent on the blanket. Even with gloves on, he was carrying the child pretty close to his chest; the dogs should have picked up something I would think. However, we'll continue searching until we find something. Until then, Detective – you're on your own."

"Thanks," David said, and then hung up.

"Well?" William asked.

David rubbed his finger across his lips then began playing with the curl on the top of his forehead. William waited until he finished twirling it around his finger. It was always like that with David. He'd stare blindly into space twirling that curl while thinking. It was like watching a chess player thinking of his next move on the board. "We'll gather up all the pictures and revisit the crime scenes. There has to be something we're missing," he finally said, letting go of his curl.

At the first scene, they walked up to the door, cut the crime tape, and walked in. William flipped on the lights. The first thing they noticed was the white powder the finger print experts had left. Everything and anything that the suspect might have touched or picked up had been dusted. The front room was a large, white room that had a wooden mantel extending wall to wall on the south side.

There were two large bookcases on either side of the fireplace and two stained glass windows in each of the upper corners over the mantel. Family pictures and small collectable dolls were displayed across the mantel. The furniture looked old, except for the piano. It sat against the half wall that adjoined the hallway leading to the kitchen on one side and the dining room on the other. They walked through and headed into the kitchen via the hallway. The floor had been cleaned, but the tape outline of the body was still there.

David noticed that the kitchen had been renovated. They had made it bigger by knocking out some walls to the back porch to add a breakfast nook and more space for the kitchen. The stove sat against the wall near the door, and beautiful pine counter tops extended across the west wall. The sink sat in the middle along with the dishwasher, which was under the counter. A round table sat in the back, which had a small TV on it. The place was spotless. Everything was situated neatly, from cookbooks, the spice rack, toaster, coffee pot, cutting boards, and a microwave oven.

David looked at William. "Do you see anything unusual?"

"Yeah, not a thing out of place. It looks too damn clean to be a crime scene."

"Right," David replied, stepping up to the counter. His eyes scanned the counter top and stopped when he spotted the knife holder in the corner. He walked over, slipped on his gloves, and pulled out each knife one at a time. They were all clean.

"So, how did he get in? The door was locked when Steward came through," William asked, checking the back door lock and striker plate.

"Maybe she knew the person and let him in, then, when she turned around, he cut her open like a can of peaches," David replied. "But then again, Kathy said that she just opened the door and was knocked back by the smell."

"OK." William said, pacing the floor near where the body was found. "So, either the door was locked, and she let the suspect in, and maybe, he left it open after committing the crime – or the door was always left open," he said, looking up at David. "You think she knew the suspect?" he added.

"All your hunches are good, but we've left one person out, the estranged husband."

"You think we'll find him?" William asked.

"I'm sure we will. Come on, let's look through this place again."

They left the kitchen and strolled through the dining room. It was clean as a whistle too. They went upstairs and walked all the rooms. Each room said the same thing. Susanne Day was as scrupulous as an army general. The Queen herself would have been pleased with Susanne's organizational skills and cleanliness.

When they entered the child's bedroom, the room still stunk to high heaven. William took out his hanky, placed it over his nose and opened the window. The night breeze felt good on his face as he looked down and noticed garbage cans and some bushes right underneath the window. "I wonder if they checked the garbage cans down there?"

David walked up and looked down over his shoulder. "Good one, Sherlock, we'll check them on our way out." He turned and walked over to the crib. His eyes scanned the small mattress, pillow and the clown face on the headboard. The smeared handprint was still there, along with the bloodstained grip on the top rail. You definitely could tell that he wore gloves. The bloodstained grip of the suspect's hand had enough pig blood on it that it had run down along one of the wooden slot boards and dripped onto the floor. The two marks showed David the sequence of events as the suspect attacked the child.

He held the pig guts in his left hand and the pillow in his right. He placed the pig guts on the child's stomach, and then reached up and grabbed the headboard as he placed the pillow over the child's face with his right hand. After the child was dead, his right hand must have come in contact with the pig guts, and he gripped the top rail with the pillow still on top of the child's face. He paused, thinking of Kim's statement. She said the mother's throat was cut from left to right, making the suspect right handed. The pillow had to have been placed down on the child with his right hand. With all things considered, they certainly had a right-handed killer. He placed that in his back pocket and turned toward William who was searching the closet.

"You ready?" David asked, walking to the door.

"Yeah, let's see what she had tossed out this week."

When they went around to the back of the house, David put his flashlight on the lid and opened the top. The garbage container was full.

"Here, use these," he said, handing William a pair of gloves. They stood there wading through each bag until William found some envelopes that had been torn up. Most were bills and junk mail, but one was a letter from her estranged husband. They searched the bag for the missing pieces and then placed them on the top of the can. When they had it all together. It read:

Dear Sue,

I wanted you to be the first to know that Mary and I are getting married in July. We are looking forward to having Robert here for the wedding. Don't worry about putting him on a plane – we'll come get him and drive back to Philadelphia.

Yours truly, Carl

"Well there's one down," William said.

"Looks like it. We need to talk to him. He might be able to shed some light on who Susanne's friends were and where she liked to hang out when she wasn't at home."

The second crime scene also failed to kick up anything new. Their Forensics team was the best in the world; they could find a needle in a haystack and had found it numerous times when faced with a crime like this. However, David and William had to check for their own peace of mind - like driving back to your house, after leaving for an extended holiday, to make sure you hadn't left the iron on. Peace of mind was all in a day's work, even for detectives.

Chapter 6

Two weeks later, after canvassing the neighborhoods, completing all the paperwork and re-reading the witness' statements a hundred times, David sat there looking at the whiteboard fully covered in crime scene photos. He leaned back in his chair, closed his eyes and thought about the funerals of the victims. That was a heart-wrenching ordeal to have to face, watching - as the small white caskets were carried into the church and placed in front of the altar. It made him sick to his stomach knowing that someone out there could take the life of a child. *How could anyone be so heartless, so inhumane?*

William, on the other hand, sat there staring at David as his own thoughts sat idling. He could only guess what part of the case David was trying to concentrate on. One has to start somewhere, and to him, David looked like a fish out of water as he watched him close his eyes and run his fingers through his hair. *His brain must be in overdrive*, he thought.

"So, where do you want to start?" he asked, trying to bring him out of his thoughts.

"Your guess is as good as mine," David murmured, keeping his eyes closed. Then, he suddenly opened his eyes and stared at William.

"Let's start at the beginning."

"The beginning, I don't think we've even made it to the plate much less seen the ball thrown over it," William replied. He knew that David wanted to go back over all the interviews and photos that sat there collecting dust faster than their wheels could spin, but he wasn't looking forward to it.

"Alright, let's do it one more time, Will. You said that none of the mental wards in the area had any reports of a missing person?"

"That's right."

"Do you think we should visit any of the neighbors again?"

"No," William sharply replied.

"So, you think we either have a religious cult or two drug-dependent sick-o's committing these crimes?" he asked, getting up and walking over to the whiteboard. "I can't say right now. Look, David, the only hard evidence we have right now is there are two of them. Hell, we can't even place them at either scene at the same time, or for that matter, know if they're even working together at all," William said.

David sat down. He picked up Jill and Kathy's statements and read them again. Nothing – not one word, sentence, or paragraph flew off the paper and hit him between the eyes. "I'm stumped for the first time in my whole career, Will. Can you believe that?"

"Well, don't tell the Captain that, my fine feathered friend, or he'll reassign this case to you know who."

David looked at him. He knew William was right. The Captain would reassign the case to those overzealous boot lickers, Tim Strong and Ted Corry, two of New York's finest bumbling detectives. "Hell," he thought aloud. "Those two clowns couldn't solve a case involving a grade school bully."

William laughed. "You're right. We need to find something quick from this pile of information and get moving."

David sat there looking at everything, but nothing was registering. Then, all of a sudden, William opened his mouth and said it, "What about looking at cold case files – you know - something that might tie into these crimes?"

David's mind reeled back. He quickly turned in his chair and looked up at the photo of the bootprint. The connection finally hit him right between the eyes! He knew where he'd seen those prints before! "Son-of-a- bitch!" his words slowly escaped his lips, standing up. "Let's go!" he continued, walking toward the door.

"Go where?" William asked, seeing David hurrying out. He got up and ran after him - catching him in the hall. "Are you gonna tell me where we are going?"

"Just like you said - cold case files," David replied, hitting the stairs.

"The basement," William yelled after him.

"Yep - the storage room, I know where I saw that bootprint before."

David turned the corner on the main floor and hit the metal door that led to the basement. The sign on the door read; Evidence Locker / Case Files - Police Personnel Only. He ran down two flights of stairs, hit the cement floor and headed to the caged area.
"Hi Charlie, I need to look at some files, please."

Charlie looked up and saw David and his partner walking up to the cage. He hadn't seen the pair in a while, but knew about the case they were working on. Being an Evidence Custodian was a lonely job, but it had its moments when evidence was passed over. It was like being able to read a card shark's hand before he would lay them down on the table and sweep up the pot. Charlie looked into David's eyes then glanced over at William. He wondered if these two could handle the heat that was about to engulf them if they did not come up with something soon.

"I haven't seen you two in some time. Go ahead - the door is unlocked," he replied.
Charlie waited until they walked in before he pulled the register logbook in front of him and jotted in their names, time, and date. Captain Clark ran a tight ship; everything

that happened down here had to be recorded for court purposes.

The file room was situated and organized like a small library. In the center sat one wooden table and four chairs. The rows of files were stacked on shelves in aisles that went around the entire room. From ceiling to the floor, the boxes were placed in rows, starting at the bottom with the first date of 1900-1910. The second row had the numbers, 1910-1920.

David walked up to the first row of boxes and knelt down. He pulled out the box marked 1900-1910 and sat down on the floor with the box between his legs. His hands held it as if it was a treasure chest.

William stood there looking down at him. He could tell that David's mood had changed; he was withdrawn. It was something William saw while people spoke of their past. Their look would change as if they stopped looking outside themselves and began looking inside. He watched David slide his hands over the box as if a genie would appear in a haze of colored smoke. He was without question reliving something in his past, William was sure of that. He sat down, leaned against the row of boxes on the other side of David, and waited until he told him what in the hell was he reliving.

David finally looked up and softly started to speak "After my grandfather passed away, my father brought me down here to show me his life's work. I was around ten at the time, and I wasn't quite sure why he brought me here until he pulled out this box. He sat on the floor and told me to sit down next to him."

William said nothing. He knew David was going to be there for a while, so he leaned back, placed his full weight up against the stacked boxes, and relaxed.

David looked into William's eyes and smiled. "That was the moment I decided that I wanted to be a cop like my father before me, and his father before him." He looked down at the box and continued. "I think that's why he brought me down here in the first place. I guess he thought when he showed me this one case that my grandfather had worked when he was a young detective, would spark a flame inside me to become one too."

William wasn't sure where this was leading. They had a major fire sitting on their desk upstairs, and time was running out. It only would take one more child to be found murdered, and it would engulf the city. His patience was being tested as he watched David looking out into space. David opened the box and flipped through the files. When his hand reached the one he was after, he looked up at William, pulled it out, and then slid the box away from him. He sat there looking like an altar boy with a prayer book in his hand. He was just about to question him when David began his story. He thought it would be nightfall before David finished, and he sighed.

Looking at David sitting there made him instantly flash back to his high school history teacher, Mr. Ross. He always had the same look on his face when he was about to give a history lesson. He was a small man with a belly that stretched across his waist like good old Saint Nick's. Mr. Ross's face would look withdrawn just like David's was now before he would start telling a story about the past. It did not matter who he was talking about; he would put you right there as if, he'd been living in that time himself.

"This was my grandfather's most difficult case," David said, bringing William back to where they were now. "The year was nineteen ten, in a little town called Ironbark in upstate New York. You ever heard of it?" David asked.

William shook his head.

"My dad said that it was what you would have called the last wilderness outpost at the turn of the century. It's not there anymore; however, it was about a stone's throw away from Rochester, New York, on the banks of Lake Ontario.

"It started off as a trading post. Hunters, trappers, and fishermen would bring in their pelts, wild game they trapped, and fish to trade. Back in those days, most of the people there were French, Canadian, Indians, or American settlers," David paused and then continued without another break.

"It was mid-October, the winter winds were already blowing in from the north across Lake Ontario. The winds off the lake could get so bad in the dead of winter that it could freeze a man to death in minutes. Many settlers just hunkered down for the winter until spring, but the ones that had to make a living during the winter months had to endure the cold in order to sell whatever they could to the trading post. They would stream down from the Great Lakes in Michigan and across from the Hudson Bay region in Canada. The trading was good in Ironbark, more so in the spring than the winter. Come spring, buyers would flood in and haggle for the pelts taken through the fall and winter seasons. Then, as if the black plague had come to town - the killings started. Four children in all were murdered in cold blood, two girls and two boys, all dead in a matter of months.

"It all started when Jamie Chamber went missing on the twentieth of April. Jamie's parents were good friends of the town doctor, Earl Thomson. And apparently, Jamie was in love with the doctor's little girl, Millie. It was reported to my grandfather, that on the day he went missing, Millie stated that Jamie went to Casper's Hill, to pick her some flowers. Casper's Hill was just a stone throw away from Marshall Lake.

"Days later - two Indians, Indian Joe and Blackfoot, found Jamie behind a log shanty on the other side of the lake nestled in a grove of pines about two hundred yards in.

The children never played there. It was too remote an area, and you only could get there by boat, or trekking around the lake, which was not an easy task even for an adult.

"The eastern side of Marshall Lake was a wooded area that was thicker than molasses and had grown right up to the lake. In some parts, you had to wade into the water to get around some of it. Jamie had been sexually molested, but that wasn't the worst part. The killers had stuck a meat hook in his back, hung him on a tree out back of the shanty and field dressed him like a deer. He was sliced open from crotch to throat.

"On the twenty fourth of April, Jill Farmer went missing. Her parents were frantic after what had happened to Jamie. A few days later, a trapper rode in carrying her little body and said that he had found her while he was out checking his traps. Her body was stashed inside a rabbit's burrow in a thicket of fallen trees - some five miles away, just west of Ironbark. The trapper was almost strung up himself. The town folks thought he did it. If it weren't for my grandfather and Sheriff Ben Coleman, he would have been hung right on the spot.

"After Doc Thomson examined the girl, he reported the killer was left-handed, which was lucky for the man who found her because he was right-handed. My grandfather and Doc Thomson held a town meeting inside the church. Jill Farmer had been murdered just like Jamie. She'd been raped and then field dressed like a deer.

"Panic swept through Ironbark like a wildfire, and anyone who was an outsider was considered a suspect. In a town like Ironbark, people came and went at the drop of a hat and the suspects outnumbered the innocent. The only ones that could be counted out were the trappers and Indians who came in afterward in their longboats.

"The settlers hardened their suspicions toward the Seneca, Erie, and Huron Indians and other natives that flooded in from Canada. Their belief was only a savage would have been capable of committing such horrors on a child. Doc Thomson believed the ranting of the small community after his examination of the children. There was something else done to them that he and my grandfather knew about, both children were missing one rib. They knew that some Indians would do that to an animal after they killed it. The Indians believed that by taking one rib from an animal and wearing it, it would keep the spirit of the animal from harming them.

"On the fifth of May, Mary Baker, the barber's daughter went missing. One of the local Indians, Chief Running Bear came forward to offer his assistance. He feared an all-out war would erupt between his people and the settlers if he did not take a stand.

"Chief Running Bear, spoke only in broken English, so Indian Joe, a half-breed, stepped alongside the Chief and spoke for him. Indian Joe was highly respected in Ironbark for his kindness toward children, especially Doc Thomson's little girl, Millie. He was also respected for his ability to track anything that moved. His senses were so keen that he could smell the fart of a butterfly from twenty-five yards and get the damn thing to land on his arm. His mother was a Huron Indian, his father a French trapper. He spoke to the folks in a mixture of French and English. *"The evil one has risen and is taking your children,"* he said. *"He is not Indian, but a white man dressed in wolf's clothing to appear like us."*

"The people in town were shocked and pressed Indian Joe about what he knew. Indian Joe folded his arms and spoke again. *"The mighty spirit of the owl has seen him. He told me in a dream that the killer runs with another."*

"Everyone stood back and gasped at Indian Joe's revelation. Indian Joe watched the faces before him fall in disbelief; he spread his massive arms and held them high in the air. *"Oh hear me great eagle, who rules the wind and sky - tell 'em I'm coming,"* he yelled, and then turned and walked away.

"The circle of people closed in tighter; they began buzzing like a beehive. They knew they were on their own and could not depend on the Indians. How could they believe an Indian talking about spirits? Search parties were formed, and areas were divided to search for Mary Baker.

"Indian Joe sought out Sheriff Coleman and my grandfather. They told him about the ribs missing from the two children. Indian Joe believed it was white trappers - that knew the hunting customs of the Seneca Tribe, and were using the taking of a rib to throw them off their trail. Doc Thomson, Sheriff Coleman, and my grandfather believed Indian Joe more so than the settlers, but tempers were mounting in the town; something had to break soon before all hell broke loose in Ironbark.

"Indian Joe had told the great eagle to let them know he was coming. He felt compelled to search for the girl and went off on his own after he spoke to the people in town. He found prints next to her house and started to track her killer, but he lost the trail when it crossed the Pinto River. He searched for several minutes on both sides until he found two sets of bootprints. He let his eyes follow them up the rocky outcrop and into the forest. He then waded out of the water, climbed the bank, knelt down and placed his fingers inside one of the prints. He smiled knowing the killer still had the child and was carrying her. As he went to stand up, he spotted something else on the ground that startled him, another set of tracks. This set was out further than the other two. He searched the ground leading into the forest and thought the outside bootprint was not with the party, but was tracking them. The spirit owl was right – the killer was running in a pack. The killer had met up with one, and another was now following.

"He could only hope the girl was still alive. Some two hundred yards inland, he froze when he saw the child sitting up against a tree. He slowly walked up to her and looked down. She was dead. He knelt down and brushed her hair aside. She still had color in her face, she hadn't been dead long. His thoughts drifted. *The killers knew they were being followed, so they left the girl here and took off.*

"He got up and searched the ground near the tree. He noticed one track heading north as if to double back toward the town, and the other two prints continued heading south toward the Forgotten Land. The Forgotten Land started at the fork of the Pinto River, which created Willow Creek. Near the rocky outcrop on the bank of the Pinto River was a stand of trees you could walk through and stand at the edge of the Forgotten Land; a valley, which was thick in scrub, pines and large boulders – some as large as wagons. Along with the rough landscape, there were large openings in the ground. One would have to be extremely careful crossing that valley. One wrong slip and you'd fall into one of those openings, and become wedged without a chance in hell of getting free. Bears, wolves, foxes, rodents and even snakes used them during the cold season, so there was no chance to of escape. The snakes were the worst. You would not see them coming, and you'd only know they were there after they sank their deadly fangs into you.

"Indian Joe stood there thinking, as he looked back toward the Pinto River. That river cut right through the Sheppard Mountains along the Forgotten Land. *Could they be using the river system to get into that rough terrain?* He looked down at the tracks and felt that the killers had to be locals to travel through there. No outsider would have known of the place.

"He wanted to go on, to continue tracking those heading south, but he knew that he couldn't leave the girl behind. He walked back over, bent down, and picked her up into his arms. On his way back to the river, he thought of the one he believed was also tracking the killers. *Who is he - and why is he tracking them?* That thought stayed fixed within his thoughts when he finally returned to Ironbark with Mary.

"After giving the girl over to Doc Thomson, he informed the Doc and Sheriff Coleman of his discovery of the two other men. One he believed, headed toward the Forgotten Land and the other he believed, doubled back toward town. He left out the third man because he wanted to seek him out if he possibly could. Sheriff Coleman told both men to keep this information to themselves, and hopefully - the murderers would return. If they did, they might just shoot their mouths off during a drinking binge.

"Then, on the twenty fifth of May, Teddy Cotton was the next to be abducted. He had gone out to the outhouse late that evening without telling his parents. This time, however, the Sheriff got lucky. Two witnesses saw the killer carrying Teddy down Hollow Trail next to Marshall Lake. Hank and Gloria Yammer were coming in their horse and buggy from visiting friends when they spotted a man carrying a bundle heading in the same direction. When the man turned and saw the buggy, he stopped, placed the bundle down, and then took off into the forest. Hank and Gloria got down and checked what the person had left. To their horror, they discovered Teddy Cotton's body wrapped up inside a blanket!"

David looked up at William sitting there on the floor across from him. He never realized that William had sat down while he was talking. William's eyes stayed glue to his then he gave David a halfhearted smile. "I'm listening – go on." David nodded and continued.

"The Yammer's thought the person who left Teddy's body on the trail was Doc Thomson because of the jacket the person had on. It looked just like the winter-hooded jacket the doctor always wore. When my grandfather and Ben Coleman went out to search the trail – my grandfather took a photo of the print. When Indian Joe saw the photo, he knew who it belonged to and it wasn't Doc Thomson. It was the same bootprint he found tracking the suspects on the other side of the Pinto River."
William said nothing watching David open the file and go through it. "Here, take a look at this," David said, handing him the photo.

William took the photo and looked at it. Nothing registered. "So what are you telling me, that this is the same bootprint?"

"Look at it!"

William looked at it again. "OK. I looked at it. Now what?"

"William, sometimes you make me wonder. That bootprint is the same bootprint on the whiteboard upstairs. Don't you get it? As soon as you mentioned old cases, I remembered where I'd seen that bootprint on the railroad tracks."

"Really?" William replied, raising his brow.

"Just hear me out before you start drawing any conclusions. After all these years, I can't believe that print has stayed in my head. It's funny, don't you think?"
William looked down again at the file in David's hands. His eyes scanned across the worn out lettering: Case File number 37 - Child Abduction / Murder.

He looked down at the photo again. *Yes, it looked similar, but it didn't have anything to do with what they were dealing with today.*

David saw the look in his eyes. He reached over and handed him the file. William looked at him and then scanned through it.

"Well?" David said, watching William's eyes roam through the pages. He looked up at David and smiled.

"Are you suggesting that the guy we're chasing is the same one in this file?"

David stood up, put the box of old files back, and then slipped the Ironbark file behind his back and into his pants. "Let's go," he said, walking out.

As William followed behind, David thanked the Charlie on his way toward the stairs. Charlie looked up from his cage, "You're welcome and good luck with that case." William gave him a simple nod and walked out with David.

Chapter 7

Back inside their cubical, David set the file down, pulled out the photo of the bootprint, and lifted it up to the photo on the whiteboard. The bootprints matched to a tee. William walked in and saw David examining the photos. He just sat down and waited - as he had all day.

"Shall I call the captain so he can come down and checkout the new evidence?"
David said nothing while examining the prints. *His blood must be thick today*, William thought, getting up and walking over to board.

"Well, what is the great Sherlock thinking? Do you think the killer up-state has come to New York City?"
David spun around and looked at him. He wasn't in the mood to be needled. "No. I'm concentrating on the boot. You must admit, it's the same print – right?"

"Well," William replied, stepping back. "Yeah, they do look similar."

"Will, they're a perfect match, and that bothers me. Who in the hell would have a pair of them today?"

William stood there dumbfounded. David had a point. "Don't know," he replied.

David rounded the desks and sat down. The puzzlement on his face was growing.
"It's more than just them boots – the whole damn case looks the same as it was up there."

"What do you mean?" William questioned, sitting down.

David placed the bootprint photo back in the jacket and handed the whole file over to William. "Here, take it home and read it, then tell me what you think."

"You already told me."

"Go home and read the damn thing cover to cover. I'm going to stick around and see if I can come up with anything on those boots."

"And if they're the same pair of boots?" William asked, taking the file from his hands.

David looked at him with dismay. "Maybe after you read that, you'll see where I'm coming from. The boots aren't the only things that match up. You had better keep the lights on when you read it, though. Now, go home."

The hairs on the back of William's neck stood up. He didn't like the tone in David's voice, or the look in his eyes when he said that. "Right," he replied, getting up. When he reached the door, he turned and glanced back at him. He hadn't seen a smile on the man's face all day, just that a look of dread.

After William got home, he finished his dinner, and kissed his wife, Sue. He then told her that he had some reading to do before going to bed.

"OK, after that is done, what are your plans?" she asked, raising her brow and smiling.

"Then," he paused to ensure he had her fullest attention. "I'll probably end up performing my husbandly duties."

"Good answer. Now, run along like a good little husband, and I'll be up later to grade you on your duties."

William swaggered up the stairs. He walked into their bedroom, rearranged the pillows on their bed and got comfortable. Opening the file, he began reading the opening case on Jamie Chamber. He was just a ten-year-old boy. His body was discovered behind a shanty near Marshall Lake on the April 20, 1910. The investigative report on Jamie was gruesome. *Only an animal could do such a thing to a child,* he thought. His eyes scanned over the name of the town. He'd never heard of it.

He got up, walked over to the desk in the corner, pulled out the New York State map, and placed it on the bed. He found Rochester and started looking at the names of the towns between there and Lake Ontario: Wilson, Medina, Albion, Greece, Rochester, but no Ironbark. David did mention that the town faded away after what had happened.

He picked up the file and continued. Reading the report, he was surprised to see the meticulous detail throughout the report. David's grandfather had a gift, a wonderful, analytical gift for detail; as if his grandfather had the eyes of a hawk and the nose of a wolf, every step in his investigation was meticulously researched. He wrote down everything he saw, touched and smelled. Day, time, temperature, weather conditions, and wind direction. *The man had been born for the job,* he thought. It wasn't until he started to read Teddy Cotton's report that David's thoughts started to reach out and touch him. The hairs on the back of his neck started to prickle once again.

Teddy Cotton: Born March 15, 1905. Murdered: May 25, 1910.

Initial report: Body found at 9:45 p.m., May 25 on Hollow Trail, adjacent to the north side of Marshall Lake.

Body discovered by Hank and Gloria Yammer.

May 25, 1910. Crime Scene depicted:

Clear night.

Temperature; sixty-eight degrees, with a light westerly wind.

Body brought in from the scene at approximately 10:15 p.m.

Body turned over to Doctor Earl Thomson, Ironbark, NY at 11:30 p.m.

William slowly read Mrs. Yammer's statement.

*May 25, 1910, 6:00 p.m. - my husband, Hank, and I
made plans to take our buggy around the lake after supper
to visit Sam and Elizabeth Howard. We spent the evening
visiting and then decided to leave before it got dark. On
our way back along the trail, we reached the curve and
picked up our pace. When we finally rounded the lake and
started heading toward town, we saw a man up ahead
walking in the middle of the trail heading in the same
direction. Hank whispered to me that he thought it was
Doc Thomson because of the long, grey hooded jacket and
red-checkered scarf. Hank called out to him, "Doc
Thomson, is that you?"*

*Without turning around, the man suddenly stopped,
tilted his head back, and looked at us. He knelt down, put
something on the ground and took off across the trail
heading toward the woods like a scared animal. As Hank
reined in the horses, we sat there and watched the man.
My mouth fell open when he jumped over the embankment
like a deer and then ran deep into the woods. That
embankment is very high. I remember grabbing Hank's
arm and squeezing it. Then Hank said, "My Lord - did you
see that?"*

*When we thought the man was gone, we climbed
down from our buggy to see what he had put on the ground.
Hank opened the blanket, and I screamed when I saw
Teddy Cotton's little face peeking out from underneath. He
looked as white as a ghost, and he had deep bluish lips.
Hank checked his pulse and his breathing. There wasn't
any sign of life in the little boy. Hank tried to bring him
back, but it was too late. Hank then wrapped him back up
and handed him to me; the poor thing was so still. We
hurried our team back to town to Doc Thomson. The Doc
took the poor boy and said there was nothing else we could*

do. I went on home, and Hank took the sheriff and the
detective out to where we found the boy.
Signed:
Gloria Yammer.

     William closed his eyes thinking back to Corporal
Carter's statement. "When he spotted me, he set his bundle
down and then took off across the tracks - leaping the fence
in a single bound, like a buck chasing a doe in heat." Then
there was Carter's description of the clothing, "He was
wearing black on black... they hung on him as if they were
hanging off a clothes hanger."

     William opened his eyes running his fingers across
his mouth. "This can't be happening. How can two people
- living in different times - give almost the same damn
description of a suspect?" He quickly flipped through
Hank's statement. It was pretty much the same as his
wife's. Hank also thought it was Doctor Thomson because
of the clothing the suspect was wearing.

     The last thing William had to brief through was
David's grandfather's investigative notes. These notes
were like a diary to an investigator. They helped in
keeping everything in its proper sequence, the initial who,
what, where, how, why and when along with the detective's
thoughts. The clothing was his first thing to check. During
his interview with Doc Thomson, he checked the doctor's
jacket, scarf, and boots. The boots matched to a tee; rubber
with five big buckles strapped across the front. However,
David's grandfather could not rely on that solely because in
those parts - everyone wore those same types of boots. He
also went out and viewed the embankment that Gloria and
Hank Yammer had seen the suspect jump in a single bound.
He figured the doctor could not have jumped it due to the
embankment being approximately six and a half feet in
height of large, jagged rocks.

William picked up the photo of the bootprint. It did match to a tee as David had said. The phone on the nightstand next to him suddenly rang. He turned and looked at it. It rang again. He knew if he picked it up, he would not be sleeping with his wife tonight. He reached over and picked it up, "Hello."

"Will, we have another one," David frantically yelled.

"Is it a child?"

"Yes. He's still alive; battered and bruised, but alive! The ambulance crew will be transporting him shortly."

"Where are you?"

"Hyde Park. We got a call from a woman who was walking her dog in the park. She said she saw the killer up close with the child. I don't know how much we can get out of her right now. She's still freaking out about the mask he was wearing. However, the rest of her description of the suspect matches the same description Corporal Carter gave us."

William's jaw muscles tightened.

"One more thing," David said. "They were both here tonight."

"Tennis Shoe and Snowman were both there together? I knew it! They are working together," William replied.

"Maybe," David said.

"What do you mean by that? They are, or they're not," William spat.

"Look, I don't want to say anything more until you get over here and see this for yourself. Just get here fast," David replied, and then hung up.

As William reached over and put the phone back, he looked up to see his wife standing at the door. Her long, drawn face made him sigh again. "I'll try to get back as soon as possible."

"I'm sure you'll try," she replied, walking over and sitting down next to him. *The pain is clearly visible in his tired eyes*, she thought. *This case was ripping him apart.* "What did David say?"

"We've got another one. They found the kid in Hyde Park, he's still alive."

"Thank God," she sighed, placing her arms around him.

"Keep the bed warm," he said, giving her a kiss on the check. She frowned watching him leave. She really wanted him to stay home, but understood why he had to go. There was someone out there killing children. They had to be stopped.

Traffic was light as William drove to the park. Just driving over the speed limit with his red interior emergency light on, gave him time to think. He liked the south side of town, with its tall oak trees that branched over the streets shading the neighborhood in thick greenery and the large houses that sat back from the road.

Hyde Park was a beautiful park, which was adjacent to the railroad tracks. On the other side of the tracks was Donny Brook high school. It was a huge, fifteen-acre complex with three large playing fields; two football fields – one for practice and one for the games - and a baseball field. Right behind the school were tennis courts. William's thoughts drifted over the area, and then his mind slammed into reverse. The railroad tracks! The same tracks that ended at the abandoned train station where Corporal Carter keeps house! *Those bastards are using the tracks!*

When William turned onto the street adjacent to the school, he drove under the railroad bridge and saw the flashing lights inside the park near the tall stand of trees next to the fence line. That part of the park was overgrown with trees and vegetation to buffer the noise of the trains that passed through the neighborhoods.

He drove his patrol car over the curb and into the park where the other vehicles were. The ambulance crew was administering first aid to the child on a stretcher. He saw another stretcher nearby, but he didn't know why it was there. *Maybe the woman fell and hit her head when she ran from the scene*, he thought. He pulled up along the yellow police tape and got out. The place was dark except for the emergency lights on the vehicles and the flashlights the forensic team were using inside the thick brush. He figured that's where David was.

A police officer approached. He flashed his badge. When the officer nodded, he lifted the tape, crawled under and stood there a second. He glanced over at the ambulance crew readying the child for transport. Just to the right of the ambulance, he spotted David's cousin, Bill Glenmore and his new partner, Mary Anne Cannon, talking to a woman and a man. There was no dog. The woman was crying, and the man was holding her.

"Careful," David said, walking out of the bushes. "There are tracks all over the place, especially in there."

William followed his finger pointing to a small path heading into the bushes. The path looked worn and muddy from overuse. It looked like an area that kids would use for a hideout. He placed his flashlight down on the path and spotted the large dog prints along with two other prints. *The woman must have had the dog off the leash, and he trotted in there*, he thought - looking at David, who was, to his surprise - rubbing Vicks up his nose.

"What gives – we have no deaths," he questioned, putting his hand out for the Vicks.

"You'll see. Are you ready?"

"No. I'm never ready for this shit," he replied, watching David turn and head down the path.

"We got the call about thirty minutes ago. Thought I'd let you see your wife a bit longer before I called," David said over his shoulder, ducking and weaving into the tall thicket. William kept his hands up to ward off the branches David was pushing apart and springing back at him. "Thanks – you could have called me in the morning."

David smiled to himself. He wasn't going to entertain William's thoughts. He figured that once he showed William the crime scene, William would forget about his wife anyway.

As David made his way around a giant tree, William saw a flash from a camera up ahead. He stood next to David when they entered the small cove. The cove was surrounded by trees and had a small pond in the center of it. Across the pond were giant rocks pressed hard against the trees. They were probably brought in and pushed down in this little gully when the railroad tracks were built. The rocks were covered in moss and old, dead tree limbs that had fallen and were sticking out. He noticed a trickle of water flowing down the rocks and into the pond. William figured there had to be an underground water table here. He wondered how many children had used the place. To them, he thought, it had to be a magical place, a place where a child's imagination could run wild and free. He let go of those thoughts, and drifted back to the scene in front of him.

He stood there watching Terry and Kim meticulously working the area; taking photos and searching the ground for more clues. Turning his head, he noticed a small hideout nestled between two trees; it was fastened together out of plywood and tree branches. Inside he could see an old sleeping bag, a few discarded pots and pans, and some old, empty cans of baked beans and tuna.

"Are you ready?" David said, glancing over at him with a smile.

"Am I ready for what?"

"This," David replied, pointing his flashlight high up into the canopy.

William's eyes slowly drifted upward following the light beam until he spotted a pair of shoes, then legs, and then a body. Thirty feet above them was a man hanging from a branch. The body was limp and slowly swinging on the wind. William followed the rope downward. It was tied onto a dead limb that was wedged tight into the large rocks on the other side of the pond. "What the hell," he said, taking David's flashlight and aiming it in up into the branches.

"You like that trick?" Kim said, standing up and walking over. "We would've never spotted him hanging up there if whoever hoisted him up there didn't tie it off over there. Now, you want some good news?"

"Good news? You got good news?" he replied.

"Well, this might steady your thoughts," she replied, pointing her flashlight on the ground.

William carefully stepped back and looked down. The footprints were deep and clean - due to the moist, muddy area next to the pond. His eyes grew wide when he spotted the tennis shoe and then the bootprint - side by side. He smiled contentedly. Seeing it first hand was better than when he heard David telling him over the phone. "David told me over the phone, but he wouldn't explain," William said.

"David!" Kim scolded, turning to face him.

David shrugged. "I had to tell him something."

William walked away from the pair eying each other up. Kim had a thing for David – he could hear it in her voice. He carefully stepped around so he would not disturb the prints on the ground and then put his light up to the shoes on the man hanging there. "You sure they're the same shoes we picked up by the ladder outside that kid's bedroom?"

"My guess, I'd say yes," Kim replied, looking up. "I won't confirm that until we cut him down though."

William glanced over at David; he suddenly felt cold.

"Well, tell me, what do you think?" David asked, waving his hand as if to say – walk the scene boy.

William stepped back even further scanning his flashlight across the entire area. His light landed on the bootprints coming into the small cove from the railroad side of the pond. *The guy must have walked through the water,* he thought, looking down on his side of the pond. There, his light shone on both prints, both the tennis shoe and bootprints, side by side on his side of the pond. By the look of it, the man wearing the tennis shoes was facing the other way – and the bootprints come up and then circled around the tennis shoe prints.

William rubbed his chin. He looked back toward the path and shone his light down on the ground. There they were; a nice clean set of prints deep within the mud. Deep enough to think he was carrying something heavy - the child. The tennis shoe prints lead straight for the hideout. Terry, who was taking samples from the hideout, caught William's light heading his way. He got off his knees, walked over to Kim and David, and watched William try to figure out the sequence of events.

Next to the hideout, William squatted down over the tennis shoe print to get a closer look. The man wearing the tennis shoes had knelt down at the entrance – *the bastard put the child in here then he stood up, and bingo - he turns around and meets Snowman right here.* From that point onward - there was no sign of the tennis shoe prints - just the bootprints spinning in a circle.

As William looked a little further out, he spotted something near the pond. It was the bootprints. It looks as if he slid into the pond. His heart was now racing - seeing the whole thing happening before his very eyes. He slowly walked across and stood next to where the rope was tied off. He quickly looked up at the man hanging there and then looked down at the pond. *I see it now... Snowman must have caught him off guard. When Tennis Shoe realized it, it was too late. He quickly turned around and bang - snowman grabs him, wraps a rope around his neck and starts to strangle him. He then picks him up, swings him in a circle and maybe tennis shoe goes limp. With that - somehow he tosses the rope up over the branch and pulls on it while walking backward - crossing the pond.*

David raised his brow at Kim and Terry. To him, William had figured it out. William nodded looking back across the pond. He then looked up at the man hanging in the tree.

"Well?" Kim asked.

William conveyed his thoughts to her.

Kim smiled. "So far, that sounds about right. However, we won't know until we cut him down."

"What about the dog?" Terry asked.

"What?" William said. "Who gives a rat's ass about the dog? He probably came in afterward, barked, and then took off."

"What about the woman, any thoughts about her?" Kim added.

"Look you two, the dog and the woman have nothing to do with this. The dog heard something. It rushed in and barked. The woman walked in and tried to call him. She didn't say anything about the guy hanging up there, did she?" William replied, pointing up.

"No," David replied.

"Alright then, let's take a closer look, shall we?" Kim said. "So far, you seem to be on the right track."

William looked up at the man hanging there.

"Just forget about him for now. Come here and take a look."

William and David walked over and looked down to where she was pointing. It was a clean dog print - slightly smeared.

"The dog stopped here in front of the pond, and then he looks as if he tried to run - or maybe it was frightened."

"So?" William replied.

Kim looked at him. "What kind of dog does she have?"

"By the look of the print, I'd say a large one." William questioned.

"It's a German shepherd. Now, what the hell could scare the daylights out of a German shepherd?" she asked, standing up. "Both suspects came in from different directions. The suspect you call Tennis Shoe had the child and laid him over there. Then Snowman walked in from the underbrush over there and came up from behind him. Tennis Shoe was facing the other way – maybe he stood up after laying the kid down and then Snowman grabbed him and then spun him around as you said. They could have struggled and ended up in the pond, and then maybe Snowman strangled him when they were still in the water. After he kills him, he puts the rope around his neck, climbs the tree high enough to toss a rope over that limb, pulls him up, wraps the end of the rope around that limb, and then ties it off."

William raised his brow.

Kim smiled and continued, "Now, let's bring in the dog and the woman. She said she let the dog off his leash after he pulled on it so hard that it almost took her arm off. Once letting go of him, he ran in here. He started barking and growling. She ran in to get him. She heard him whimper, and he bolted out between her legs. She did not see Snowman at first, but saw the child lying there. Snowman stood up, and she froze. She said that the man

startled her, making her almost drop her flashlight. She then put the light on his face. She could not see him because of his hood. It wasn't until Snowman turned and looked at her that she saw a bit of his face and screamed. With that - she bolted out faster than the dog."
Everyone stood there digesting Kim's analysis.

"Is there anything else running through your thoughts?" William asked.

"Yes, he never went after her - and he left the child."

"So why have we waited all this time to put our own blood hounds on his trail?" William asked.

"Go ahead, bring in the dog team. We've got everything we need now," Terry said, walking out. He turned around. "Oh, one more thing, I'd like to know what the woman tells you after you interview her."

"We will," David replied, walking out with him.

When they reached the yellow tape, they saw Bill and Mary Anne standing by the couple.

"Bill, before we cut him down, have your dog team run the area and see if they come up with anything."

"Right, Cuz. Let's do it boys," Bill ordered. The canine team went in.

Kim, Terry, William and David stood there by the couple and waited. Fifteen minutes later the team came out.

"Nothing. The damn mutts just went around in circles."

David looked at William. "That's why we waited. The dogs didn't find anything at the tracks, and I figured they wouldn't find anything here either."

"Great, let's get these two back to the office," William replied, turning toward the couple. "Where's your dog now?" he asked.

The woman started to cry. Her husband put his arm around her. "He's gone. After he ran out of here, my wife could not find him. Normally, he would just head to the house. We live right over there. But I checked a while ago, and he wasn't there yet," the man said.

Kim and Terry looked at one another. They turned and walked back toward the ambulance crew.

"Hey, before you two head back, you might want to call the fire department to get that guy down from the tree," David yelled.

Terry turned and nodded.

Chapter 8

Back at the precinct, William settled the couple down in the small interview room.

"Would you like something to drink?" he asked.

"Water would be fine, thanks," the man said.

William walked out, grabbed two bottles of water and headed for his office. David was at his desk when he entered. "What do you think?" he asked.

"Don't know, Will. Let's just see what she has to say."

When they walked back into the room, the woman was crying again. William placed the water bottles down on the table, reached over, and grabbed the box of tissue. *It was going to be a long night,* he thought, handing her the box. William took the opportunity to look the pair over. They looked to be in their mid forties – both showing a little grey in their hair. "I am Detective William Hall, and this is my partner, David Bradshaw."

"I'm Bob Goldsmith, and this is my wife, Caroline."

"Would you like to tell us what happened tonight, Caroline?" David asked, taking out his pen and setting on the table.

Caroline rubbed her puffy eyes, blew her nose, and looked up at the big detective.

"Just relax and take your time," David said, folding his hands together.

"Well," she said. "Where would you like me to begin?"

"When you entered the park," David replied.

"Well, every night around seven, I walk our dog. It's been a ritual since he was a pup. He's a German shepherd. His name is Titan."

William and David both nodded.

"After we finish our two laps, I always let him off the leash and he high tails it home," she said and then paused, taking a sip of water. "But tonight, when I started to walk him, he kept tugging on the leash toward the thick grove of trees near the tracks. I yanked him several times and we kept walking. On our second lap, he did it again. This time, he was barking and growling. I didn't know what got into him - so I let him off - hoping he'd head for home. Once he was off the leash, he ran straight into that grove. I thought it would be a pain to get him out of there, so I ran in after him. When I got down the path, I could hear him growling. I thought maybe he had cornered a cat or something. I turned my flashlight on and walked in. As I got deeper into the thicket, I heard Titan start to yelp and then he bolted out between my legs. I wanted to see what frightened him, so I took a few more steps and shone my light around. I almost died right there when I saw the infant in the blanket and this man sitting on a log, leaning over the poor child. It looked as if he were rubbing the infant's forehead with his finger. I must have startled the man with my light because he turned to look at me. I could not see his face at first because he was wearing a hood. He suddenly stood up and faced me. I tried to scream, but nothing came out. When I went to turn and run, it felt as if my feet were glued to the ground. I just froze standing there.
I don't know why I pointed my flashlight upon his face, but when I did, I thought," she paused and sighed. She started to cry; tears rolled down her cheek.

"Now – now, sweetheart," Bob said, leaning over and placing his hand around her shoulder.

"Did you see the man's face?" William asked.

"Yes. But…" she replied, sniffling.

"Yes, but what?" David asked.

"He was awful looking and very tall. He had to stand well over six feet, and that face, that awful face of his," she cried.

"It was a stupid mask, Caroline – that's all it was," Bob said, reassuring her.

"How do you know that, Bob?" William snapped.

Bob took off his glasses and squinted at the detective. "It had to be. No one looks like that."

"Go on, Caroline, what about his face?" David asked.

"It was like looking at death. The man looked dead. His face was unusually white. That's all I can remember. It happened so quickly. I was scared. I ran as fast as I possibly could. I just wanted to get away from him."

"Do you think he was wearing a mask?" William asked, glancing over at Bob.

"It had to be a mask."

"It was a Halloween mask, for Christ's sake," Bob barked.

"Mr. Goldsmith, did you see the guy?" William shot back.

Bob sat back and folded his arms. "No."

"Alright then, let your wife tell us what she saw."

"OK – OK let's all just settle down. Will, let's take a walk," David said, getting up. "More water?" he asked, walking to the door. They both shook their heads.

After closing the door, William asked, "Do you believe her?"

"Yes," he replied. "Look, Will, you're not helping by pressing her like that. She'll never remember anything if you keep it up. She said she saw a guy wearing a mask, so let's find out what kind of mask."

102

"Mask my ass. Her husband has hammered that into her head," William snapped.

David grabbed a cup of water from the drinking fountain and splashed some on his face. He hoped William would just cool it so Caroline could remember.

When William walked back inside the room, he saw them hugging. To him, she looked as fragile as a little girl. *She's probably has been pampered to death her whole life by the lug,* he thought. He sat down when they let go of one another and waited for David. When he walked in and sat down, William continued the interview. "OK, Caroline, what kind of mask was it?"

"It was half flesh, half skeleton, I think."

"Did you see the opening for the eyes?" David asked.

Caroline closed her eyes thinking. She opened them and replied, "There were no eyes, just large dark holes where the eyes should have been."

"So there were no eye holes in the mask?" William asked.

"I guess not."

"So after you ran out, did he come after you?" David asked, leaning up and putting his elbows on the table.

"I don't know," she replied. "I just ran and ran - screaming my head off, hoping someone would hear me. I don't think he followed me, though. I didn't hear any footsteps coming from behind."

William sat back and sighed. The room went silent for a moment.

Then suddenly Caroline blurted out, "Wait... the man did say something before I ran out." She paused for a moment closing her eyes. William leaned up. He raised his brow at David.

Without opening her eyes, Caroline continued, "He was leaning over, then when he stood up, he said something. It's there, but I can't recall what he said."

David leaned back. He glanced over at William. With pen and paper ready, William looked like he was just about to place a bet on a horse. They sat there looking like restless stockbrokers, waiting for the numbers to roll up on the board.

"Children, he said something about children. Yes. It was when I tried to run but was too scared to move. The man stood up and looked at me. It was frightening the way he spoke. He said, "Children must be protected." After repeating what the man said, she opened her eyes.

"Anything else?" David asked.

"That was it I think," she replied, looking at the two of them sitting there.

Bob smiled. "That's good, Caroline. You're doing great."

"No, there's more. It's coming back to me, now. Children must have protectors. Then the man knelt back down, placed his finger on the infant's head again, and then he looked up at me. That's when I shone my light upon his face. He said something like - I wish I could have saved them like I should have in iron something – iron beck, iron brook."

David's face went white. He could not believe what she just said. Her mind was trying to untangle it, and he did not want to hear. William sucked in a ton of air feeling tiny ripples shooting up his neck. Without realizing what he was doing, William drove his pen into the paper. *You're not going to say it,* his thoughts screamed.

"No, that wasn't it," Caroline, said. "It sounded like Ironbark. Yes, that's it. He said Ironbark, whatever that means."

"What the hell is Ironbark?" Bob asked.

David glanced over at him; dazed.

William felt his heart pounding as his thoughts raced right over a cliff. *This can't be happening. I just read the Ironbark case. I must be in the Twilight Zone.* Bob could see their faces go from pale to stone white. "You two look as if you know what he was saying," he asked.

William looked at him shaking his head. David quickly stood up. "I think that's all we need for now. Leave us your number so we can reach you if we need to talk some more."

"I'll be in Ohio. I'll leave you my sister's address and phone number. You can reach me there if that's alright with you," Caroline replied, clutching her purse.

Bob quickly glanced over at her. "What in blazes are you talking about!? We're not going to your sisters, we're going home."

Caroline beaded her eyes on him. "You might be going home, but I'm not going back there tonight! I'm not going home until they catch this bastard!" she replied, standing up and locking her eyes on the detectives.

"I'll be at my sister's place. Here's her phone number and address."

David saw them out and then walked back into their office. He stood in the doorway watching William pacing back and forth in front of the whiteboard. He walked in and sat down. He could tell that William was rattled.

"What the hell is going on?" William asked, stopping and looking at the photos.

David said nothing. All he wanted to do was, think. William turned and looked at him sitting out there in the abyss of space. He walked over and poured himself a cup of coffee. "Want one?" he asked.

"Yeah, I might, as well. Make it strong; it's going to be a long night," David replied, sitting back in his chair and staring at the whiteboard. His mind was like a blank screen, the screen you see on your TV at the end of the

night when the TV guy pulls the plug and goes home.
William walked over and handed David his cup. David's
eyes never blinked. *Unusual*, he thought, sitting down
"This isn't the time to be playing chess in your head," he
said, trying to snap him out of his thoughts.

David glanced over and smiled. "I think we have a
copycat killer. It has to be someone who knows about the
murders that took place up in Ironbark at the turn of the
century."

"You think?"

"Yeah, or maybe it's the guy's great grandkid doing
it."

He watched David's eyes - none of his remarks
were catching fire. He seemed to be out there past Pluto.
"Alright then, what's your thoughts?" he asked.

David turned in his chair. William looked like the
runt on the baseball team who wanted to get out there and
play.

"You read the case?"

"Yes."

"The entire report?"

"Yes," William replied again, picking up his
briefcase and tossing the file on David's desk.

"He isn't the killer," David calmly said.

William's expression went limp. "What the hell do
you call someone who strangles a man and then hoists him
up in a tree thirty feet in the air?" he shouted.
David rubbed his face; pulling the skin back tight. "That's
not what I meant, Will. Snowman didn't kill the children.
Tennis Shoe did."

"So you're saying that you don't think they were
working together, or perhaps, something went bad between
them? Maybe Tennis Shoe wanted the kid to himself and
Snowman whacked him for it?"

David tossed that over and shrugged. "Then why
didn't Snowman kill the child? And what about Snowman

106

carrying the other child on the tracks and putting him down when he spotted Carter? Does that make any sense to you?"

William sat there confused. He had it nailed that those bastards were working together, and now David was taking the eggs and scrambling them all up.

"Let's take a look at the Ironbark case. How many children were killed?" David asked.

"Four, I think," William replied.

"Tell me the report on Teddy Cotton."

William's throat went tight. It had all the hallmarks of what was happening now.

"Two people spotted a man walking toward town with a bundle in his arms, and when he heard the horse team from behind him, he dropped the bundle and took off into the woods."

"Anything else grip you about Mrs. Yammer's statement?"

William could see where David was heading. Hell, even a blind horse could follow this line of questioning. "Yes, in the woman's statement she said that the guy knelt down and put the bundle on the ground then took off like a scared animal."

"And?" David pushed, rubbing his finger back and forth over his chin.

"He jumped a six foot embankment in a single bound and was gone before they could get down from the buggy."

"If I recall, that sounds about right," David replied, standing up and leaning over the table. William saw the look in his eyes, and he wasn't going to buy into it. "You've got to be kidding me! You don't think for one minute," he started to say, seeing David's facial expression go slack - no smile, no gleam in his eyes - just that dead, straight stare. William crossed his arms and leaned back.

"Alright then - we'll stake out all the old folk's homes. Our suspect has to be in one of them. Don't think he'll put up too much of a fight, though. We'll probably find him heavily sedated and receiving lots of oxygen - after all the running around he's been doing the last few nights."

"No. He won't be there," David interrupted. "But, I think I hit the nail on the head when I said copycat killer. However, I could rephrase that," he continued, rounding his desk and walking over to the whiteboard. "How about, copycat protector?" he said, turning around.

William's brain switched on. That thought was intriguing.

"Caroline stated that Snowman said he wished he would have saved all of them in Ironbark. Maybe she didn't hear him right. He could have said, *Just like they should have in Ironbark,*" as if he was talking about his great-grandfather or someone else he knew. And... I'd even bet my pension that our man knows the whole story because no one in this day and age would have any clue that Ironbark ever existed at the turn of the century. It faded away sometime after those murders. Are you with me on that?"

William nodded.

"Alright, we should go on the presumption that Tennis Shoe is the killer. Now that he's dead there should be no more killings."

William nodded again. "Let's hope."

"If I'm right, the killings will stop. And if that's true, we'll never catch Snowman. He'll just fade into the background until someone tries to harm another child." William pondered that. It sounded right. Snowman wasn't stupid.

"So, what's our plan?"

"We let him walk."

108

"What? But he killed a man! Captain Clark and the mayor aren't going to let him go. The press would be all over them like flies on shit!"

"That's not what I'm proposing. We'll tell Captain Clark everything he wants to hear, but we won't be going after Snowman," David replied.

"No?"

"Well, not yet anyway."

"Then when?"

David sat down, folded his hands on his desk and smiled. Here we go, William thought, seeing David's brain spinning a hundred miles an hour through those scheming little eyes of his.

"We need to find someone who's still alive that lived in or near Ironbark."

"You can't be..." William's voice trailed off.

"I'm serious! Snowman must be a relative. He has to be. I'll even bet if we find someone still alive from there, we'll find Snowman."

William's face showed uncertainty.

"It's either that, or we spend the rest of our careers on a witch hunt to find him."

"How about we bait him with a hoax murder of another child," William said, raising his brow.

"You must be kidding. You'd really want to try and bait this man? I wouldn't touch that with a fifty-foot pole, Will. We'd end up thirty feet up a tree ourselves. This man is not stupid, and from what we've seen and heard so far, I wouldn't want this guy pissed off at me. He has to have some kind of specialized background and training – Army Ranger, Navy Seals, Delta Force. Someone like that would be skilled enough to strangle someone and hoist them up in a tree. That killing looked to be right out of a military manual. You know; how to slowly torture your enemy into talking."

A chill went up William's back as he recalled Carter's comments on what he thought of the man. 'I wish he was in our unit in Nam.' *Bait him! How stupid, was that?*' he thought.

"So, what's our game plan?" he asked again.

"Simple, we do what you said. We stake out all the nursing homes, hospitals, retirement villages - until we find someone who lived up there."

"And what if we come up with a blank?"

"We'll start the witch hunt," David replied, grinning.

"What about Clark?"

David pondered that while playing with his short little cruel hanging down from his forehead. *His thinking cap is on*, William mused.

"OK, tomorrow we'll walk into the captain's office with Kim and Terry, and let them fill him in," David said.

"Then we tell him that we're on the trail of Snowman," William added.

"Yeah, we'll then tell him that we think he's running the tracks, and we're setting up a stakeout." David added.

"If you say that just like you said it now, David, the Captain just might go along," William replied, nodding.

Chapter 9

The week that followed was frantic. The press camped out on the steps of the mayor's office waiting for news of the latest killing in Hyde Park and the safe return of little Beth Matter to her parents. The FBI then stuck their nose in to see if they could polish up their name brighter than a ship's bell by taking over a case that was all but solved. With that - Captain Clark was now feeling the heat on both sides. It all started when Terry and Kim came into the precinct with their autopsy report on Tennis Shoe, and the evidence obtained at the scene.

Jack Straw, head honcho of the New York FBI division sat waiting outside Clark's office with Terry and Kim when Clark, David, and William walked out of the investigation department down the hall. William elbowed David when he saw the agent sitting there looking as smug as a wino in an alley with his favorite bottle of Gin. Clark strolled past with a nod to the agent and then smiled at Kim. "Come on in, we got a lot to go over."

The group filed in and sat down in the small, plush office. Clark closed the blinds for privacy. The first thing he did was to welcome Jack and state the reason he was there. Afterward, he got right down to business.

"So, why don't we start with the findings," he said, looking at Terry.

"Certainly, Captain," Terry replied, leaning back. As the group sat there, Terry went over the results of what they found at the crime scene. "When we took Tennis Shoe down, we discovered his own knife stuck in his back," Terry said and then paused, pulling a knife out of the evidence bag and setting it on Clark's desk. "We believe that Tennis Shoe was surprised from behind and a struggle occurred. Snowman somehow got the knife from him. He then wrapped a three-strand, nylon rope around his neck and hoisted him up into the tree. We think he was probably still alive at that point. The knife, even though it cut his vitals inside, held everything together. If Snowman had pulled it out, Tennis Shoe probably would have bled out as he was being hoisted up into that tree. My guess is Snowman left the knife in to make sure he'd stay alive long enough to feel his own neck snap. I suspect he died soon afterward."

Clark leaned back and looked at the pair. He couldn't imagine a death so cruel.
"You got a name on this guy?" he asked.

Kim leaned up and shot a glance over at Jack Straw sitting smartly in the high backed, leather sofa with one knee over the other. His pen was resting on his pad, waiting to take notes. She thought he looked like Paul Newman. He was a Yale graduate and held a Master's Degree in Criminal Law, but she didn't like him. He was shrewd and arrogant to the core. She took her eyes off Jack and let them in on the identity of Tennis Shoe.
"The finger prints taken matched a lowlife named Kevin Downer," she said. "He had a rap sheet as long as your arm. He's been in and out of jail most of his life; drugs, petty theft, and armed robbery. The knife was used in both crimes."

Clark stretched out his arms and pulled his hair back. "What about Snowman? Where does he fit into this?" he asked.

"Snowman, you got a name on him?" Jack asked, slipping his shiny, gold pen into his top pocket.

"No, not yet," David replied, looking over at him. "We believe Snowman and Downer were working together and somehow it all went south. We think Downer took the child for himself and Snowman whacked him for it."

"Can I read the report?" Jack asked.

William clutched the case in his hands. That was the last thing they wanted. Clark nodded for William to hand the case file over. Jack took it, smiled, and then flipped it open.

The room fell to small talk as everyone waited for Jack to catch up. Jack combed through the report then flipped to the last page, and read the detectives investigation notes slowly. He had to give the detectives an 'A' for spelling and punctuation, but he was getting a different picture on Snowman.

Years of investigating the criminally insane leaned him in the opposite direction. Snowman, whose clothing description and the fact that he wore a mask, was a sign of an insane mind wanting to feel like a warrior. He was not the killer – no, Snowman was, in fact, the hunter and he was hunting Downer. Jack knew deep down inside that detective Bradshaw and Hall were covering something up. *Why - what could they possibly know?*
Jack handed the report back to William; keeping his poker face. He thought about the next card he should toss onto the table. "Caroline's statement was pretty vague. What do you make of what the suspect said to her?"

"Childlike and uneducated," Kim replied. She did her lessons in profiling too, and figured she'd shoot that across to him. Jack nodded as all eyes fell on the two detectives.

"Look, the woman was out of it," David said turning in his chair. "When we questioned her about that, she said Snowman said something about children needing protectors, then he went on to say something about iron, iron beck, iron bay, and then she came up with Ironbark."

"What the hell is that?" Jack asked, interrupting.

"We don't know," William replied. "It could be a thing, or a place. We checked on it being a place, but could not locate it in the state of New York. However, since you guys are planted like weeds all over the country, how about tossing it out there and seeing what your men can come up with."

Jack's eyes narrowed on the detective. *A real smart ass*, he thought.

"I plan to, Detective. We'll run the name and see if anything comes up. I'd like to see the body before you toss it into a coffin, that's if you don't mind?" he asked, looking at Terry.

"Sure, come around this afternoon."

Jack stood up. Clark stood up with him and walked Jack to the door. "You taking the case?" he asked, opening it.

"Nope, we'll hang back for now. See you two this afternoon," he replied, walking out.

They waited until he left, and Clark sat back down. "Smart one, Detective Hall," he said, looking at him.

"Come on, Captain. You wouldn't have let that one slip by."

"Sometimes you have to. You know Straw won't let that slip by – he'll be on you two like flies on shit from here on out until we solve this. How soon do you think that will that be?"

William looked at David. David knew that masked gaze with no facial expression. He saw it enough times when they interrogated suspects.

"Well, we think this guy is running the tracks. Every hit was within a stone's throw away. Thought we'd plant some undercover winos and bums along the tracks and see if we can discover any hidey holes he might be holed up in. William and I will be visiting Kevin Downer's place and checking out all his acquaintances."

"And?" Clark asked.

There was a long pause on the Captain's '*And.*' He said it enough when digging for details and wanting more information. It was one word David hated hearing from him. It made him feel like a detective in diapers. He smiled back at Clark.

"And, we'll stay tight to Jack's coattail and see if the FBI can come up with anything on Ironbark if it's a thing, or a place - at all."

"Good," Clark replied, turning his attention on the Crime Lab.

"Great work, you two. Make sure you place enough doughnuts out for Jack when he arrives."

Kim smiled. She knew the Captain would have loved to have pitched William's line to Jack himself.

Chapter 10

Snowman was just out of sight when it all went down in the park that night. Kevin Downer had finally paid the piper for his murdering ways. Mr. Bones, dubbed, 'Snowman,' by New York's finest, sat high up in the trees waiting for the police to arrive.

When the woman gained her footing and screamed down the path leading back into the park, Mr. Bones covered the child. He stood up, turned on a dime, and slipped into the thick underbrush near the trees on the trackside of the pond. There, he made his way back up the incline to the fencing. He looked up at the top of the fence and saw the tree limb he used to climb over and rescue the child.

Mr. Bones jumped up, caught the branch, and climbed up. From there, he stood on the branch and then jumped up to a higher limb; continuing upward into the tree. When he reached the level where the bastard he just hung and was now dangling, he stopped and glared at him. His face was blue, his tongue was hanging out, and his eyes were never more to be seen.

He looked down *I better climb higher,* he thought. Nearing the top, deep within the tree's canopy, he sat on a branch next to the thick trunk and caught sight of the woman running through the park screaming. He wasn't going to leave the infant unattended until they came.

He looked out at all the houses nestled along the street on the other side of the park. They all sat as quiet as empty churches in the night. Except for the woman frantically screaming, there wasn't a sound to be heard.

Porch light after porch light went on when the people inside heard the desperate cry for help. He cocked his head when he heard another terrorizing scream coming out from the last house on the corner. A woman and a man came running out. The woman was screaming that her child was gone.

"Don't cha worry none. Your little one is safe with me," he whispered, looking down at the child lying there, all bundled up.

The pair stopped in the middle of the road when they saw Mrs. Goldsmith running through the park toward the street. They thought Mrs. Goldsmith's screams were about their child. They ran toward her in the street. The woman missing the child grabbed her and spun her around. Mrs. Goldsmith tried to speak, but she was completely frantic. She just stood there screaming as she pointed over to the grove of trees and bushes then lifted her hands into the air and yelled out, "She's over there with a mad man!" The woman missing the child looked like she fainted when she heard the awful news. Her body just crumbled underneath her, and she hit the pavement. Then, Mrs. Goldsmith went down with her. People came running from every direction like a swarm of bees to aid the women now sprawled out in the street.

Mr. Bones leaned against the tree trunk watching the people carry them both inside one of the houses. He looked down again when he heard the infant cooing, she was kicking her legs and moving her arms.

"Stay still little one, they'll be here soon. They always come," he whispered, looking out from the cover of the canopy and scanning for the lights.

He rested his head against the trunk and looked up at the starlit night. A full moon hung just over the horizon. He cocked his head and looked at it intently. He knew the moon would be making its full appearance around midnight, and then start it's slow decent around 2:00 a.m. Like a mother and child, he knew the moon's positions and cycles throughout the year. From season to season, he had followed it and could tell where it would be, or if it wasn't coming that night. It was all he had to guide him and aid him in his timing. It never failed him, and its position in the night sky tonight, told him his time was coming to get back. His thoughts faded backward. He began remembering all the times he sat watching the moon. He felt at first that the thing was watching him, and then he realized that it was watching over him. It became his keeper, his time watcher. From full moon to half moon, to quarter moon, and then to complete darkness on the nights it wouldn't come out, he used it like his father's silver pocket watch. His timing had to be accurate when he searched, attacked, slipped away, and escaped into the night.

He came out of his thoughts when he heard the wailing sounds cut through the night like a knife through a melon on a hot summer's day. He looked out through the branches and saw the flashing lights.

"They're here, little one," he whispered down to the infant. The wailing sound got louder and louder, and then he saw the people from the houses coming out onto the street to meet the police. One after another, patrol units pulled up, and the people gathered around. Officers got out and stood listening to their cries for help. He saw the people pointing in his direction. The officers ushered the folks back to their homes, got back into their cars, and slowly rolled into the park. He knew it was time to go.

He stood up, raised his arms over his head, and just dropped through the canopy. His long slender frame descended downward through the branches like a monkey. As he fell through the branches, he kept his gaze on the flora below - and then spotted a nice thick limb to grab onto. His timing had to be just right. His lower body shot past the limb in a split second. With his arm already extended above his head, he reached out for it. His arm made contact with the thick limb. He felt it slide quickly toward his glove. He then grasped the limb with his long fingers and hung there. His glove slipped, and he almost let go. He quickly reached up with the other hand took hold of the branch. Wood chips from the bark splintered past him as his hands circled the limb and locked together. He held on tightly dangling there. With one strong pull upward, he climbed onto the branch.

He stood there for a second frantically looking down and searching for another limb to jump to. Just below him and to the right, he spotted a large limb. He jumped toward it, grabbed on, and pulled himself up. He quickly checked the distance of the cars rolling into the park. The lights were coming nearer to the grove of trees. He had to work fast. With arms stretched out at his side, he walked along the big limb until he could jump to another branch that would take him around to the backside of the tree for his escape.

As he made his way around, he looked down to see the limb that brought him across from the tracks. It was a lengthy limb - that arched clear across the fence line. He stepped off when he spotted it right below him and then dropped onto it like a feather landing on a pond. He walked the short distance, dropped to the ground and stood there. The tracks were dark and empty in both directions. He darted across and started down the slope until his feet were parallel with the top portion of the fence on the other side. He leaped high into the air over the fence and landed on his feet in the large playing field at the back of the school. *I must get back before they know I'm gone,* he thought, running like a deer.

With his long poncho streaming out on the wind, he ran across Donny Brook high school's practice field toward the back of the building. He passed the tennis courts and headed along the side of the building on Stanley Street where the tall bushes obscured the engineering room's heavy metal door. Slipping inside the tall bushes, he walked up the small path, opened the door and stepped inside. Once the door closed, he opened the security key pad, punched in the security code, and walked past the large boiler and electrical boxes toward the hallway.

He stood there in the dark looking up at the clock. It was 3:00 a.m. The doors to the school would not open until 7:00 a.m. He walked down the hallway toward the janitor's locker room. There were eight janitors in all - each had his or her own locker. The room was divided, men on one side - women on the other.

Mr. Bones opened the main door, stepped in, walked to the men's side and entered. He walked over to the corner, stripped off his clothing and placed them in a box he had left on the bench.

He picked up the box, stood up on the bench, and opened the false ceiling overhead. After placing his box on a large metal beam, he lowered the ceiling back into place. Back in the hallway, his thoughts drifted over finally catching and killing the murdering thug. He only wished he could have saved them all. It made him sad.

He wondered about Millie. *She must have heard the news. Would she be happy, as well?*

She was always worrying about him - always asking him what he was doing. They had been together all their lives, and she was happy that he finally found a new place to stay that was near children. Millie lived in an old folk's home just less than a mile away from him.

He walked down the hallway toward the science room and entered. He loved it here as the science teacher's assistant. Mr. Bloom was a good man. He loved children too. Mr. Bones looked up at the clock, then out the window, and knew the sun would be coming up soon. He walked to the front of the room and took his position in the corner.

Chapter 11

Jack Straw kept his promise as he entered Terry and Kim's office, which sat just off the cold room and slabs. He never liked walking into the lab always smelling of medicine and disinfectant. It was like a freezer down there; keeping the bodies stabilized so they could work on them. He stood there observing the white coats ambling around the tables. They appeared to be as cold as the stiffs on the metal slabs. They showed no emotion and went about their business as if they worked in a car garage as grease monkeys; just lifting hoods and diagnosing what the problem was.

It won't start, dirty carburetor, dead battery, electrical problems, but it wasn't that simple down here. This was a human dissecting station. The vehicles that were brought in here had been shot, stabbed, had their skulls crushed in, or worse - were found dismembered. The diagnostics of the person were pretty much known before they were brought in. The white coat's job was to gather all the facts and subtract the who, what, where, why, how, and when - to come to the final analysis - *who was the killer?*

While standing just outside the door, Jack spotted Terry and Kim walking around a table with New York's Chief Examiner, Doctor Su Lin - who was working on a dead young female. The girl looked as if the entire defensive line of the New York Giants had crushed her. Before he made his entrance, he glanced over at the far slab along the wall. Underneath the white sheet were two large feet sticking out. He could not read the toe tag from that distance, but suspected it was his man.

"Pssst..." a young intern whispered to Kim, nodding his head toward the door.

"Hello, Agent Straw, please come in," she said, turning and lifting her surgical mask. "We left him out just in case you kept your promise."

"Thanks. I won't keep you long," he replied, looking past her at the dead female on the slab. "Just wanted to view the body and ask a few more questions."

Kim caught his eyes staring at the young female. "She was found inside a dumpster on Twenty Fifth and Main. We think she's one of the Salvation Gang ladies. My guess is she probably got caught double dipping on the price of her wares."

"Such a high price to pay," Jack replied.

"Here, slip this on and cover your face with these," she said, handing him a mask and a pair of gloves.

"No thanks, I won't be examining him that close. I just need the details."

"You're not one of those agents that get a little white around the gills when looking at dead bodies, are you?" she teasingly replied.

"Yes, ma'am. Now let's get on with it."

Terry looked over, nodded at Jack, and then continued his tape recording analysis of the battered female. Jack smiled, turned, and focused his attention back on Kim.

"OK, let's take a peek here, shall we?" she said. "I think you'll find some unusual things on his body," she continued, sliding the white sheet off.

Jack stood there looking down at the dead, naked man. He noticed a small cut just over his upper ribs and some bruising around the heart area. His skin was a bluish white except where the rope had dug in around his neck; it was deep purple.

"Look here," Kim said, leaning over and pulling the body up. "That wound was made by his knife. It went right through his upper back here and came out there."

"What about the three small bruises around his heart?"

"Those were made with fingers. Probably when our boy picked him up and lifted him off the ground," she replied, demonstrating the grip by taking her fingers and putting them over the marks on Kevin's chest.

Jack scratched his head. "You'd have to be pretty damn strong to pull a man up like that with only one hand."

"Yes, especially when you're defending yourself from a knife coming at you."

"You sure it went down that way? The struggle, I mean?"

"By the marks left there, it wasn't hard to decipher. Snowman caught him off guard and grabbed him from behind. You could see that Kevin's shoe print was turned, and Snowman must have seen the knife coming around. He must have grabbed him with one hand, and then blocked the knife coming at him with the other. At that point, we lose Kevin's print all together. That's where we believe that Kevin is no longer standing on the ground – he's dangling in midair. Somehow, Snowman gets a hold of Kevin's knife and drives it into his back with such force that the tip breaks through the front. We think, after Snowman stabbed Kevin, Kevin was probably still alive. Seeing that he was - Snowman left the knife in him and started hoisting Kevin up into the trees - then tied off the rope."

Jack walked around the body trying to picture the struggle. "It's hard to imagine the man Corporal Carter described, being able to do that. I think his statement read that the man was so thin that his clothes hung on him like they were hanging on a clothes hanger."

"Drugs maybe," Kim replied.

"Yeah, someone on PCP might be able to do that, but he wouldn't be able to sneak up on someone like that."

Kim looked at him. He was certainly at the top of his game. *He probably could beat you in a game of Scrabble while watching TV at the same time,* she thought.

"Was there any fragile evidence found?" he asked, looking at the large wound around the neck area.

She understood his question completely. Were there any small items or particles found on the body. "Nothing, he's as clean as a whistle."

"Can't be," he questioned.

"Sorry, Agent Straw, we went over him with a fine toothed comb. We even went over his clothing twice and found nothing. The way I see it is either Snowman is just too damn smart – or he never thought about the protection he was affording himself by wearing all the clothing he had on. His gloves, long poncho, the mask and the hood have certainly saved him thus far. We did not discover any trace evidence such as hair, saliva, or sweat. We know he wasn't cut during the attack either because all the blood we found was Kevin's."

"Too clean," Jack mumbled underneath his breath. He turned and looked at her. "What about the rope?"

"There's nothing unusual about the rope. It's just your average three strand, nylon rope."

"Color," he asked.

"Blue. Here, take a look," she replied, turning around and pulling it out.

"Nothing found in the fibers?" he asked.

"Yes, we found some items; fish guts, motor oil, and salt."

"Well, it's possible that we have someone who owns a boat, maybe?"

"That's possible. However, we have about a million of them all along the coastline," she quipped. "And, a million fishing outlets too," she continued.

He looked at her. The lines at the side of his mouth turned up. She smiled back.

"He could be on one, you know," he shot back.

"Or, it was one of Kevin's instruments to access the houses," she volleyed back.

He raised one eyebrow looking at her.

He sure is handsome, but what an idiot, she thought.

No question about it, she's easy to use, he thought - *like playing a violin with nothing but sweet music coming out of it.*

"Well, if it was Kevin's rope then I suspect that you're holding something back. Kevin should have those same trace elements on his person, don't you think?"

"Hmm… never thought of that," she replied, keeping the verbal game going.

"Then it wasn't Kevin's?"

"It could have been, Agent Straw."

Jack stepped back. He liked what he saw. Not only smart, but pretty too. Slim and shapely, just the way he liked them.

He slowly circled Kevin's body one more time. His mind turned over in several directions looking down at it. He had lots of questions and no answers. He looked up at Kim. She had a brain and she was skilled at using it. He figured all he needed was a scent trail, and he hoped that she would provide it. "A million boats you say?"

"Yep, maybe more," she replied, waiting for his next volley.

"You have to start somewhere, and the marinas might be the first place to look. Other than that, the rope gives us a back up down the road," he said.

"What do you mean?" she asked confused.

Even a good brain can't see the future, he thought. "Snowman wasn't thinking when he used it. It has to be all over his clothing."

She smiled trying to hide her stupidity. *Jack is thinking miles ahead of me.* The fish guts, motor oil, and salt would nail him to the scene.

"You got to catch him first," she said.

"We'll nail him sooner or later."

"Does that mean you're taking over the case? If you are, you'll have to inform Doctor Su Lin."

"We're going sit back for now, but there is just one more favor I need to ask."
"Shoot."

"Mrs. Goldsmith, I'd like her sister's address in Ohio."

Kim smiled. She had something he wanted after all. "Cost you a dinner," she replied and then panicked. "I mean..." she started to say.

"You meant just that," he interrupted. "How about tonight around eight at Pier Thirty Nine? I hear they serve a fine sailfish steak with a Greek tossed salad," he continued, smiling.

She sighed looking over at Terry. She knew that she was playing with fire and she could already feel the heat. "Sure," she replied, turning back and looking at him with an air of showmanship.

"Good, see you then."

The evening went well with Jack. It was a lot of small talk and some intrigue as each of them told the other about the cases they had worked. After dinner, she gave him the address and he left. *Thank God, he didn't try to kiss me,* she thought, knowing he wanted to conduct some 'under- the- cover' work with her. She wasn't going to entertain Jack in that fashion; there was someone else she

126

was interested in. She called him the very next day with some interesting news.

"Good morning, Kim," David greeted her.

"Morning, Detective. I'm calling in regard to Agent Straw."

"What-cha got on the bum?"

"Well, he came over and viewed Kevin Downer's body. I then swindled a dinner out of him when he asked me for Mrs. Goldsmith sister's address. I thought I could do some undercover work of my own and see what he was planning to do on this case."

There was a long pause.

"Not that kind of undercover work, Detective, if that's what you're thinking," she replied to the long pause.

"I see. So what did he have to say or will it cost me a dinner to find out, too?"

Kim pondered that. *Get a box, tie a piece of string to a stick, lift up one side and prop the box up. Then toss in some birdseed and wait for an unsuspecting bird to land inside - then pull the string. Bingo - I just caught Detective Bradshaw!*

"Dinner at my house around seven?" she replied, waiting for his answer.

David smiled. "Is this more undercover work?" There was a long pause on Kim's side. *Sure I want him, hell - every woman wants him*, she thought. "A bird in the hand is worth two in the bush. I'll see you at seven - don't be late," she quickly replied, and then hung up.

David looked over at William, rolled his eyes, and hung up the phone.

"Who was that?"

"It was Kim. She called to say she had dinner with Jack. She said that she had some information and wants to tell me over dinner at her house tonight."

William leaned back in his chair and smiled. "She's not a bad looking bird," he quipped.

David looked at him oddly. *Bird,* he thought. *Now I've heard it twice in less than a minute.*

"You know, I could save you the trouble of going over there tonight and finding out. Jack is going to sit back and let us clean up this mess," William said.

"He might, but I suspect his boss in Washington isn't going to let him sit back on this one, not after we just got done buring a few children."

"Even with Kevin Downer now lying down in the lab and being dissected?" William asked.

"Yep, you know Washington wants the bastard who killed him."

"You still think it's a copycat?"

David stood up, walked over to the whiteboard and looked at the bootprint.
"I think it is, and I want you to start looking for relatives," he said, turning around.

William leaned back in his chair and slowly ran his fingers through his hair. *This was madness,* he thought. *Even though the cases look similar, there is no way we're going to find anyone still alive who lived up in Ironbark.*
"OK, so how long do we look, one week – two weeks - a month, and then what?"

David walked over and sat back down pondering that. *How long should we keep looking?* He knew Snowman was not involved with the abductions or the murders. Snowman was hunting Kevin. How Snowman did it - he surmised that only the Good Lord knew that one. Good or bad, he wanted no part of it. He dropped his thoughts and looked over at William.

"Let's just start checking. I'll see Kim tonight and find out what Jack is up to."

"OK, boss, but I think we're wasting our time. I'll start with the senior citizen homes. Are you taking off?"

"Yeah, it could be a long night," he replied with a wink.

"Right, just watch your ass, I am sure she has large carving knives, and knows how to use them."

Chapter 12

David drove through the plush neighborhood of Pleasant Ridge, which looked like a miniature forest, with clean streets, manicured lawns and gardens, and lovely big houses - if you could call a twenty-room estate a house. He pulled into Kim's driveway and walked up to the door feeling a little foolish and apprehensive about having dinner with her. She was way out of his league. When she opened the door, the first thing he noticed was the elegant, red evening gown she was wearing and was thankful he decided on a suit coat instead of jeans.

"My, my - are we going to the Governor's ball or having dinner here?" he said, casting his eyes down her dress.

Kim smiled. *At least he's observant*, she thought. *However, he could have just said, "You look beautiful tonight." You'd certainly win more points by telling a woman she's beautiful rather than passing it off with a lame line like that.*

"I guess you approve. Please, come on in and make yourself at home. What's your drink?"

"Whatcha got?" he replied, walking in.

"I'm having a glass of red wine."

"I think I'll have Whiskey - that's if you have any?"

"That I do."

"I'll have that with Coke, on the rocks, please."

Kim nodded while escorting him into the front room. "Please, have a seat, I'll be right back."

"Tonight," she said from the kitchen, "I've prepared Spanish duckling, string beans, Caesar salad, French rolls, and for dessert - we're having German pudding."

"Maybe I'll switch my drink to a red wine too, if you don't mind," he yelled.

"I thought you would," she replied, walking out with two glasses of wine.

He smiled as she handed him his glass and took a seat next to him. "Your house is really lovely, very worldly too. You have things from all over the place."

"Thanks. I bought some of this stuff overseas," she replied, looking around the room. She turned and looked at him. It was the very first time they'd been alone in the five years they'd worked together. In that awkward moment, as they looked at each another, neither knew what to say next... His thoughts were drifting; *she's absolutely gorgeous.* Her thoughts spun; *I certainly could past up dinner and go straight for dessert.*

David seemed to untie his tongue first. "Tell me, what seems to be on Jack's mind these days?" he asked, lifting chin.

She let the question linger while looking into his eyes. *He's going to be all business tonight,* she thought. "Let's talk about that over dinner, it's ready."

He nodded, stood up as she got up, and followed her into the dining room. He took a seat at an elegant table for two; candles and all. He watched her light both candles, smile teasingly then stroll back into the kitchen. *No man could have sat there and looked at the paint on the walls,* he thought, eying her up. *What a knockout!* You'd never believe just by looking at her that she earned her living as a criminal forensic scientist, who worked down in the lab, dissecting dead people.

After bringing each dish out, she sat down, folded her hands, and closed her eyes. He quickly realized she was going to say grace. He folded his hands and listened. With that over, she opened her eyes and smiled at him.

"You ever had Spanish duckling before?"

"No. But I must admit I'm in awe of your abilities. I knew you were well educated in many subjects, but I never thought that culinary art was one of them."

She leaned up on the table and looked at him with a childlike smile. "My maid is from Greece, she's the cook around here. She doesn't mind teaching me how to cook after cleaning a house - that actually doesn't need to be cleaned. I even make my own bed."

"I see," he replied, laughing.

They spent the next few minutes eating. The duckling was mouthwatering, and the French rolls were superb. Kim picked up her napkin, wiped her mouth and started talking about Agent Straw.

"I guess you took Jack's word that he was going to sit on the fence with this case."

"Kim, we've both dealt with him before. You know he only takes on the big cases, and this is a big case. His statement did throw me a bit, but I know his boss in Washington probably has a torch up his ass. Maybe he didn't want us to see the flames coming out of his ears."

She smiled. "Well, first off, the reason I had you over tonight was to inform you that you have a tag. He sits out front waiting for your vehicle to pull out. The other thing is, we have one small problem with this case, and I think Jack is way over his head."

"Why do you say that?" he curiously asked.

"Snowman, that's why. You must admit he has us all stumped. I have never seen anything like him before - have you? I mean, our dogs can't track him, and he finds Downer before we do. So who is he? Some kind of elite military man, or is it possible that superman is actually real?"

David sat back thinking. He remembered the night in the park; Kevin Downer hanging thirty feet up in the air with his own knife stuck in his back. *Only a superman could do that,* he thought. *I'd even wager a bet there wasn't one trained military elite who could do that by themselves, no matter how strong they were.* Kevin was still alive when he hoisted him up in the tree. The knife made sure of that. If he wanted to kill Kevin quicker, he would have pulled it out so he'd bleed out like a stuck pig. "I'll have to confess, I've never seen anything like it before either. The other problem I have is – I don't think he's on drugs. He's too precise. This guy thinks like a marine sniper, and they only take the cream of the crop in that field."

He watched her spinning that thought around as she buttered her roll, sampled the gravy, and then cut another slice of her duckling.

"You have any angles?" she asked, taking bite.

"Yes I do, but I need you to promise that you'll keep this information between us."

"Sure – shoot."

"My grandfather worked a case up in Ironbark, New York - back in Nineteen Hundred and Ten."

Kim put her utensils down and stared at him; the name of the town took her by surprise. "Does the captain know this?"

"No, only William knows. He thinks I've lost my mind, but listen to this. The bootprint we found matches the bootprint in that old case. Now I'm not saying it's the same person – how could that be? He'd certainly be well over a hundred years old by now. However, if you look at that case and compare it to this one, there are so many similarities - it's unbelievable."

"Were there children involved in that case?"

"Four children murdered over a two month span, and the suspects were killed just like Kevin Downer, but there deaths were much worse. That guy seemed to have enjoyed killing them bastards, just like this one. I think Snowman has done this before."

"What? Are you telling me that you think Snowman goes after murderers?"

"Yes. I think he goes after those who hurt or murder children. That's just my hunch."

"Let's finish our dinner and then go and sit in the front room, OK?" she replied, gathering her thoughts. *Could this be true?* She figured that once they sat down, David was going to tell her that he believed it was a copycat killing. *But how? Who ever heard of Ironbark? No one alive today – that's who.*

After their meal, Kim poured two more glasses of wine and joined David in the front room. "So, tell me your thoughts," she said, setting her drink down and moving closer to him.

He noticed her posture - she was more laidback and relaxed now. "I have this gut feeling that he's a relative or someone who had heard stories about those crimes up in Ironbark. Maybe he likes the idea of helping children. That might seem strange, but that's what I think."

"That's a possibility," she replied, sliding closer to him.

David took a sip of his wine watching her getting closer. He swallowed and replied, "The other thing that has me stumped is the bootprints. They match to a tee. And, if that doesn't lift the hairs on your neck - in both cases the guy runs and hurdles something no human can jump. I mean really, a six foot embankment... an eight foot fence?"

Kim nodded. She picked up her drink, drank it down, set the glass on the table, and then slowly crossed her legs. David sat there watching her. He started feeling warm around the collar. *She certainly has all the right moves.*

"I would love to read that case in Ironbark. I might even find something on the computer - maybe do a little research, and see what I can come up with," she replied, resting her hand behind him on the sofa.

David set his glass down and leaned back. "I'll give you the file tomorrow, but I must warn you – it's not your average murder case. Some of it is gruesome."

Kim looked into his eyes. She slowly reached over, took hold of that sexy curl of his between her fingers, and then started twirling it. "I'm sure I'll find it quite interesting, David. However, I don't think you and I will be solving this case tonight. So…" her voice softly trailed off. She let go of his curl and then ran her finger over his lips. "Would you like to see my gun collection? I'm sure you'll find it stimulating, and I'm quite certain that it will take your mind off things for awhile."

David thought his heart stopped beating. *This isn't a suggestion or come on line - she's asking me to go to bed with her.* Before he could answer, Kim stood up, reached down and took his hand. After he stood up, she slowly waltzed him up the stairs. She was right on both accounts; her gun collection was the finest collection he'd ever seen, and he completely forgot all about the murder cases they were discussing.

Two weeks had passed without another murder and no sign of Snowman. Because of that, David felt his hunch was right. Snowman would not strike unless a child was injured, or worse. William, on the other hand, had checked twenty nursing homes without any luck.

Kim too, was now putting in a lot of time helping with the case, which meant she was seeing a lot of David. Captain Clark felt satisfied having surveillance teams out there and was giving the mayor daily reports of their findings. The heat was settling down.

Over the next two weeks, William noticed the closeness between David and Kim. They may have thought that no one could see it, but he could tell that something was going on between them. Every time she stepped into their cubical, or he went to visit her down in the lab, it was blatantly obvious to him - they were seeing one another.

That morning was no different as she walked in. There was a soft, underlining cooing in her voice. "Good morning, gentlemen. Any luck, yet?" she asked, looking at David and smiling.

William saw the smile and the gleam in her eyes when David stood up and greeted her.

"Morning, Kim. Right now, it's the same old, same old. We've got nothing so far. How about you, have you picked up anything yet?"

"Maybe," she replied, brushing past him and lightly touching his hand.

William smiled. His hunch was right.

"Well, I've been on the computer for the last three days looking up cases where super human strength was used to save a person's life. There was a man in Germany who lifted the back end of a car off his son after the jack had slipped out. Then, there was a woman in Canada who lifted a fully loaded refrigerator off her husband after their house exploded from a gas leak. The weirdest one was a woman in Australia. She killed a large kangaroo with her bare hands after it attacked her child. Kangaroos, you know, can be over six feet tall, and they have a kick that could knock down a man."

"So, you're saying that Snowman's adrenalin kicked in when he grabbed Downer - slammed the knife into his back and then hoisted him up into that tree?" William asked. "And while we're on the subject," he added. "What about jumping an eight foot fence with barbed wire at the top?"

Good question, she thought, walking up to the whiteboard and staring at the bootprint. *It was the same print alright.* She turned and looked at William.

"I told David that only Superman could do that."

"Superman," William spewed, shaking his head.

"You got some time?" David asked, pulling up a chair for her to sit down.

"Sure."

"Have you heard from Agent Straw?" William asked her, dropping his thoughts.

"He stops in at the lab from time to time. However, I think he's working the Captain. He knows we have nothing so far," she replied.

"How about we start calling the last twelve nursing homes we have on our list?" David said.

"OK, that gives us four calls each," William replied, pushing a phone across the desk for Kim.

They all sat there asking the nursing home staff the same question on each call they made. David and William finished their calls then sat back and watched Kim dial her last number. It was to the Sunny Village Nursing home on Fourth Street and Sterling, located on the south side of the city.

"Sunny Village Nursing home, this is Pam, how can I help you?" the staff member said.

"Good morning, Pam. I'm Kim O'Malley - criminal lab technician for the state of New York. I am working on a case with the One Hundred and Tenth Precinct's Investigation Division. We need to know if anyone living at your facility was born, or lived in a town called Ironbark. It was located in upstate New York in the early 1900s."

"Well Kim, our policy doesn't allow us to give out such information about our residents to anyone over the phone. Is there some way I can verify your identity?"

"I understand, Pam. Please call the Precinct and asked them if a Kim O'Malley is down in the Investigation Division right now." Kim replied, raising a brow to her comrades.

"OK, can you hold for a minute, please? I'll call on the other phone."

"Sure." Kim replied, rolling her eyes as she waited. A moment later, Pam hung up the other phone and came back on the line.

"OK, Kim, I called, and they verified that you are there. If you can hold for a second longer, I'll check the files."

"Thank you," Kim replied. She waited a few more minutes before Pam came back on the line. "Kim, we do have a resident that listed her place of birth as Ironbark, New York. Her name is Mildred Thorn. We call her Millie. She's one hundred and six years old, and surprisingly, she's still all there if you know what I mean."

Kim's jaw hit the desk. Millie's name was all over that case file on the murders that took place in Ironbark. However, her last name was Thomson and not Thorn.

"Hello, are you still there?"

"Yes…" Kim replied, staring at David.

"What?" he mouthed.

She shook her head. "Do you have her maiden name?"

"Her last name was Thomson."

Kim looked at David and William. "We have someone," she mouthed.

"You said that she's all there, can I then assume that you mean Millie is responsive and knows who and where she is?"

David sat back looking at William. They both sighed hearing Kim say that name.

"The only thing wrong with Millie is that she's old. She keeps telling us that she'll live forever."

"What are your visiting hours?" Kim asked.

"Visiting hours is between nine in the morning until eight at night. Just so you know, Kim, Millie hasn't had a visitor since she's been here. However, and this may sound funny

- seeing that she still is smart as a whip - she tells us that she has an imaginary friend that she talks to."

Imaginary friend, Kim thought. *She must be awful lonely.* "Thank you, Pam, you're a gem," she replied and then hung up. "Can I have a glass of water, please?"

William got up and poured her a glass.

She drank the water and set the cup on the table. "They have a resident there, her name is Millie Thorn. Her maiden name is Thomson - she was born in Ironbark, New York.

"Doc Thomson's daughter," David whispered, looking up at William. William quickly sat down. "She can't be Doc Thomson's daughter, can she?"

"It has to be her, Will," David replied.

"OK," Kim said. They both turned and looked at her. "Now, think about this. The nursing home is on the south side, about four or five blocks from the park where Snowman hung Downer. She must have heard about it," she continued, looking into David's eyes. He looked back at her as if he just saw the Titanic resurface.

"David?"

"I'm still here. I'm just thinking."

"Well?"

He sighed, looking up at the whiteboard. "You might be right," he said, getting up. "Everything happened in this one location," he continued, pointing at the map. "The mother and son were found inside their house here. The boy was abducted from this house here. Then Snowman somehow gets the boy and takes him to the tracks here. Then there is Kevin. He's found here."

William and Kim looked at the small circle David made on the map. "If that doesn't blow your mind - Millie is living here. What are we looking at, a six block radius?" David said, turning around.

"Wait a minute," Kim replied, standing up and walking over. "There's one more thing."

"What's that?" William asked.

"It may be nothing, but when I asked Pam if Millie ever had visitors, she said that Millie hasn't received any visitors - just her imaginary friend."

They immediately locked eyes, as if reading each other's thoughts.

William stood up. It wasn't because he wanted to. His spine was tingling. "Now, you're freaking me out," he gasped

"Me too," Kim agreed. "So what now?"

David could see they were jumpy – so was he.

"Visiting hours are nine to eight. William and I will go see her tonight. I think it's time to sit down and meet Millie and see what she has to say."

"Don't forget, gentlemen," Kim said, "Jack has people watching you. You can bet they'll be following you tonight. I really don't think you want him, or any of his goons near Millie Thorn."

"I don't think Jack is that smart," William replied. "If he or any of his goons see us walking into a nursing home, they'll think we're visiting a friend or relative."

Kim nodded looking over at David.

"I'll call you when we come back," he said.

"Thanks, best of luck," she replied, strolling out of the room.

William looked up at David; he was still watching Kim walking out the door. When she was gone, David looked down at him. He smiled like a school boy - that just caught his best friend drooling over a female classmate.

"I see that look in your eyes," David ribbed.

William quickly glanced around the room. The coast was clear. "You two are seeing one another, aren't you?" he whispered.

David laughed reaching over picking up the piece of paper Kim had written the Sunny Village address on.

"You're not going to answer that question, are you?"

David placed the paper inside his top pocket, sat down and leaned back in his chair. "One day, I'm going to marry that woman."

"No…"

"Does that answer your question?"

William shook his head. David was more than seeing her - he was over the moon with her.

"You have a best man lined up?"

"Nope," he replied, laughing. "Let's get back to work. Tonight just might be our night."

William shook his head leaning back in his chair.

Chapter 13

David and William left the precinct at five thirty. Both men had only one thing on their mind, who was watching them. Was it Jack, or was it one of his goons? When they drove out of the parking lot, they spotted a car pulling off the curb on the other side of the street. It was Jack in his shiny, black unmarked car. He was alone.

"I think we'll just go with the flow of traffic and let the bum follow us. Once we drive into the Sunny Village nursing home, Jack might pull up and sit a spell and then think we're just visiting a relative," David said, glancing up into the rearview mirror.

William shrugged his shoulders. He could care less if Jack was following them. However, he wouldn't mind having a little chit chat with the agent once they pulled into the parking lot.

He glanced over at David. "Let's just concentrate on Millie Thorn. All I want is to hear her story."

"Me too. I couldn't imagine what she went through back then," David replied, tossing him a glance.

He turned at the corner of Washington and Fourth Street. Just a quarter mile up Fourth Street, he pulled into the Sunny Village parking lot. The home was a mundane, brick building with a cross above the front entrance. There were entrances in the front and around the back. The walkway leading to the back entranceway had a sitting area with picnic tables, umbrellas, and a large over-hanging tree for shade. There were beautiful manicured bushes that sat along the building's brickwork.

David sat there for a few minutes waiting for Jack to pull in, but he never showed up. They figured he'd just drive past the nursing home and then double back, once they left their vehicle. They got out, grabbed their briefcases and entered the rear entrance. A nurse was sitting at the receptionist desk, which was situated in the middle of the corridor to accommodate the doctors and visitors that came in from either direction.

"Good evening, I'm Detective David Bradshaw, and this is my partner, Detective William Hall," David said, walking up to the desk and showing his badge.

The receptionist looked at the badge, and then up at the two men. "Is something wrong? No one called the police to my knowledge."

The head nurse, Pam Gibbons stepped out from one of the rooms. She saw the two men standing there and approached the desk.

"Hello, gentlemen, can I help you with something?"

"Yes, we're here to see Mrs. Mildred Thorn," David replied.

Pam looked up at him and then slowly glanced over at the receptionist who mouthed 'cops'.

"Oh, yes, I do recall. I spoke to Kim this afternoon." Pam said. "My name is Pam Gibbons."

"Hi, Pam," David greeted her. "You're here pretty late."

"I'm the head duty nurse for the next four days and during those days the duty nurse sleeps here."

"I see. You work shifts."

"Yes, the elderly here like it this way. With so much going on around here - if we swapped out every day - this place would be a nut house."

David looked over at William. He was nodding his head as if he was interested in what Pam was saying.

"We certainly appreciate the work you all do. Now, how is Millie these days? Does she know we called?" David asked, turning his attention on Pam.

"Yes. We informed her, and she's looking forward to seeing you. But remember now, she's one hundred and six years old. If she gets too tried, we'll have to ask you to leave."

"We understand," David replied.

Pam turned toward the receptionist. "Jill, please write their names down in the Visitor's Log. OK, gentlemen. Follow me, please."

William looked over at David and raised his brow as they followed Pam down the corridor. William's facial expression displayed a bit of excitement. He was excited too.

When they had Pam alone in the corridor, David stopped her. "Before we walk in, Pam - please tell me something."

"Sure, what is it?"

"You mentioned to Kim this afternoon that Millie has an imaginary friend. What did you mean by that?"

"Well, I think it would be better coming from Millie. She can tell you better than I can. Don't get me wrong, but some elderly patients have no one left in this world, so they make them up."

They both nodded.

"Shall we?" she said, turning and walking down another corridor toward the rear of the building. Millie's room was the last room on the left. It faced the rear picnic area.

Pam knocked on the door.

"Come in," a frail, shallow voice came from within.

Pam opened the door and let the two men in. They stood there just inside the door as she walked over to Millie's bedside, reached down and touched her hand. "Evening, Millie. Do you remember the call I told you about this morning?"

Millie leaned up and frowned. "Yes, I remember. I remember yesterday's breakfast, too. I had two eggs, a slice of ham and some orange juice."

Pam smiled. She loved Millie. For a woman her age, she still had a quick mind and a wicked sense of humor.

"You're a whip, Millie. These two men are detectives. They'd like to ask you a few questions."

Millie looked over Pam's bent frame and caught the handsome eyes of David. "Here, help me prop myself up," she said. Pam hit the button; her bed went up. She then fixed her pillows behind Millie's head. "How's that?"

"Fine, now let me take a look at these two. Would you like something to drink?"

"Water would be good," David replied. "May we sit down?"

"Yes, please. I don't want to be looking up that high if I don't have to."

They moved the two chairs from the small table in the corner, and placed them on either side of her bed. After sitting down and getting comfortable, David formally introduced themselves. "I'm Detective David Bradshaw, and this is my partner, Detective William Hall. We're happy to meet you Millie, may we call you Millie?"

"You can call me anything you like, David."

"You have a very nice room Millie," he replied, allowing his eyes to drift around the room. He looked at the big sliding window next to her bed. There were white blinds and drapes hanging down on both sides. The blinds were pulled down, but slightly open. He then noticed a welcome mat on the floor right in front of the window. *That's an odd place to put a mat*, he thought. When he turned and looked at her, he smiled.

Pam came back with two bottles of water. "You ring when you're done, Millie, and I'll see the detectives out."

"Thank you, Pam. Can you close my door, please? I am sure these gentlemen must want to talk to me about my days when I worked for the CIA," she teased, winking.

They all laughed. Millie was a whip all right.

After Pam left, David turned and looked at her. "Millie," he said. "I'd like to tell you why we're here to see you. Are you aware of what's happening out there?" he continued, pointing toward the window.

"Yes," she replied, glancing up at her TV in the corner.

David and William's eyes followed hers over to the TV. David looked back and noticed her remote sitting on the nightstand. He nodded with dismay knowing she had lived through this before.

"Pretty sad, isn't it?" David said.

"Yes. It sickens me to know there are humans who act like wild animals. For the life of me, I can't understand why someone would want to harm a child. So, why do you want to talk to me about this?"

David looked over at William. He knew he was going to hang back and just listen. "We're here because this case resembles a case that happened a long time ago," he replied.

She said nothing.

David let it go and continued. "I see from your files here that you were born in Ironbark, New York?"

"Yes I was. I lived there until nineteen hundred and fourteen, and then my parents moved."

"Well, Millie, this case we're working on now has been one of the hardest cases we've ever dealt with. But we know what happened in Ironbark when you were a child, and this may sound weird, but we have a bootprint on this case that's similar to the bootprint that was taken from the crime scene in Ironbark." He stopped there to observe her facial expression. She looked at him odd and then slightly turned her head and looked over at William.

"How did you find out about what happened up in Ironbark?" she asked, looking back at David.

"My grandfather worked that case with Sheriff Coleman."

The color in her face disappeared. She pushed her head back into the pillow. The look in her eyes was of shock as if she was flooding back in time.

"I remember your grandfather. He came to our house with Sheriff Coleman after Hank and Gloria Yammer thought they saw my father carrying Teddy Cotton down Hollow Trail next to Marshall Lake."

David felt a lump forming in his throat. It was one thing to read an old case and imagine the carnage, but this was something totally different. To actually sit and talk to someone who had lived it - was frightening, to say the least. "My grandfather knew that it wasn't your father, Millie," he replied.

"I know that."

"Well, if you'd like to take a look, I have photos of two sets of boot prints - one from Ironbark and one from a crime scene here in New York."

Millie knew she did not have to look at the photos – she already knew they matched.

"Sure, I'll take a look, if it helps you."

David reached inside his briefcase and pulled out the two photos. He showed her the old photo first and then the one taken from the railroad tracks. "What do you think?"

"It's amazing," she replied, closing her eyes and drifting back to that awful time.

"Is there something wrong?" William asked.

Millie opened her eyes. "You can talk," she replied, looking at him.

They laughed. "Yes, ma'am, but I didn't want to talk over you."

"You're a polite one. Now, I know you both did not come down here just to have me look at the photos, and then tell you want I thought. I'm sure you'd like to hear the story?"

"Yes we would," David replied.

Millie nodded. She looked down at the photo, sighed, and then drifted back to childhood days in Ironbark.

Chapter 14

"The year was Nineteen Hundred and Ten, just before the cold snap of winter was letting go and giving way to spring."

David glanced over at William. He sat back in his chair knowing this was going to take some time. William did the same. He would have sat there until the sun came up to hear what she had to say.

"The winter ice was just breaking up along the shores of Lake Ontario. It would be a full month before the longboats would be able to glide across the Great Lake, bringing the trappers, frontiersmen and a mixture of Canadian and American Indians back into the small town of Ironbark.

"In eighteen hundred and forty five, Ironbark was established; it was not long before people from as far away as the Hudson Bay, Pennsylvania, Ohio, and northern Michigan, heard about the trading town called Ironbark in upstate New York. They came by the droves trading their wares.

It was created by unscrupulous adventurers that made their home in the wilderness; carving out a living from their hunting and fishing skills. They built shacks for skinning and tanning their pelts, and for cleaning and packaging their fish, which was all then prepared and transported south. They did a fair bit of trading with the Southerners back then.

"Summer after summer, they continued cutting a swash of trees from the dense forest that had grown right up to the shoreline, and slowly the path they carved out of the forest became Ironbark.

"My father earned his medical degree from Calvary University in Maine. He came to Ironbark in nineteen hundred. He'd heard about Ironbark from a friend of his whose son had ventured north and wrote home about the place.

"After my father arrived in Ironbark, he settled in and never looked back. He met my mother, Mary Fletcher, the first year he arrived. Her father, Daniel owned the Fletcher Hardware and Supply Store in town. They married that same year.

"I was nine years old when the devil came to Ironbark. It all started one day in May. I think the twentieth if I recall. I remember it was Friday because we always had fish on Friday. I was home that day when Mrs. Chamber came by to see if her son, Jamie, was over visiting with me. We were always together. He was my dearest friend. I guess you could say we were childhood sweethearts, and everyone knew it.

"We'd spend our summer days on the shores of Lake Ontario, fishing off the shore, or from the pier where the longboats came in. Sunfish, bluegills, and if we got lucky, a nice sized perch - we'd catch them by the bucketful; taking them home so our moms could fry them up for dinner.

"Sometimes, we'd skip stones on the lake, look for pretty rocks, or just sit on the beach and watch the waves roll in. There were occasions that our parents would allow us go out to Marshall Lake, so long as we stayed together. There were still bears, snakes and other wildlife living in and around Ironbark, so we had to be careful. Those were great times.

"My name for Jamie was Jimmy. He sure liked that; me having a nickname for him that no one else used. It was fun to have secrets that were just our own. He wanted to surprise me with something that day, but I knew what he was up to. He loved to sneak out to Casper's Hill, just a stone's throw away from Marshall Lake, to pick wild flowers to give to me. He left our house that morning when he said that he wanted to surprise me with something. I thought he'd be back shortly, but he never came back," she said and then paused. "Did I tell you that the Chamber's lived right next door," Millie continued. She looked up from the old photo to see the detectives sitting there as if they were in church. They simply nodded. She smiled, looked down at the photo, and continued.

"Mary, is Jamie here with Millie? I haven't seen him for over an hour." Mrs. Chamber said, walking through the door.

"Why no," Mary replied, coming out of the kitchen and wiping her hands on her apron.
"Millie, dear, please come down here."

Millie heard her mother calling. She put down her pencil and jumped off her bed.
"Yes, Ma," she yelled, dashing down the stairs and landing right between the two women.

"Have you seen Jamie today?"

She looked up at her mother, and then tossed a glance at Mrs. Chamber. She could see that she was worried. "He was here twenty minutes ago. He said that he wanted to surprise me with something and then he left."

"Millie Thomson!" her mother scolded. "Don't tell me that boy is out picking you more flowers!"

Millie looked down at her shoes, and then at her mother's shoes, and then at Mrs. Chamber's shoes.

"Millie, you answer me now!"

"I told him that he didn't have to," Millie replied, still looking at everyone's shoes.

Mrs. Chamber knelt down and lifted up her chin. "You told him that he didn't have to do what?"

Millie looked into her worried eyes and knew trouble was on the way if she didn't spit it out. "I told him that he didn't have to give me a surprise. I wanted to just sit up in my room with him and draw the birds that landed in the tree out back, but he wanted to go. I think he went out to Casper's Hill."

"Casper's Hill!?" Mrs. Chamber gasped, quickly standing up. "Mary, where's Doc?"

"He's in town looking after Ted Billing's wife. She came down with some kind of bug."

"Oh Lord, Walt is in town too, picking up supplies. Come, we have to hurry into town and get someone out there before Jamie gets snake-bitten or worse."

While Millie was talking to the detectives, Mr. Bones looked up at the clock in the science room. He wanted to leave, but the principal had notified all the teachers that he was holding a conference when school let out that afternoon. He had no choice but to wait.

When everyone finally left, he walked down to the janitor's room, pulled out his box from the ceiling, and put on his clothes. He made his usual exit via the metal door and stood there behind the bushes. Before stepping out, he checked the street to make sure it was clear. He then casually walked down the side of the school toward the playing fields.

After passing the tennis courts, he walked up behind the football stands and made his way to the fence. Jumping over it, he headed up the small incline to the railroad tracks. He glanced up at the tall oak tree; the same tree where he hung Kevin Downer. He dropped his thoughts and proceeded down the tracks toward the abandoned railroad station. When he got halfway between the school and the railroad station, he walked down the incline on the other side of the tracks. Through the underbrush, he walked up to the security fence. There was an opening large enough for him to slip through the fence. He knew the route by heart; he'd been using it every week for over a year now to see Millie at the nursing home.

When he slipped through the fence, he stood there on the dead end street for a moment to ensure no one was out. All was quiet. He pulled his hood over his face and started down the street. Halfway down, he turned left into an alley and walked toward the nursing home's rear parking lot.

At the end of the alley next to the rear parking lot, he climbed a tall tree and looked down over the area. He had to make sure there was no one around before he climbed out onto the limb and jumped into the next tree that hung over the picnic area near Millie's window. After he jumped over, he climbed high into the canopy and sat for a while, looking down at the cars sitting there. After so many visits, he knew every car, the staff, and most of the visitors that came to see their loved ones.

As he scanned the cars below, he noticed one car he'd never seen before. It was a big, brown car with a high antenna on the rear trunk and a smaller one on top of the roof. He puzzled over it for a second then switched his thoughts to Millie. He stood up and made his way toward the rear of the building where the bushes were. Jumping down, he stood up behind the bushes and crept over to Millie's window.

When he peeked through the slightly closed blinds, he was startled to see two well-dressed men sitting on opposite sides of Millie's bed. When he looked down at the one closest to the window, he could see the butt end of a gun sticking out of his suit coat. He glared at the man. His eyes began to glow like bright red flames within his dark sockets. *It's the police*, he thought. *How? How could they know?* He stood there trying to listen through the closed window as Millie was telling them her story.

"We lived just west of town, in the section known as Tall Tree Pocket on Sugar Bottom Road. We only had to walk down Sugar Bottom to Elm Street and then take the Hollow Trail to get into town. The pier was just north of us. Hollow Trail started at the pier and ran south toward Marshall Lake, crossing over the Willow Creek Bridge near the Forgotten Land, and it ended in Rochester; which was a half day's ride by horse and buggy.

"They hurried me out of the house and down Sugar Bottom Road all the way into town. I liked going to town. There were usually all kinds of people there selling their pelts or game meat. My favorite people were the Indians. I just adored Indian Joe. All the children loved him. He always had time to play or tell us stories. He was a bear of a man and had the smoothest, golden brown skin you ever seen. His hair was jet black like a raven, and he always wore it in a ponytail. He wore buckskin boots, deerskin pants, and homemade shirts; he was exceedingly handsome. However, it wasn't his looks that people took to, it was his spiritual side. He always spoke of the great white eagle and the spirit owl, and he certainly had a cunning way of saying things. His talent of tracking was, without a doubt, remarkable.

"If you wanted to catch Indian Joe in town, all you had to do was stop by the sheriff's office. He and the sheriff were like two pumpkins in the same patch, and they liked spending time together. The sheriff was as big as Indian Joe, and he always stood proudly - just like George Washington did; while standing in that boat while crossing the Delaware River during the Revolutionary War.

"When we got into town and headed down Main Street, Indian Joe and the sheriff were standing out front of the sheriff's office. When they saw the look in Beth Chamber's eyes, they started to walk toward us.

"Indian Joe, do you see what I see?" Ben asked, tilting his head toward the women coming down the middle of the street.

"I do, and it looks like trouble."

"Sheriff, have you seen Walt?" Beth asked, walking up.

"I just saw him walk over to Bowman's Stables. Is there anything wrong?"

"It's Jamie," she replied. "Millie told us that he went out to Casper's Hill to pick wild flowers for her, but he's been gone for quite some time now, and I'm getting worried."

Ben looked at Millie. She shyly looked down to the road to avoid his eyes.

"Millie," Ben said, looking at her studying her shoes. "This isn't your fault. We all know Jamie loves you like a sister."

Millie looked over at Indian Joe's boots, then she looked up at him, and he smiled. *He knows too*, she thought. She reckoned everyone knew how she and Jimmy felt about each other. It made her feel ashamed of their feelings as if they'd been caught kissing. As much as she wanted to kiss Jimmy, neither of them ever tried.

Ben looked at Mary. She looked as worried as Beth. "OK, Beth, let's go and see Walt. Indian Joe and I will ride out with him and fetch Jamie for you."

"I'd really appreciate that, Ben," she replied, taking Mary's hand. Mary gave her a reassuring look and then put her arm around Millie. "We'll wait here for you," she said.

As Ben, Indian Joe, and Beth walked down to Bowman's Stable, Millie started to cry. She tried to wipe her tears as fast as they streamed down her pretty little face.

"Now, Millie," her mother whispered, kneeling down. "No one is mad at you, or Jamie. He just needs to let his mother know where he's going, and what he's doing, so she doesn't worry about him."

"I just don't want him to get in trouble, that's all."

"He might get a scolding, but you two must understand that you have to let us know where you're going."

By the time Mary stood up, she saw Beth escorting Walt back. She was scolding his ear the whole way as Ben and Indian Joe walked behind them. The three men unhitched their horses and rode off down Hollow Trail to Casper's Hill.

"Everything is going to be just fine, Beth. Heck, they'll probably meet up with Jamie on the way," Mary said.

After watching the men turn the corner and disappear down Hollow Trail, Beth turned and looked at her. "I pray you're right. The knots in my stomach won't go away until I have my little boy back in my arms."

Mary nodded knowing she'd be out of her mind too if it was Millie that was missing. She wanted to comfort her, and the only way she thought she could get her mind off Jamie was to take her to Jane's and pick out some fabric she needed to make a dress for Millie. She asked if she wanted to go. Beth nodded, looking down at Millie. She gave Millie a brave, half-hearted smile.

When Ben, Indian Joe and Walt got to the trail in the forest that led up to Casper's Hill, Indian Joe took point as they slowly entered the woods in single file. Indian Joe spotted some tracks right away. He put up his hand, halting the men behind him, and dismounted. Ben and Walt followed his lead and got down from their horses.

It was a beautiful location; covered in high grass, and thousands of wild flowers that covered most of the hill. On the other side of Casper's Hill, the forest took over once again. You could take a path through the forest down to Marshall Lake. If you stood at the top of the hill the lake was not visible, but on horseback, you could just catch a glimpse of it through the trees. From where Indian Joe stood looking down at the tracks, he could smell the water.

He followed the tracks from Hollow Trail to the hill. He stopped before the high grass took over, allowing his eyes to scan the hillside. He could see where someone had walked into the grass; the blades were slightly bent over. At the top of the hill, he stopped and halted the men behind him. From his position, he could see another set of tracks that came up from the lake. Indian Joe knelt down, cleared the grass away, and saw a larger set of prints. He felt the nape of his neck go cold. From the size of the bootprint, he reckoned the man had to stand at least six feet tall.

"Well," Walt asked, looking at him kneeling there.

"Something looks strange here," he replied, scanning the ground.

Walt looked at Ben with anger in his eyes. Ben put up his hand to calm Walt as they waited to see what Indian Joe was looking at. Indian Joe was a highly skilled tracker. He could not only follow prints - he could tell many things about the person or animal he was hunting just by the way they walked; how tall they were, how much they weighed, or if they were carrying something.

Ben and Walt stood there watching him walk down the hill through the tall grass toward the lake. When he reached the bottom of the hill, he stopped once again. He could see the print clearly now. It was deep and heading down the path toward the lake. He waved his hand for the Ben and Walt to follow. When they got down the hill, Indian Joe did not have good news for Walt. He knew when he told Walt of his findings - all hell was going to break loose.

"Indian Joe, where's my boy?" Walt sternly asked.

"Walt, look here," he replied, pointing down to the single bootprint.

Walt looked down. The print was too big to be Jamie's. He looked up at Indian Joe and saw the devil in his eyes. He knew what he was trying to say. He shook his head in disbelief before Indian Joe told him.

"Your boy came up on the other side of the hill. This one came up from the lake. I think Jamie's been taken. Look at the tracks, this man is carrying something."

Walt's heart stopped, he could not breathe. "No, no, no – this can't be!" he screamed, looking at Indian Joe. The look in Indian Joe's eyes told him that it was true. In his anger, Walt quickly turned around, pulled out his rifle, and chambered a round. Indian Joe quickly grabbed the barrel.

"Get out of my way. I have some killing to do!" Walt spat, trying to it pull it away from him.

"Walt, if you go down that trail you'll destroy our chances of catching the devil!" Indian Joe yelled, looking him dead in the eyes.

Walt pulled his rifle away from Indian Joe. Indian Joe shook his head. Walt stood there fuming. He knew Indian Joe was right, he could see it in his eyes. "OK, lead the way, but understand this, if I get that man in my sights, he's a dead man for sure!" Walt spat, looking hard at both men.

Ben saw hell in his eyes. "I'll shoot the bastard myself, Walt. You know that. Now let Indian Joe work his magic and find him before harm comes to your son," he replied, looking at Indian Joe. "How long?" he asked.

Indian Joe knelt down, placed his finger inside the bootprint, and then looked toward the lake. "One hour, maybe more. That's plenty of time to run, but with an eight year old boy on your shoulder, and hopefully fighting for his life – he'd be short on distance. We may have one problem, and I won't know that until we get to the lake. Stay back and let me search."

Ben put his hand on Walt's shoulder. "We'll get him back Walt, as sure as I'm Sheriff of this town."

"I hope you're right, Ben," he replied, keeping his eyes focused on Indian Joe. "Anything happens to my boy, I'll not stop until the bastard's dead!"

Indian Joe walked along the path leading down to the lake. He wanted to see if the track veered off in another direction. However, his instincts were telling him different; this animal was heading straight for the lake. *Will I find Jamie down there floating in the water?* He knelt down every so often to check the track. He knew for certain, that the man had Jamie over his right shoulder. The right heel was much deeper than the left. He looked behind him; both Ben and Walt had their rifles drawn and ready. He stood up and moved forward.

When he reached the lake, he spotted the markings from a keel of a canoe dug into the thick mud. He knew by the sign that the man carried Jamie back to the lake and put him in a canoe.

Walt walked up and looked down; his blood ran cold when he saw the marking that the canoe had left. He wasn't intelligent in the ways of a tracker, but he knew what he was looking at; whoever took his boy had put him in a canoe and took him out on the lake. "He's got my boy out there somewhere, doesn't he?" he asked Indian Joe.

Indian did not look at him; he was scanning the lake and the coastline off in the distance. The area around the lake was thick with trees and vegetation, and he knew they'd be hell bent in finding him now. He turned and looked at Walt. His eyes were disappearing into darkness. He had seen that look a thousand times before - when a man's heart grows so cold, and nothing matters anymore until the shooting is over. "He has him alright, and only the great white eagle can track a man over water. We need to get back to town and round up some men. We'll try cutting his path off across Hollow Trail to the west - if he is heading that way. And also, we need to get a boat down here to start searching the lake. There's no telling which way they went. If they headed south into the wetlands and through the forest, we're going to have a hard time tracking them."

Walt knew Indian Joe was the best tracker in the world. If he couldn't track a man through that terrain, then no one could. "What do you think, Ben?" he asked.

"Indian Joe is right. We need to get back and get more men. The longer he's on the run, there's no telling what will happen."

Walt gripped his rifle and stared at him. Ben wasn't going to say another word. He knew by the look. Walt kept his stare and then turned toward the lake, and screamed, "You harm my boy and I'll skin you alive! I'll cut you into a million pieces and feed you to the fish, you rotten bastard!"

Chapter 15

By the time the three got back into Ironbark, everyone knew Jamie was missing. Word had spread like wildfire throughout town. Deputy Daniel Harding heard their horses racing up out front. He heard the hard pounding of their boots coming up the wooden steps. He walked over and opened the door - his eyes searching for Jamie. He wasn't there. His skin felt cold, looking into Walt's dead eyes. "You didn't find him?" he sullenly asked.

"He's been taken by a lowlife snake. When I get my hands on him, I'll cut his throat from ear to ear!" Walt spat. "Where's my wife?" he continued, walking into the sheriff's office.

"She's with Doc's wife and Millie. They're down at Jane's," Jim Picket replied, sitting there.

"Dan, go see Jake Fuller and have him hitch a longboat to a wagon. Walt, you stay with me. Someone run down and get Beth," Ben ordered. He had children too and knew what Walt was feeling. He'd like to string up the bastard as well, but he was the law around here and he knew that was not an option. He also knew when they caught the bastard, he'd have to put him in jail and then take him to Rochester for trial; that's unless Walt got to him first.

Ben turned toward the crowd gathered outside. "Listen up, everyone! Jamie's been abducted. Indian Joe tracked him to Marshall Lake. Whoever took Jamie, they placed him in a canoe and headed across the lake. I need volunteers."

Six men stepped up. "We're ready! What do you want us to do?"

"Get your horses, grab some gear and bring your guns. We ride out in twenty minutes."

Indian Joe spotted his two friends, Chief Running Bear and Blackfoot, coming out of the supply store. He looked at Ben and nodded his head toward them. Ben gave him a nod. He walked down and met both men in the middle of the street. "Jamie's missing. He's been taken by a white man."

"Are you sure?" Chief Running Bear asked. "It had to be a white man, you know the Indians around here. They would never take a child. They know their spirit would never rest," he replied, glancing over at Blackfoot. "Will you go with me in the longboat?"

Blackfoot nodded. He had tracked his share of killers in the northern forests with the Canadian Mounties. He looked over Indian Joe's shoulder seeing the crowd standing out front of the sheriff's office. He saw their anger, and knew whoever had taken Jamie - wouldn't make it out alive. *The white skin would see to that,* he thought. "Where did he take him?" he asked.

"They got into a canoe on Marshall Lake near Casper's Hill. We'll start our search on the eastern shoreline."

Blackfoot knew that part of the forest. The vegetation was so dense that not even a black bear would venture in for a log full of honey. He looked into Indian Joe's eyes. "You think a white man would take a child in there?"

"I don't know what to think, but the canoe left the shore just past Casper's Hill. He wouldn't head west; a lot of the settlers live on that side of the lake."

"You've both been there, and you know there isn't a place on that shoreline to pull a canoe ashore," Chief Running Bear questioned.

"You're right, but my spirit tells me different. The crazy is in there somewhere."

Chief Running Bear was worried. He knew his people would be signaled out and blamed. "You know where this is heading," he asked.

From the look in Chief Running Bear's eyes, they knew what he was thinking.

"Ben and Walt don't see it that way. They know it's a white crazy. Our people will not take the blame for this," Indian Joe replied.

Before Chief Running Bear could respond, the crowd started yelling and accusing the Indians. Chief Running Bear raised his brow to both men. He stepped out and walked toward the crowd. They turned and watched him make his way toward the sheriff's office.

Indian Joe and Blackfoot followed. The crowd hushed and waited to hear what the Indian Chief had to say. Before he could speak and settle the crowd, Beth, Mary, and Millie came running down the road.

Beth started screaming for her husband. The crowd turned and stared. "Walt, where's our boy?" she yelled, running through the crowd. Walt looked into his wife's eyes and broke down. Tears rolled down his cheeks as he grabbed her. "Oh my God, where's our boy? Where's Jamie?" she screamed.

Ben placed his hand on each of their shoulders. "Someone took him from Casper's Hill, Beth," he sighed.

Beth's knees gave way. She slid down Walt's body and collapsed on the walkway. Walt went down with her. He held his wife in his arms and then looked up at the crowd. Anger rushed through the crowd. They all started screaming for revenge. Some spit words toward the Indians.

Bill Miller, the town bully, who was as big as a horse and liked to push his weight around, set the crowd on fire. "Every man here grab your guns, someone get a rope. Before this day is over, we'll have the bastard hanging from a tree!"

"You heard him!" another yelled out.

"Hold up, Bill!" Ben screamed above the crowd, waving his hands in the air.

"No, Ben!" Lance Simmons shouted. "We're not waiting for the law on this one. He has Jamie. You mess with our children – you're a dead man!"

Chief Running Bear stood there watching the crowd turn into a bloodthirsty mob. He wanted to speak, but knew they'd go after him and his people. Then it happened. All eyes fell on the three Indians standing there alongside Ben.

"It's them!" someone yelled, pointing toward Chief Running Bear.

Ben had heard enough. He knew if he did not get this under control, he'd have three dead Indians on his hands. He pulled one of his six shooters, pointed it in the air, and fired off a round. The crowd went dead quite. "Now listen up! No one here is going to take this upon themselves. Indian Joe tracked the man's prints. It was a white man's bootprint. Now those of you who can help us find this bastard, get on your horses and let's ride. The rest of you go home. We'll find this bastard and bring him in."

"We'll bring him in alright, dead or alive!" Bill Miller yelled.

"Yeah, dead or alive!" another shouted.

Ben looked at the crowd. He knew how they all felt. Most had children of their own. "Alright - dead or alive, I don't care how he's brought in!" He looked down at Walt and Beth. They looked like children sitting on the walkway sobbing. He looked up and over the crowd when someone yelled out that Doc Thomson was coming. Doc Thomson raced up and grabbed his wife. She fell into his arms and began to sob.

"Doc!" Ben yelled. "Can you and Mary take Walt and Beth inside?"

Doc nodded. He gathered his wife and walked through the crowd.

Millie stood there watching as her parents waded through the crowd. She was shaking feeling all alone. Jamie was her best friend and no one cared that her heart was broken in two. She stood there with tears rolling down her little cheeks. It was all her fault and no one cared about that either.

The crowd in front of the sheriff's office kept getting larger as more men volunteered to help find Jamie. Millie watched her parents comforting Jamie's parents and then they all went inside the sheriff's office. She wanted to go to but couldn't. She knew they would probably all yell at her because she was to blame. As she stood there, she felt a hand on her shoulder. She turned around to see Mary Baker, the barber's daughter.

"Millie, what's going on? The whole town is buzzing like bees."

"It's Jamie. Someone took him from Casper's Hill. He went there to pick wild flowers for me," she replied, sniffling.

She hugged Millie and shook her head. "It's not your fault, Millie. We all know how he feels about you. Now, don't you go worry none, they'll bring him back, you'll see." Millie looked at her and saw tears welling up in her eyes. She hugged Mary while watching the angry men saddling up.

When they were mounted, they sat there and waited for Ben to give the next order. "Bill, you ride out with Deputy Harding. Phil and Luke, search the forest just south of Willow Run along the lake. Lance, you take Carl, George, and Kent and go talk with the settlers in the valley; see if anyone saw a boat on the lake. The rest of you - follow me out to Casper's Hill. We'll search the forest to the east. Indian Joe and Blackfoot will take the longboat and search along the shoreline."

They all nodded, turned their horses, and rode off. Indian Joe and Blackfoot rounded up their horses and tethered them to the back of the wagon. Jake Fuller would go with them and stay with the horses and wagon.

Before Ben left, he walked inside the office and spoke with the Walt and Beth. "We're leaving now, but you hear me, we'll get him back."

"I want to come, Ben," Walt replied, standing up.

"No." Beth scolded. "I'm not losing both of you today."

"But, honey."

"Our child is missing. I can't lose you too. Ben and the men can handle this."

"She's right, Walt," Doc Thomson said. "Why don't the two of you come and stay with us for the night? That way they can bring Jamie there and I can examine him."

Walt looked at everyone and then noticed Millie and Mary Baker standing in the doorway. The look in their eyes said it all; the whole town was in shock.

"OK, we'll stay with the Doc and wait. But you listen and listen good. I want that bastard slung over a horse dead when you bring back my boy. If you don't kill him out there – I'll do it the moment I get a chance, law or no law!"

"Just bring my boy home alive, Sheriff," Beth cried.

"We will. Doc, take 'em home," Ben said, turning and walking past Millie and Mary.

When the wagon pulled up at the trail leading to Casper's Hill, Jake brought the team of horses to a halt, and the men got down. Indian Joe and Blackfoot untied the longboat and hauled it down. They took the paddles and secured them to their saddles. "Jake, we could be in there all night. Stay until the sunsets, then leave. If we find them, we'll carry them out," Indian Joe said.

"Good luck. I hope you find that boy."

Blackfoot nodded, thinking the boy was already dead, and the man that took him was probably long gone. They picked up the boat and hoisted it over their shoulders. Indian Joe gave the horses three clicks, and they followed the two down the trail.

After climbing Casper's Hill, they made their way down the other side to the path leading to the lake. Indian Joe showed Blackfoot the tracks and the markings left by the canoe. He bent down, stuck his finger inside the bootprint, and then looked out over the lake.

"You're right, Indian Joe. The child taker is six foot, maybe more. He was certainly carrying something heavy," he said, standing up.

Indian Joe looked at Blackfoot studying the lake. *Blackfoot is as keen as a fox,* he thought, turning around and grabbing his hatchet and rifle off the side of his horse. Blackfoot walked back and pulled out his rifle, powder sack, and lead balls. He checked to make sure his bowie knife was in his boot. They put their gear inside the boat, walked back, retrieved the paddles, and then tethered their horses to a tree out of sight.

They pushed the boat off the shore and got in. The sun was drifting down in the sky, which gave them an hour or so before nightfall. If they didn't catch the landing site before the sun went down, they'd have no chance of tracking Jamie's captor. The boat glided silently through the still waters. Both paddles hardly made a sound as they dipped them in, pushed back, and then brought them up and dipped them again.

On this side of the lake, the forest came right up to the shore. Some trees grew in the shallows among the deadfall, rocks, and boulders. The shore was clear in some parts, which gave just enough room for a man to haul a canoe ashore, wade through the thick brush and enter the forest. Neither man said much, they never did when they were hunting. They used birdcalls, hand signals, nods - or facial expressions while stalking their prey.

About a half hour into their search, Indian Joe, who was sitting in the back of the canoe, noticed a fallen tree lying in the water up ahead. In the center of the huge trunk, there was a pile of limbs. It looked as if beavers had cut them, and stacked one on top of the other. Indian Joe gave a soft birdcall. Blackfoot stopped rowing and looked back. Indian Joe pointed at the tree. Blackfoot turned and looked. He slowly nodded.

They paddled over to the downed tree and maneuvered the boat alongside. The two carefully lifted the branches and discovered an empty canoe. Indian Joe cast his eyes down the long trunk toward the shoreline. Just past the tree's high roots that stuck up in the air, he saw a path. Blackfoot set down his paddle and readied his rifle. Indian Joe slowly canoed the rest of the way to the shoreline. In the shallow water, he spotted the canoe's securing rope running up toward the bank. It was tied off to a portion of the submerged tree trunk.

Indian Joe took hold of the large trunk, steadying the canoe as Blackfoot slipped into the water and pulled the boat ashore. Indian Joe grabbed his rifle, stepped out into the shallows, and waded ashore. Once they pulled the canoe up, they tied it off and knelt down on the bank searching for tracks.

Blackfoot spotted them first. He raised his hand with three fingers up; showing he saw three sets of prints - two adults and one child. They looked at each other knowing that they had two men to deal with before they could rescue the boy.

Indian Joe reckoned that one of the men must have seen Jamie while paddling ashore near Casper's Hill. He then abducted Jamie and brought him here. *So where were they now?*

Blackfoot stood up, loaded his rifle, and walked into the forest with Indian Joe right behind him. About twenty yards in, they came to an opening in the forest. There was hardly any sunlight due to the thick canopy overhead. The terrain was hilly, covered in thick moss, grass, large rocks, and rotting trees. The only thing they had to go by was the deep, rich soil which showed the bootprints of the men and the child walking alongside them - traveling east over the rough, hilly terrain. Another hundred yards into the forest, they smelled a hint of smoke. Indian Joe reached over and touched Blackfoot's shoulder. Blackfoot looked back, showing a sign that he smelt it too.

"Let's wait until nightfall. We'll take care of them then," Indian Joe whispered.

Blackfoot looked through the forest at the next small hill up ahead. He cast his eyes up through the thick canopy above. "We have one hour before nightfall. Are you sure you don't want to cut their throats and take the boy now?"

Indian Joe pondered that. He knew Ben wanted them taken alive. He looked into Blackfoot's eyes. They were lifeless. He had seen that look before. He nodded in agreement to killing the two - but he still wanted to wait and kill them in the dark. "No. With the sunlight - they have the advantage. We've never been in these parts. We'll wait until it's dark to kill them both, and then take the boy." Blackfoot nodded. He knelt down and hunkered next to a tree. Indian Joe did the same.

While the two Indians waited for nightfall, Boone Davenport and Darrell Cobb were taking turns raping Jamie Chamber. When they finished, they took Jamie around the back of the makeshift shanty, drove a meat hook into his back and hoisted him up on a rope over a low hanging limb. Boone then took out his knife, and slit him up the middle like a deer; letting his insides fall out onto the ground. Jamie was still alive. The meat hook had severed his spinal cord. He lived long enough to bleed out before he died. When the boy was dead, Boone opened his chest cavity and cut out one of his ribs.

"What did ya do that fur?" Darrell asked.

"If the animals don't get him, and the people lookin' for him find him first, they'll think the Indians killed him. Indians take a rib out of animals they kill for some reason. This should throw them off our scent, and start hunting for Indians, instead of us."

The two men grabbed their gear from inside the shanty and headed toward Willow Creek. There, they clean themselves off. After they finished, they used the shallow creek to travel west toward the Forgotten Land - just three miles away. They figured a bear would come along, pull the boy down, and drag him off. If they came back and he was still hanging there – they'd bury the boy deep in the woods where no one would ever find him.

They waded through the creek, so they did not leave any tracks. Their plan was to get back to the Forgotten Land as soon as they could. It was a mountainous region surrounded by rich vegetation and forests. Before man had stepped foot in this part of the county, there was a massive landslide that cut a mountain in half, which left the landscape covered in large boulders and deep ravines. Over time, the forest grew back and covered the ravines, leaving the unsuspecting traveler many unforeseen holes to fall in. One foolish step, you'd find yourself trapped, and it would be a nightmare trying to get out. No one would hear your cries for help because no one ever ventured into the Forgotten Land - not alone, at least - and not often.

Boone and Darrell chose this section of the forest for just that reason. They were loners, drifters - that wanted to escape the dredges of society. They came up from southern Georgia after being wiped out by the floods down there.

"Did you hide the canoe good?" Boone asked, wading through the shallow creek.

"Yeah, I always cover it good."

"Tie it off good?"

"Yeah, Boone. Why you ask me that all the time?"

"I want to make sure. Did you like the boy?"

"Yep. I never thought I'd like a boy. You know I like girls."

"Right – but wasn't he tight?"

Darrell glanced over at him while navigating through the creek. Boone never said much, and now he was chattering more than the birds. "Yeah, but I'm glad we had some bear grease. I'd rather have a girl though."

"We could go to Sue's. She has lots of girls to choose from."

"They scare me, Boone. You know I have a hard time talkin' to them. Been shy all my life. That's why I like little girls. They cry when I take 'em, but then they just lay there and let me have my way."

Boone stopped in the middle of the creek. "You know, she even has a few squaws up in them beds. Nice, brown skin, soft as a peach - with big, doe eyes, they are. Heck, they just lie there too just looking up at the ceiling - as if they were watching the moon rise high in the sky while you have your way with them. You should've come in with me last month. I had two at one time."

Darrell titled his head.

"OK, OK," Boone replied to his drawn expression. "We'll take a little girl next time, but you mind me now if I give her to you first, you better leave enough for me."

Indian Joe opened his eyes to see that dusk had settled in. He tapped Blackfoot on the shoulder. Blackfoot opened his eyes and looked at him. He cast his eyes upward looking into the canopy. *The moon would be rising soon*, he thought. "Best we move out before the moon rises," he whispered.

Indian Joe nodded, stood up with his rifle, and walked up the hilly terrain. Blackfoot followed with his rifle ready. They navigated toward the smell of smoke as if they were wolves smelling the blood of a wounded deer on the wind. When they reached the top of another hill, Indian Joe crouched down when he saw the small, wooden shanty sitting between two large trees. The smoke was coming from a fire pit in front of the shanty. The place looked deserted. He looked back at Blackfoot and then gave Blackfoot a hand signal for him to circle around the back; leaving the two no escape. He then knelt down watching Blackfoot slip silently through the forest around the back. Once Blackfoot was in place, he would call out like an owl, telling Indian Joe that he was ready.

Indian Joe lay there for what seemed longer than it should have taken Blackfoot to navigate through the rough terrain around the back. After a few more minutes, he gave a woodchuck warning call, "Chip, chip, chip." Nothing came back. He called out again and waited. Nothing, it was dead quiet. He knew something was wrong. He lowered himself to the ground and started crawling along the path Blackfoot had taken. When he finally made his way to the back of the shanty, he spotted Blackfoot lying next to a large log and looking through the brush. He slipped up beside him. "What's wrong?" he whispered.

Blackfoot pulled the brush aside and pointed. Indian Joe leaned up and looked out. His eyes filled with terror when he saw little Jamie Chamber's naked body hanging from a meat hook off a low limb near the rear of the shanty. His blood began to boil. All he wanted to do was to take the meat hook out of Jamie's back, stick it into those murdering snakes, and then slowly peel their skins off while they were still alive. He stood up, chambered a round, and started down the small slope. Blackfoot grabbed his leg. Indian Joe shrugged it off and kept moving. Blackfoot got up and followed with his long rifle at the ready.

When Indian Joe reached Jamie, he did not look up at the child. He kept his rifle pointed at the shanty and then headed toward the left side toward the front. Blackfoot slowly crept down the right side. They met in the front and slipped up to the door. Blackfoot nodded. Indian Joe kicked in the door and pointed his rifle inside. The place was empty. They walked in and looked around. Blackfoot spotted a lantern on the floor. He set his rifle down, picked it up, and lit it.

In the small, one room shanty, there was a table in the center and two make shift bunks on opposite sides next to the walls. A kettle and some can goods were stacked in the corner. The whole structure looked as if it was hobnobbed together from dead wood from the forest floor. Without looking at Blackfoot, Indian Joe said, "You stay till morning and track 'em. I'll take Jamie home."

"You want me to kill them and bring back their scalps?"

Indian Joe turned and looked at him. "I want more than their scalps - bring me their heads," he fumed. He grabbed an old blanket from one of the beds and walked outside.

Blackfoot stood there in the glow of the lantern. He spit on the floor, grabbed his rifle and then lantern, and walked out. They went around the back to where Jamie was hanging. Indian Joe went numb looking up at the boy. The poor boy's hands were tied behind his back, and a piece of cloth had been shoved into his little mouth. Another cloth was tied around his head to hold the one inside his mouth; so he could not scream.

As Indian Joe stood there looking at the boy, Blackfoot walked around Jamie, pulled out his knife, and cut the rope. He slowly lowered the boy's lifeless body to the ground, took the meat hook out of his back, turned him over, and removed the cloth from his mouth. The next part was rough - even for an Indian. He painfully shoved the boy's organs back into his stomach, pulled his chest cavity together and then bundled him up inside the blanket.

After wrapping the boy up, they leaned back on their hunches. Jamie's head rolled to the side toward Indian Joe. A smile slowly appeared on Jamie's face. Indian Joe froze. Blackfoot quickly stood up. He looked down Indian Joe. Indian Joe said nothing. Blackfoot sat down and watched him take off his deer skin pouch from around his neck, pull out one small eagle feather, and stick it in his hair. He then pulled out a sack of white powder. The powder consisted of crushed bear claw, a wolf's tooth, and a portion of a hawk's skull. He sprinkled it over his head. Afterward, he took a small pouch containing yellow pollen, smeared it across his nose with two fingers, and then smeared two lines down each of his cheeks. He looked up into the night sky and began chanting.

Blackfoot knew Indian Joe was praying to the great white eagle. It was something he had never seen Indian Joe do before; it worried him. Something was coming; he could feel it on the wind. When he was done, Indian Joe opened his eyes and looked over at Blackfoot. Indian Joe's eyes were dead and lifeless.

"What did the white eagle tell you?"

"He hasn't left. The boy is still here with us."

Blackfoot lowered his head and closed his eyes. The nape of his neck felt suddenly cold. *You can't run from the spirits. If they want you – you're a dead man no matter what you do.*

"Fear not, Blackfoot," he whispered. "The spirit is not here for us. We must cover the boy's blood so no animal can take his spirit."

"What about the shack and the canoe? Should we burn the shack and sink the canoe?"

"No. We leave 'em. They are not to know we've been here. We will make it look like the animals took Jamie."

Blackfoot nodded.

Indian Joe stood up, picked up Jamie's body and hoisted him over his shoulder. Blackfoot handed him his rifle. They stood there for a moment looking at one another. "I'll see you when you get back to town. Your horse will be at the stable. I want their heads if you catch them." Blackfoot reached out with both hands, grabbed Indian Joe's arm and squeezed. Indian Joe turned and headed back toward the lake with Jamie.

Chapter 16

After putting Jamie's body in the boat, Indian Joe shoved off. He paddled around the eastern shoreline and came to the bank where their horses stood tethered to the tree. He stepped out into the shallow water and pushed the boat toward the muddy bank. He gathered Jamie into his arms, carried him to Blackfoot's horse, and then gently placed his body across the saddle. After securing him to the horse, he touched the boy's head.

He then walked back to the boat, picked it up, and carried it into the forest; where he covered it pine branches next to a stand of trees. Indian Joe untied Blackfoot's horse, tethered the reins to his own saddle horn, mounted his horse and slowly rode off through the forest toward Casper's Hill.

When he got back to Hollow Trail, he looked south toward the open meadow around Marshall Lake - where Sheriff Ben Coleman said they would be searching for Jamie. He knew they must be back in town by now; it was too dark to be searching. He turned his horse north and headed for Ironbark. He wasn't looking forward to bringing Jamie back to his parents in the condition he was in.

When he entered the quiet town, he noticed a dozen or so horses tethered out in front of the sheriff's office. *They're waiting up for our return.* He prodded the two horses down the road. When he got to the sheriff's office, he dismounted and stood there in the glow of the light streaming out from the window. He decided to leave Jamie on the back of Blackfoot's horse and walk inside.

Ben heard him coming up the steps. He stood up and waved the men to be silent. Every eye was staring at the door waiting to see Jamie run in with Indian Joe and Blackfoot. The door opened and Indian Joe walked in looking sullen and pale. Ben stood there frozen. His heart sank. "Where's the boy?"

Indian Joe shook his head looking down at the floor.

"Don't tell me - don't tell me that you found him dead? He's not dead, is he?" Ben yelled.

Indian Joe looked up at him then glanced at the men sitting there. What could he tell them? Jamie was more than dead; he'd been raped and butchered.

Ben shook his head. He started for the door. Indian Joe grabbed his arm. "Wait," he said, blocking his path. Ben looked up at him, looked directly into his eyes. There was something in them that he'd never seen before. "What is it?" he asked.

"Ben," Indian Joe softly replied, looking over the group. "I have him; what they did to him... was..." his voice trailed off.

"What?"

"It was inhumane," he replied. "I just wanted to warn you before you look at his body."

Ben stood back; the rest had choices, he had none. He turned toward the group.

"Everyone, stay put," he ordered. "Where is he?" he continued, turning around.

"He's out front draped over Blackfoot's horse."

Ben walked out with Indian Joe. His eyes caught the boy lying over the saddle. Before going down, he stopped at the steps and looked at Indian Joe. "How bad is it?"

"Ben," he replied, and then paused. "The bastards raped him, hung him on a meat hook and then gutted him like a deer. The boy never stood a chance."

"My God," he whispered.

"We found him hanging in a tree, his guts spilled all over the ground."

Ben's stomach lurched into his throat - his jaw muscles tightened. *What kind of evil could do that to a child?* "Where did you find him and where's Blackfoot?"

176

"We found a canoe along the eastern shoreline. There's a shack about two hundred yards in. There was no one there but Jamie. Blackfoot will stay out there tonight. He'll pick up the tracks in the morning. I must tell you - there are two of them."

"Two?"

"Yes."

Suddenly the door to the sheriff's office opened. It was Carlson. "Carlson, run over to the boarding house. Tell John that we have Jamie and we need a room on the bottom floor. I don't give a damn if it's occupied. Tell John to kick them out," he ordered.

Carlson raced across the street, jumped the wooden steps and entered the boarding house parlor. The rest of the men stepped out and gathered on the porch. None of them wanted to look underneath the blanket, so they stood there and waited for Ben's next order. It didn't come until Indian Joe told them that Jamie was fully naked. Ben turned around and looked up at the men. "Kent, go to the Wilson's and ask Dorothy to put an outfit together. I believe her son is about the same size as Jamie, now hurry. If she asks any questions, just tell her that we found Jamie, and he needs new clothes because we don't want his parents to see him like this."

"Right," Kent replied, running off.

Ben turned when he heard John Fisher, owner of the boarding house, come out.

"Sheriff!" he yelled, taking the steps down. "What gives you the right to tell me to kick out one of my boarders?" The group of men who were milling about the sheriff's office gathered in the road around Ben and John.

"I'm sorry, John, I need the room." he replied, pointing over to Blackfoot's horse. "That's Jamie. I'm not going to take him to Doc Thomson's while the Chamber's are staying there. Not in the condition, he's in now. If you want me to pay for the room, I will. But if word gets out that you turned me down, you might as well pull up stakes and

leave town. I don't think you'll be getting many boarders."
John stepped back looking at the men. Their eyes were as
cold as steel. He turned and looked at Ben. "OK, OK, I'll
remove the couple near the lobby. Bring the boy in," he
replied.

Ben watched him leave, and then turned toward
Indian Joe. "Grab the boy and take him inside, I'll fetch Doc.
I just hope Doc gave Walt and Beth enough sedatives to last
the whole night."

Indian Joe nodded and then gave his own order as
Ben went for his horse. "Sheriff, make sure Doc brings
enough thread to stitch him up."

"I will. Now the rest of you men – go home, please.
We won't get word back from Blackfoot until tomorrow."

"Sheriff, where is he?" one man yelled out.

"Yeah, we have a right to know," another spoke up.

Ben mounted his horse and spun it around. "They
found Jamie on the eastern shoreline, two men took Jamie.
Blackfoot is staying out there tonight, and he'll be tracking
them in the morning. There's nothing we can do until we get
word."

Bill Miller stepped out of the pack and looked up at
Ben. "Sheriff, this town will be armed to the teeth until we
catch those bastards. I'm telling every man here to carry a
gun and to escort their wives and children everywhere."

"Bill, do you want my badge?"

"No. Just do your job, Ben, or we will!"

Ben shook his head. He knew Bill was going to set
the whole town on fire. There was only one way to stop him.
"Deputy, run inside and grab me a badge." Daniel looked up
at him.

"Go!" Daniel raced up the steps and came back out with a
badge.

"OK, Bill. You think you have the guts for this job. Raise
your right hand."

"What are you doing?"

"I'm making you a deputy right here and now."

"I don't want to be a deputy, Ben."

"If you don't want to be a deputy, then leave me be."

Bill stepped back from Ben's horse. He did not want to look at the faces around him. However, he wasn't going to allow Ben to have the last word. "You're the Sheriff, but understand this, Ben Coleman, every man in this town will be out for blood!"

Ben nodded, turned his horse, and raced toward Tall Tree Pocket. When he got to Sugar Bottom Road, he rode up to the house at the end of the street and dismounted. He stood there allowing the cool air to wash over him. It felt like a sedative. He turned and headed toward the back steps. He gave the door three hard knocks and waited.

The door opened. Ben looked into the eyes of Doc Thomson. The moment could have lasted a lifetime; as neither man had to speak. Doc saw the writing in Ben's eyes; Jamie was dead. "No?" was all Doc Thomson could say.

"I'm sorry, Doc, are the Chamber's awake?

"No. I gave them enough juice to keep them out all night."

Just then, Mary walked up behind her husband and looked over his shoulder to see Ben standing there. By the looks of him, she knew it was bad news. "Ben," she said. Doc Thomson let Ben in and closed the door. Ben looked at them and shook his head. Mary's knees gave way; she crumbled to the floor sobbing in her hands. "Oh, sweet Jesus, how are we going to tell Walt and Beth? What are we going to tell Millie?"

Doc knelt down and helped his wife to her feet. "Let's pray they stay asleep, we'll think of something in the morning. Now, keep the doors locked, I'm going into town with Ben."

Ben placed his hand on Doc Thomson's shoulder. "Grab your medical bag and bring plenty of thread."

Mary looked up at Ben through her swollen eyes. Their eyes met. She shook her head, she didn't want to know what happened to Jamie; she knew he was dead - that's all the mattered. Ben mounted his horse and waited for Doc.

Doc settled his wife in the front room, walked into his office, and grabbed his medical bag. He placed three spools of thread inside his bag and headed for the back door. As they rode into town, Ben filled him in on what had happened to Jamie.

When they arrived at the boarding house, Ben saw the people still gathered in the street. None had taken his orders to go home. They dismounted and stood there looking at all the people. The news had spread like wildfire. He'd have to be a fool to think otherwise. *This wasn't like setting a match to a bale of hay - this was like tossing kerosene over barrels of gun powder. Once word got out on how Jamie was murdered, the whole town would explode,* he thought. "Alright, please move aside and let us through." Ben ordered.

"What did they do to that poor boy?" a man shouted.

Ben spun around. "We won't know until Doc here checks him out. So please, just stand back and let us through."

"How do you know that it wasn't Injun's who did this?" another man yelled.

Ben turned again. He looked into the crowd; allowing his stare to do most of the talking.
"Do you really want me to answer that?" he replied. "Y'all know the Indians don't commit crimes against children."

"Yeah, what about out west, those redskins kilt many women and children," another yelled.

"Butchered is more like it," someone else yelled.

"YEAH," the crowd erupted.

Ben looked at Doc. Doc raised his brow. He then took the steps up and stood there. Ben knew he had to face this before all hell broke loose. "How about you all give Doc the chance to check the boy before you make up your minds on who killed him."

Just then, Indian Joe stepped out onto the walkway with his Winchester slung over his shoulder. Ben and Doc

Thomson turned and looked at him. His eyes were dark and menacing. Indian Joe stepped forward scanning over the crowd. "Who found the boy?" he shouted.

The crowd went silent.

"Blackfoot and I found the boy. He is still out there searching for whoever done this. If it was Natives, he'll bring them in so you can see for yourself. If it was white men, he'll bring back their heads. Now, let the Doc do his job." With that, the three turned and walked inside. Carlson walked up to Ben with the clothes he got from Dorothy Wilson. "Which room?" he asked John. John pointed down the hallway. "Use the last room on the right."

When they entered the room, Ben closed the door, locked it, and then turned around to see Doc place the small, bloody bundle on the bed. He looked so small. Doc pulled the blanket off Jamie. He stepped back losing his breath. Jamie was fully naked and sliced open from crotch to throat.

Ben stepped forward and froze. "My God, I can't believe what I'm seeing! What kind of animal could do such a thing to a child?" he gasped. Indian Joe looked at Ben, and then glanced down at Jamie. "You're right, Ben, only an animal could do this to a child, and when we find them, they will pay for what they did to this boy!"

As the two spoke, Doc Thomson opened his medical bag and started to examine Jamie. He opened up the chest cavity and looked inside. He saw something odd. "Here, take a look at this," he said. They both stepped up and looked down.

"He's missing a rib. Don't Indians do that after they kill an animal?" he asked, looking up at Indian Joe. Indian Joe looked at him, turned, and looked at Ben. He could read it in their eyes. They were waiting for an answer. "Yes, but understand one thing," he said, and then paused. "We don't rape children. Go ahead and check. I know this child was raped!"

Before either man spoke, Doc Thomson rolled Jamie to one side and checked.

"You're right, the boy has been raped. How did you know that?" he asked, rolling Jamie over onto his back.

"I didn't, but I suspected he had. I didn't think they would just kill him without torturing him first."

"OK," Ben said. "This information will be kept in this room, understand, gentlemen?"

Doc and Indian Joe agreed. If the killers murdered anyone else, child or adult, they'd know it was the same men.

"Alright, let's get him cleaned up, and we'll put these clothes on him," Ben ordered.

"Before I can stitch him up, I'll need some bed sheets to tuck inside his chest. He won't look right unless I do."

Ben looked down at the bed. "Pick him up; we'll use the sheet on this bed."

After they had Jamie cleaned up and ready, Ben made one more request. "I don't want to tell Walt and Beth what actually happened to their boy. We'll tell 'em that he was strangled and leave it at that."

"Do you think they'll buy it?"

Ben weighed that up. *That wouldn't make sense, would it?* "OK, we'll tell Walt and let him take it from there. Whatever he says is how it will be." They agreed.

As they walked out, Ben thanked John, and then noticed Neal Clancy, the undertaker, standing in the parlor. "He's all yours, Neal," he said, nodding his head toward the room down the hallway. "I'm counting on you. I don't want another soul to know what actually happened to that boy, Neal. If anyone finds out, I'll know who told."

"You can count on me, Sheriff. I won't tell a soul, you have my solemn word. I'll make him look nice, you'll see," he replied, heading down the hall.

Make him look nice, Ben thought. *How nice can you make someone look after they'd been mutilated and murdered - especially a child?* The three of them walked out and stood on the walkway. Most of the crowd had gone home, with the exception of Bill Miller, Deputy Harding, and Jake Fuller.

"Look, Sheriff," Bill said, leaning against one of the pillars. "I was way out of line tonight."

"Forget about it, Bill. We all want to catch these bastards and there's no one here who'd like to see their heads on a pole more than me. Now… how about we all get some sleep. "Doc," he continued, "I'll be up early. If Walt and Beth are up, go ahead and tell 'em. If not, wait for Daniel and me. I think the more people we have standing there - the better. Those two will need all the support we can give them."

Doc Thomson didn't need that bit of information. He wished the whole town could be there when they broke the news to the Chamber's.

Chapter 17

The morning rolled in with overcast skies. The sun seemed to know the heartache that was to come as Sheriff Coleman and Deputy Harding rode out to Doc Thomson's house in Tall Tree Pocket. It was going to be one of those days; dark cold and grey - just like the clouds drifting in from Lake Ontario - when Walt and Beth were told the news.

After riding up, they went around the back and tethered their horses to the fence. They stood there for a moment looking at one another; as if to gather strength.

"Maybe they're already up, and Doc told 'em," Daniel said, hoping.

"It wouldn't matter if he had, we still have to face 'em," Ben replied, walking toward the back steps.

Daniel followed as Ben walked up to the door. Before they even knocked, it opened. It was Mary. They could tell she had not slept at all. Her eyes were swollen and wet with tears.

"They're not up yet. Doc's checking on them now. C'mon in."

"How's Millie?" Ben asked.

"She won't come out of her room. I'm worried. Doc thinks she's in shock. You know…" Mary said and then paused, turning and facing them. "This may sound funny, but those two children loved one another. I know that they're only eight years old, but they do."

Ben nodded. He understood. His parents met when they were twelve. They knew then that they'd be together forever. "We all know how they felt about each other. It's just so sad to think he was out there picking flowers for her when this happened. I guess we'll have to be more aware of who's in town and where our children are at any given time."

184

"After this, I'm sure that every mother and father living in this town will have their children on a very short leash. It's so sad that it has to be that way, but now we have no choice. Would you like some coffee?" she asked.

"Yes, black, please. We'll wait in the parlor," Ben replied, stepping past her and heading down the hallway.

They both took up seats and waited. Mary came out with their coffee. A moment later, they heard Doc coming down the stairs. They both stood up.

"Morning, gentlemen. Please have a seat," Doc requested.

"Morning, Doc," they replied, sitting back down.

"Mary, may I have a cup?"

"Sure, Dear. Please, excuse me, I'll be right back."

The three men just sat there looking at the floor; none wanting to confront the Chamber's with the news. "Are they up yet?" Ben asked, cutting the silence.

Doc nodded. "They're washing up now."

"Have you told them?" Daniel asked.

"No. Y'all know Walt. I wanted to wait until you two arrived."

Millie looked up at David and William. "Before the Chamber's went downstairs, I was in my bedroom. I wanted to stay there forever. My parents told me that morning. I knew when they both came in. My mother always did that you know," she said.

David and William nodded.

"I loved Jamie. I thought in time that I would get over losing him, but I never did. I still love him to this day."

David looked over at William then back at her. He sighed, not knowing what to say. He just nodded.

"You know, he never minded that I did marry. It was so nice of him," she sighed.

David quickly shot another glance over to William. The look in William's eyes was of shock. "Who are you talking about?" David asked.

Millie looked up at him. She said it without even thinking. She was still drifting on the winds of time. "What?" she questioned startled.

"Who never minded you getting married?" William asked.

Mr. Bones stood there looking into Millie's window. He sighed hearing her speak of her love for him. He loved her too. He always had and always would. He saw tears begin to roll down Millie's cheeks. He looked at the two detectives sitting there. It made him mad! The only person he ever cared for was now crying. He had made a promise to himself a long time ago. He'd always protect her, and now these two men were causing her grief. He stepped up to the window with the intentions of going in and grabbing them both by the throat, but he stopped when Millie started talking again.

"I'm sorry, I must be getting confused. It happens when you get old, you know. Now, where was I?" she said, trying to throw them off track.

William looked at David. David's eyes said - let it go. William raised his brow and let the frail woman continue. "You were telling us about the Chamber's."

"Oh, yes. Now… where was I? After my father went downstairs, I heard Mr. and Mrs. Chamber's going down the stairs. It was the only time, besides Jamie's funeral, that I left my bedroom. I walked out and stood at the top of the stairs. It was awful."

Walt stopped at the bottom step when he saw the two lawmen sitting there with Doc and Mary. His heart sank when Ben looked up at him. He could see it in his eyes; Ben did not have good news. Beth saw it too. "My boy, my boy, where is my boy?" she shouted.

No one said a word. Walt's sadness turned to anger in an instant. "I'll kill the bastard! I'll kill the son-of-a bitch!" he yelled, walking toward the front door.

"Walt, wait. Hold on," Ben shouted, running over to him. He grabbed him by the shoulders and spun him around. The anger, hatred, and sadness were all sitting there in Walt's eyes. Ben looked at him and said it. "He's gone Walt. Indian Joe and Blackfoot found him last night near Marshall Lake. He's dead; he been strangled."

Walt's body melted. He crumbled to the floor. Beth screamed. The grief was so overwhelming; she passed out and fell to the floor. Mary ran to her side and held her in her arms.

Blackfoot was just passing Tall Tree Pocket at the time, unaware of what was happening inside Doc Thomson's house. He was alone, on foot, and heading back to town. It had been a long night and a hard day of tracking the two men that killed Jamie.

That morning, he fixed it so it looked like an animal had come and taken Jamie away. He cleared all the tracks, leaving no trace, and walked toward Willow Creek following the bootprints. He stopped at the water's edge where the tracks disappeared into the water.

He crossed the creek looking for signs were they might have gotten out. He found none; which meant they were using the creek to hide their trail. Being from these parts, he knew the creek and river systems like the back of his hand. Willow Creek started at the Pinto River just south-west of there. It ran perhaps a mile and a half on the outskirts of Marshall Lake. From there, it emptied into Lake Ontario. The Pinto River also emptied into Lake Ontario from its north end. Due North, the river cut through the Sheppard

Mountains and then traveled along the Forgotten Land - were it continued onward to Lake Ontario.

Blackfoot knew the killers would not head north - using Willow Creek, because that would lead them straight back toward the town. He waded into the creek and headed south. From there, he would skirt around Marshall Lake, come up on Hollow Trail where the Pinto and Willow Creek emerged - right before the Forgotten Land.

After three hours of searching the creek's bank, he stopped at the Willow Creek Bridge just before the Pinto River. His gut instinct told him that they never left the creek. They headed straight into the Forgotten Land after crossing the Pinto River. He waded out of the water, walked up to the bridge and looking towards the Forgotten Land on the other side of the Pinto River. He knew they were in there, or hiding out in the Sheppard Mountains just beyond. *That could take weeks of tracking,* he thought. With that, he turned and headed back toward town - a six-mile hike on foot.

When he got to Main Street, Jack Burns, the owner of the grocery store, stopped sweeping his steps to look up and see Blackfoot. "Blackfoot!" he yelled.
Blackfoot tossed his head in Jack's direction, nodded, and continued walking toward the sheriff's office. From the nod of his head, and the drawn look on his face, Jack knew that Blackfoot did not find the men who murdered Jamie Chamber. He also knew that all hell was going to break loose once word got out.

"Hey look," Kid Carlson said, pointing up the road. The men all turned to see Blackfoot walking in by himself. They walked off the steps and stood there. Blackfoot approached the men. He looked into each of their faces with silent anger.

"Where are they?" Bill Miller asked, resting his rifle over his shoulder.

"They're running the river systems. I followed their tracks past the shanty to Willow Creek. I headed south and then west until I got to the Pinto River. My gut tells me their hiding out in the Sheppard Mountians."

"What if they headed north and came back into town? Hell, the bastards could be holed up inside Sue's right now with some soft flesh next to them," Jake Fuller spat.
"I searched Willow Creek. I saw no signs of them coming back this way. They're too smart to come into town."

"Who are these bastards? Where did they come from, and how would they know how to navigate through the Forgotten Land or the Sheppard Mountains?" Kid questioned, without wanting an answer.

Where they came from, was anyone's guess. There were so many drifters, hunters, and Indians in town at this time of the year, any one of them could have done it.
As they milled about waiting for Ben and Deputy Harding, Indian Joe, along with Chief Running Bear and ten braves, walked into town carrying rifles.

"I think Indian Joe knew you'd come back empty handed," Bill Miller said, looking down the street.

"Is that a war party?" Kid asked.

"Yes," Blackfoot replied, stepping away from the group.

Blackfoot approached Chief Running Bear and told him what happened in their native tongue. Chief Running Bear's jaw muscles tightened. He wanted to see scalps; not hear words.

As the two men spoke, town folk started streaming into the street wanting to know what was happening. The news of Jamie had struck at the heart of the town like a hot branding iron. No one dared to go out at night. Women and children were forbidden to go out alone. Doors were locked, and the small schoolhouse was closed.

Bill Miller thought of what Kid Carlson had said, 'the killers could have doubled back and were hiding out in town.' He thought that might be true and he worried that whatever was discussed on the street right now, could be to the advantage of those murdering thugs.

"Chief Running Bear," he said, looking at the crowd of onlookers. He quickly nodded his head toward the sheriff's office.

Chief Running Bear nodded and then followed Bill through the crowd. When he climbed the steps, someone yelled out, "We all know that only a cold-blooded savage could do something like this!"

The ten Indian braves following Chief Running Bear stopped and turned toward the crowd; rifles at the ready. The group of white men did the same. The tension in the air thickened.

Bill Miller stood at the door with Chief Running Bear. The Chief then gave an order in his native tongue to his braves to lower their rifles. One of them turned and looked at him; no words were spoken, they lowered their rifles. The white men followed suit and the standoff settled down. Everyone turned when they heard the sounds of horses and a wagon. Doc Thomson had Walt and Beth in his wagon. Ben and Daniel were following behind. The crowd went silent as the wagon pulled up. The women gathered around Beth as she started to cry. Ben dismounted and waded through the crowd. He saw trouble in their eyes.

"Doc, take them to Clancy. Daniel, you go with them."

They nodded. Doc snapped the reins, the horses moved forward, and the women folk stepped aside. Everyone stood there watching Walt and Beth being escorted over to the undertaker's. It would be the last time they'd see their boy.

Once they were out of earshot, Ben took the steps up and turned to face the crowd. He wanted this information kept secret, especially from the Chamber's. To say what he was about to say would most certainly get back to them, but he knew if he kept silent and did nothing – the whites and the natives would start killing each other. "Everyone gather around and hear me out," he shouted. They all stepped up. "Now, I want this kept to yourselves. If word gets back to Walt and Beth, I'll have your hides. Jamie Chamber was raped, and then strangled," he continued; not conveying everything that was done to the boy.

The crowd stepped back. The women gasped, the men felt their guts tighten. No one dared to pin that on the Indians. They all knew that Indians would never do that to a child.

"What are you going to do?" a woman shouted, startling the crowd.

"Were going to find them and bring them in," Ben replied.

"Yeah, well what the hell do we all do now, just go on living as usual?" a man shouted.

"Yeah, Sheriff," a woman added.

Ben raised his hand. "Listen, we all must stick together. I don't want any fools trying to take this on themselves. Leave it to the law and these men here. We'll catch these murderers. In the meantime, watch your families, your houses, and don't go out alone. You women folk, get with Beth, she needs you. The funeral is tomorrow morning. Now, please, let's get on with this. Go home and remain alert." With that, he turned and walked inside with Chief Running Bear, Indian Joe, Blackfoot, Jake Fuller, Bill Miller and Deputy Harding. "OK, so what happened out there?" Ben asked Blackfoot, sitting down at his desk.

"They're using the river systems to get around. I tracked them south down Willow Creek and stopped at the bridge before the river's fork."

"Why did you stop there?"

"The water there is rough. I believe they swam across the Pinto and headed into the Forgotten Land or the mountains beyond."

Ben looked at the men thinking. *If they had a hideout in there, it would take every soldier from Fort Mason to try to find them - and I'd lay odds that they'd come out empty handed.* "What if they headed north down Willow Creek toward Lake Ontario, if they did, don't you think that they could be walking the streets right now?" Bill Manning asked.

"You think they're foolish enough?" Chief Running Bear replied.

"Yes. Why, they could be here right under our noses while we're out there chasing ghosts."

"If that's the case," Deputy Harding spoke up, walking to the center of the room, "then they'll never know our plans from here on out. We keep everything in this room, understand."

"That might be to our advantage," Indian Joe agreed.

They all looked at him.

He shrugged his shoulders and continued. "Look, if those murderers are in town, let them think we're continuing our search out there. A rabbit won't come out of its hole until it feels safe thinking the wolves are gone. We can send half the posse to search out there and keep the rest here in town."

"OK, who stays and who leaves?" Ben asked.

"We send my braves out," Chief Running Bear replied. "Leave your men in town. Have them congregate at the saloon, the boarding house, and at Sue's. If they're in town they're bound to spill it to someone," he continued.

Blackfoot figured if these cut throats would spill their guts, it would be at Sue's. Men talk more freely when in bed with a woman. "I'll talk to Wild Flower. She'll spread the word at Sue's. I'm sure all the women there will be happy to lend a hand," he suggested.

Ben nodded. "OK. We'll try it. Have your braves ride out. Bill, get the men in town to meet me behind the stables tonight. We'll wait until then, and hopefully, if those cut throats are here amongst us, they'll be in the saloon chasing the girls or they'll be down at Sue's."

Bill nodded and headed for the door.

"Oh, one more thing before you all go," Ben said. "Clancy is burying Jamie tomorrow morning. Please be there. We all have to take care of Walt and Beth now."

"How are they?" Indian Joe asked.

"Bad. I've never seen such sorrow. I don't know how they're going to get through this terrible tragedy."

"You know," Millie said, stepping out of the past. "I was not aware of all this happening until I was much older. But what they had planned after Jamie was murdered backfired on them."

"What do you mean?' David asked.

"Well, those men never were in town. Blackfoot was right. Boone and Darrell were using the river systems to get around. And... they were in fact, hiding out in the Sheppard Mountains. I look back now and wish Ben had wired your grandfather sooner, maybe things would've turned out different."

"Well, he did come up after Ben dispatched the wire after Jill Farmer went missing," David replied.

"Yes, and I am glad he came," she replied, looking up at the ceiling. *Even though he did came - he would have never found Boone and Darrell, not where they were hiding out. It was Mr. Bones. He's the one who caught them in the end,* she thought. *My beautiful friend,* her thoughts continued. *If you only knew just how close, the police were to discovering you.*

She stepped out of her thoughts and focused here eyes on David. "Well, as you know, while everyone turned their backs and headed off to Jamie's funeral, those two struck again."

"We know Millie," William replied. "Go ahead and tell us what happened."

Millie leaned her head back and started where she had left off. "Boone was certainly the smarter of the two. He was the one who worked out the plans and got to know the area as well as the trappers and Indians. He proved that with his navigational skills through the rough terrain of the Forgotten Land. Not many would have even attempted it," she said, looking at William. He nodded. She smiled, looked up at the ceiling and closed her eyes.

"It was early morning when my parents woke me up. I had not been out in days, and it seemed like years to me. After losing my beloved Jimmy, I did not want to do anything; I was so lonely without him. My parents wore dark clothing to the funeral, but I did not have anything dark or black to wear, so I wore a blue dress. Jimmy's favorite color was blue.
The wagon ride seemed to take forever.

"My only thought while we rode to the funeral was watching them lowering his casket. It was heart wrenching, to say the least. The church was located on Forest Street near the school. The cemetery was at the end of the street. As we pulled up, my father got down from the wagon and tethered the horses. It seemed the whole town showed up; everyone was there. Not one shop in town was open that day, not even Sue's boarding house. Beth and Walt were in the front. They sat together, devastated. Their world would never be the same again. Both of them were inconsolable at that time, and everyone could see that Walt was slipping over the edge. Devastated; he never recovered. He went to drinking soon after. Beth had a hard time keeping him out of the saloon.

"I guess the saddest part, besides Jimmy's funeral that morning - was Jill Farmer. She lived on Mansfield Lane. Funny, it was actually their driveway leading up to the farmhouse. She just liked calling it that. It was a beautiful farm; sitting right in the center of the meadow along the Hollow Trail. She stayed home that day because I guess she just could not get up the nerve to come. Her parents requested their maid to stay back to keep her company. It was a grave mistake. Mr. and Mrs. Farmer never suspected the murderers would strike again while the town was in such mourning. Sadly - they did."

Chapter 18

"Hey," Boone grumbled, kicking Darrell's bunk. "Y'all get out of that bed and get that fire going. I want to eat and get movin'."

Darrell moaned, opened his eyes, and then yawned - sitting up. "What-cha gettin' me up so early fur, it's not even daylight yet. We can check our traps when the sun comes up."

"We're not checking our traps today, Spud."

"What? Then why we getting' up so early, and quit callin' me Spud. You think I'm a potata or somethin?"

Boone laughed, opening the cabin door. "Hurry up," he shouted over his shoulder.

While Darrell was getting dressed, Boone stood near the cabin looking through the forest. He looked straight up at the sheer peeks and bluffs of the Sheppard Mountains right behind the cabin. It took them well over a month cutting trees down and constructing the small cabin in this little inlet next to the base of the mountain. He felt safe with the mountains right behind them knowing that there was only one way in. It was a small path they created, which led along the base of the mountain through the forest and ending at the Pinto River.

It would certainly take a good tracker to find them on this side of the mountains. Most hunters and trappers would stop at the Forgotten Land on the other side.
Their secret was simple. They never ventured into the Forgotten Land. They used the Pinto River to head into the mountains. As the river cut through it, it pooled in a small inlet where they could swim to a rocky outcrop. From there, they followed the path along the base of the mountain range. Hidden deep within the forest, at the base of the mountains,

they never even worried about having an open fire at night. It was impossible for anyone to see or smell.

Darrell came out with his shirt half tucked in. He walked over to the woodpile, grabbed a few logs, and walked back in. After kicking up the fire, he sat at the table cutting up leftover porcupine. He placed the slices near the fire, walked outside and stood next to Boone. "What you got planned in that head of yours today?" he asked.

"I think it is time to go back into town."

"What, are you crazy? You know those people will be lookin' for us after we took that boy."

Boone looked at him then down at the ground. He took two steps and kicked a rock across the dirt. "Yeah, but they have to find him first," he replied, turning around. "I think while they're looking for that boy we can slip back in and no one will even know we're there."

Darrell walked over to the rock Boone just kicked and kicked it back to him. He then looked up into the morning sky. It looked like a good day ahead. "Maybe you're right," he said, looking back at Boone.

"When have I been wrong? Every time I say the time is right, it worked," he replied, walking over to him. "Look, how many have we taken since leaving Georgia?"
Darrell could not remember. He was glad Boone did all the thinking. He never went to school. He couldn't read or write, and he knew he hadn't the brains to make decisions.

"Well? Don't you know?" Boone pushed. "We've taken ten kids since leaving Georgia. Can't you remember anything?"

"Guess that's why you're the boss. OK, let's eat and get ready," Darrell replied.

Boone walked over and kicked the rock back to him. Darrell picked it up, tossed it into the woods, and followed Boone inside.

After packing their gear, they headed down the path toward the Pinto River. When they came to the fork where the Pinto River split - creating Willow Creek, they waded out of the water and headed west, continuing down the Pinto River bank toward the small farming community.

A half mile down the bank of the river, Boone stopped. He looked across the river, through the trees, at the farmland. "Let's cross back over," he said, wading into the river.

After crossing, they knelt down in the dense scrub, looking out at several farms just off in the distance. "Hey," Boone whispered.

"What?"

"You notice something strange?"

"No."

"Look out there and tell me what you see."

Darrell looked through the dense foliage. He didn't notice anything strange. It all looked normal to him. "I don't see anything wrong."

"That's the problem, you don't see anything."

Darrell shook his head. "That's right, I don't see anything. So, what should I be seein'?"

"People, damn it! There's no one around out there. There's no one tending their fields, or their livestock, nothing."

"Yeah, you're right. Maybe they're all out searching for that boy."

"Wait! Look at that farmhouse over there. You see what I see?"

Darrell looked in the direction Boone was pointing. His eyes lit up like a Christmas tree. "Well, if that don't beat all. Look at that little filly heading for the outhouse. You think she's alone?"

"No. You kiddin' me? Who would leave her all alone? Her parents have to be there, and if there not, someone else is there watching her."

Millie opened her eyes. She looked over at David sitting there with his legs crossed. "You know how Jill Farmer was found?" she asked.

"Yes."

"Those two monsters took Jill from that outhouse, carried her back across the Pinto River and did all kinds of horrible things to her. After their horrible fun, they stuffed her body down a rabbit burrow."

David and William sighed, shaking their heads. "You know, this old report here doesn't say anything about the maid that was watching Jill," William questioned.

"Her name was Gloria Wilson. She never recovered. She felt so guilty and responsible for what had happened to Jill that I don't think she ever forgave herself. She left Ironbark soon after and returned to her parents in New York City. Martha and Ben Farmer never blamed her, though."

"I can only imagine," William replied.

Millie sighed, thinking of that horrible time. "After they buried Jill, the whole town went crazy. All they could think about was killing Boone and Darrell. Some however, still blamed the Indians. There are some folks out there who just need an excuse to seek revenge on those they hate."

"Sadly, that still applies today, Millie," David replied.

Millie nodded. "I think that's why Ben Coleman wired your grandfather for help. He knew things were going to get out of hand. So your grandfather and his partner... what was his name?"

"Jim Dole."

"Yeah, that's it. When they showed up, it seemed to settle the town a little. They saw that your grandfather was a smart man. He was so thorough in everything he did trying to solve those murders."

David laughed. "You're right."

She smiled. "However, soon after your grandfather showed up, my father's dear friend, Mr. Bones came to town. And, if it wasn't for him, those two monsters would probably have never gotten caught."

David sat back. He slightly glanced over at William. William looked puzzled.

"Mr. Bones?" David questioned, looking back at her. "There's no one by that name in this report."

"Oh, I'm certain of that, Detective. I called him Mr. Bones for so long back then, that I've forgotten his real name. You see, I used to whisper that name to my dolls when I lay in bed at night. He was tall and skinny, so I called him Mr. Bones."

"He was your father's friend?" William asked.

"Yes."

"Where did he come from?" David added.

Millie's head went back and forth as if she was watching a tennis match looking at the two of them. "Mr. Bones was a trapper. Best darn trapper in them parts at the time, too. I think he was better than Indian Joe and Blackfoot if you can believe that."

"What did he look like?" William asked.

"Like I said, he was very tall and thin. He had dark brown hair, a long nose and wore a moustache. I don't know why he was so skinny with all the wild game he'd catch. He was a very shy man, though. He liked his own company. I guess you'd get that way living in the woods all alone. When he came to town and heard what had happened to Jimmy and Jill, he went after those two murderers."

David remembered the report stated that, after Indian Joe had discovered Jill Farmer's body, he tracked one of the bootprints along the west side of the Pinto River. The tracks lead to the Forgotten Land. There, he decided to go back and take Jill's body back to town.

Once he turned her body over, he and Blackfoot went back out to continue their search. When they reached the Forgotten Land, the two decided to split up. Indian Joe headed east back toward the Pinto River. When he reached the riverbank, he allowed his eyes to drift down the river toward the mountains. It hit him right there. Those two were not crossing the Forgotten Land to hideout somewhere in the Sheppard Mountains - they were using the river, just as Blackfoot suspected.

Indian Joe rode his horse straight into the river. In several sections, he had to get off and swim alongside holding onto the saddle. Approximately a half mile down, the river started to bend. It was there that he spotted a small rocky inlet and shoreline. He guided his horse over and waded out of the water. After tethering his horse, he walked into the dense forest and started searching the ground for signs of tracks. To his surprise - he discovered several leading deeper into the forest at the base of the mountain. He quickly returned to the river, gathered his horse and ventured in. It wasn't long until he came upon a small cabin - and then shockingly discovering Boone and Darrell hanging from the trees.

When he returned with the bodies, he informed Sheriff Coleman and my grandfather that their bodies had to go on display for all to see. When they asked why - he said that a spirit had spoken to him out there. The spirit told him it was the only way to rid the town of evil.

As David stepped out of his thoughts, he looked at Millie. *She knows the man who killed those two, which means - Millie's father and her mother must have known the man too. So, why did they hide this information from my grandfather?*

He needed to find out. Because whomever he was that Millie was talking about, he now believed that the man's relative was the one who killed Kevin Downer. "Millie, are you sure you can't remember the man's name?" he asked.

Millie could see it in his eyes. He not going to let it go. *I should have never mentioned Mr. Bones,* she thought. She had to think fast. "Wait a minute," she said and then paused, trying to throw David off track. "I think his name was Remington. Remington, hmm…." she continued. "Yeah, that's it. His name was Samuel Remington."

David glanced over at William. William wasn't buying it either. *Why was she lying?* he thought. *What reason could there be? She's certainly trying to cover up something, but why?* Then something struck him odd. He looked down at the old photo of the bootprint and had an idea. He picked it up, turned it toward Millie, and asked her, "Is this Mr. Remington's bootprint?" Her pause gave him caution. He knew the answer was yes, but she caught him off guard with her reply. "No, those boots belonged to my father."

David's mind twisted. "How could that be? Those prints were discovered at the crime scene. Your father was accused and then eliminated because," David said and then paused when Millie interrupted him. "That's right. He was too old to have leaped over that embankment. Is that what you were getting at?"

"Yes. You seem to remember everything," David replied.

"You're right, I do. Mr. Remington liked wearing my father's boots. He said they were a nice fit."

"OK, so now that we know that Samuel Remington was wearing your father's boots, how about finishing your story."

"Where do you want me to begin?"

"When did Mr. Remington arrive in town?"

"It was right after Jill Farmer was murdered," she replied, looking at the two detectives sitting there waiting.

She closed her eyes and began again. "As I said before, right after Jill was taken, Ben Coleman wired your grandfather. Mr. Remington came a day or two before your grandfather arrived with his partner. It was late one evening when I heard a horse coming around the back. I looked out my window to see who it was. I watched Mr. Remington get down from his horse and tethering it to the hitching post next to the barn. When he walked up the steps, my father opened the door."

"Hey, Mary, look who's come to town. How are you Sam? It sure has been awhile. Come on in. We just finished dinner, are you hungry?"

"Shh, you two," Millie whispered to her dolls, hear Mr. Remington coming in. "Mr. Bones is back." She got out of bed with her dolls, slipped into the hallway, and sat down at the top of the stairs. She heard her mother greeting Mr. Remington and then asked him if he wanted something to eat. He said yes. Then she heard her father speak up - asking Mr. Remington if he had heard about the murders.

"Sadly, yes. I was hunting just west of here for the past two months. I had some Frenchmen paddle up in a canoe while I was cleaning my pelts. They told me what had happened in Ironbark. They said they left right after they took the second child. Said it was too heart wrenching to stick around. After hearing that, I thought I'd pull up stakes and come in."

"I was so glad he came," Millie continued. "He liked children. He would sit with me in my room and draw the birds just as Jimmy did. I was surprised how well he could draw. I guess when you live in the wilderness the animals become your friends. I sure liked his company even though he was shy."

"Did he ever speak to my grandfather when he was there?" David asked.

"No. He did not talk to anyone. He said he had no need to and knew how to deal with people who hurt children."

"Did your father tell my grandfather about Mr. Remington when he was accused of being the person who put Teddy Cotton's body on the trail that night?"

Millie could feel the noose getting tighter. She knew her story was so far out there that you would need a telescope to see it. She made her answer short. "No. My parents never mentioned Mr. Remington because he asked them not to."

"So, you're telling us that Mr. Remington actually jumped that embankment after putting the dead boy down on the trail?" William asked.

"Well," Millie replied, and then paused. "If the Yammers said that they saw it, I guess he did."

"But you said he was tall and very thin. I would guess by that description that he wasn't a strong man, you know, well built," David asked.

"No. You're right. But he sure had a pair of legs on him. I would think anyone who lived in the wilderness all his life would have to be a good runner, wouldn't you?"

David weighed that up and thought of track athletes. They were skinny and long legged men and women. However, was it possible for one of them to jump a six-foot embankment?

"I guess you may be right," he replied, picking up the old file. "Do you mind if I read a bit?" he asked.

"No, go right ahead."

David opened the old file and re-read the part on Mary Baker, the barber's daughter, who was the next child abducted. This part of the investigation was interesting because Indian Joe spoke of a third person who was involved.

He looked over Indian Joe's testimony, which stated; he discovered a set of bootprints at the back of the Baker's home and followed them to the Pinto River. While there, he found another set of prints and figured the second suspect was waiting for his partner to return with a child. Indian Joe then discovered another set of prints that he suspected was following Boone and Darrell. The prints were about a yard away from the other two sets of prints. He looked up at Millie. "It says here in Indian Joe's statement that he discovered a third set of prints on the west side of the Pinto River after Mary Baker was abducted. Can you tell me about that?"

"Those were Mr. Remington's tracks. He came back and told my parents that he had found Mary sitting against a tree. That's when he started searching which way Boone and Darrell went. He figured they dropped her there because they knew someone was following them."

"So why did he leave Mary there?" William asked.

Millie looked into his eyes. She knew that she was really messing her story up. "Mary was already dead. He was mad and went after them."

"OK, so after he tracked the one set of prints to the Forgotten Land – he came back to where Mary was and brought her back to town, is that correct?" David asked. "Well I might be a little confused. I think I said he did in my story. However, Indian Joe actually brought her back into town. Indian Joe said that a spirit told him where she was, and he went and got her. He spoke to the great owl and the white eagle all the time."

David sat there thinking about Millie's story. It was too hard to believe because her parents never told anyone about this "Mr. Remington" during the entire investigation, or even after Boone and Darrell were dead. *Millie's story is so baffling,* he thought. *If Mr. Remington killed those two as Millie said he did - he certainly wasn't from the*

spirit world. Indian Joe said that a spirit had told him what to do with Boone and Darrell's bodies.
With that, he knew Millie's story had too many holes in it. She was hiding something or someone. *What else can I ask her that would make her trip up?* A question popped into his head. "Tell me then. Did Indian Joe know Mr. Remington?"

She looked at him. He saw a slight waver in her eyes. He slowly glanced over at William. He could tell William had caught the look.

"I'm not really sure. However, he might have. I did not know many men like Mr. Remington. He was a great frontiersman, a great tracker, and I guess I could say; he was as much a part of the wilderness as cactuses are to a desert, so Indian Joe may have known him. He knew many fine hunters back then."

"I'm a bit confused. It states here that Indian Joe told my grandfather and Ben Coleman that the spirit told him to hang them both in the big oak tree – when actually, I think you're now telling us that it was Mr. Remington who told him to do that?"

"I think after Indian Joe met Mr. Remington out there and saw what he did to Boone and Darrell at that cabin, he was scared. With that, it's my guess that Mr. Remington then told Indian Joe to take them back and hang them in that tree. Indian Joe did what he asked and probably just made up the spirit talking to him out there."

"So it was Mr. Remington who threatened him?" William asked.

"Yes, he damn well threatened Indian Joe! We lost four children; Jamie Chamber, Jill Farmer, Mary Baker and Teddy Cotton - all dead. Mr. Remington was going to make an example out of Boone and Darrell. He was going to make damn sure no one in Ironbark would ever harm another child again."

206

"So, what happened to Mr. Remington after he killed Boone and Darrell?" William asked.

"He left in the middle of the night after those two were strung up down by the lake. He never returned to Ironbark. I missed him very much. Now, do you have any more questions? I'm getting tired."

"Just one more thing, if you don't mind," David said.

"Yes, what is it?"

David lifted up the photos of the bootprints so she could see them. "You say this old bootprint is from your father's boots and Mr. Remington borrowed them while he hunted those two down?"

"Yes, they are."

"Then who do you think is wearing these?"

She looked at her father's bootprint and then at the new photo. They were the same boots. She shook her head. "You know, I'm just as shocked as you are. They certainly look the same. But I wouldn't have a clue."

As Mr. Bones stood in the shadows of the bushes listening to Millie's story, he spotted a black car pulling into the parking lot. It parked right behind the car the two detectives drove in. He glared at the driver sitting there. He knew it was another lawman. He quickly looked back at Millie as the two detectives were about to get up and leave.

"Well, Millie, I want to thank you for your time. I hope with all this talk of the past," he said, and then was abruptly cut off.

"Detective Bradshaw, it happened a million years ago. I'm very old now and don't have much time left. Dwelling on it now will not help me."

David and William stood up. They bid her a good night and headed for the door.

"Detective Bradshaw," Millie said.

David turned around. She waved him back over. David looked at William and nodded for him to leave. David waited until William stepped out and then walked back to her bedside. Millie waved him down to her level. He bent over close to her face.

"Detective Bradshaw, I'm warning you, whatever you're chasing – you don't want to catch. Leave it be. Your suspect is dead. Go home to your wife and children, if you have any."

David felt a lump in his throat. He slowly raised his head to meet her eyes. Her eyes never wavered off his. From her look, he knew deep down inside that, her story was just that, a story to lead them off the path. He smiled, took her hand, and gently squeezed it. When he stood up, he let go.

"Thank you, Millie. I think I'll take your advice." She smiled and closed her eyes. He turned and walked out.

Chapter 19

David slowly shut her door and stood there in the corridor. Her last statement or more so, warning, sat within his thoughts. *"Whatever you're chasing - you don't want to catch. Just leave it be and go home."* His mind felt like a house of cards ready to fall in on itself. William looked at him. David's facial expression looked as if his whole world just changed. David put up a finger. He nodded. He could see that his partner was in a minefield of thought. David stood there for a second pondering the last part of Millie's story. *Who was Samuel Remington then? Or - did Millie just make him up?* His thoughts circled back to Indian Joe. He was the only one who saw the person that tortured and killed Boone and Darrell. Up to that point in Indian Joe's life - he wasn't afraid of anything until that encounter. He said it was a spirit who ordered him to take Boone and Darrell back. David had no answer, but one thing was certain - *Indian Joe did in fact have an encounter with someone or something within the Sheppard Mountains.* He sighed and then looked at William.

"What did she have to say?"

He raised his brow. "She said that we don't want to catch what we're chasing, and to just go home."

William slowly nodded, observing the look within his eyes. He knew Millie was lying the whole time. Or maybe, just the part about Samuel Remington to try and cover up the real person who murdered Boone and Darrell. "Here, let me see that old report," he asked, coming out of his thoughts.

"What are you looking for?"

William shook his head while shifting through the file. He pulled out Indian Joe's statement and read it again. "You were right."

"I was right about what?" David asked.

William pointed down at the page. "Indian Joe said that he was told by a spirit to bring them back."

"Yes, I was just thinking of that."

"She told us that it was Samuel Remington."

"We both know that's not true, Will."

"Yes, I know that."

William cocked his head staring into his eyes. "I know this might sound crazy, but if it wasn't Samuel Remington who told Indian Joe - then do you think maybe just maybe that it was an actual spirit that told Indian Joe? Could it be possible that we're chasing a spirit, and that's why Millie told you to leave it alone?

David stepped back. "Where are you?"

"Passing Mars, I think."

David reached up and rubbed his chin. *He's losing it.* William caught the look.

"You think I'm crazy?"

"Are you talking about a ghost? You think that's what we're chasing?"

"Maybe, I'm not sure. However, we cannot explain how a person can jump an eight foot fence or hoist someone thirty feet up into a tree, can we?" Besides that, you know as well as I do that it would take the strength of ten men to have done that to Boone and Darrell. That goes for Kevin Downer, too."

David stood there listening still deep in thought.

William stopped talking seeing his partner standing there drifting on the wind. He decided to shoot another idea across his bow. "What do you think about the welcome mat sitting under her window? Most people put them at their door."

The welcome mat, David thought. *I almost forgot about that. Pam did mention something about Millie having an imaginary friend who would come to visit her.* He looked at William standing there waiting for an answer. "Alright, let me play judge's advocate here. What about Corporal Carter and Caroline Goldsmith actually seeing the guy?"

William pondered that. "I don't know. You think ghosts can run around with clothes on?"

"Would you like me to take you to a hospital?" David remarked.

"Alright, that might have sounded stupid, but this whole thing is getting a little weird, don't you think? What other explanation can you come up with besides a spirit or ghost?"

David had no comeback. He saw the look in Millie's eyes. They were dead and lifeless. *People don't look that way unless,* he thought, *unless they're telling you the truth.* He'd seen that look before. Victims of violent crimes always had that look. They would talk as if they were dead people reliving a horrific act. "How about we get some fresh air?" he replied. "Maybe that would help."

"You're right. Let's get the hell out of here. We can talk back at the office when our heads are clear."

Outside Millie's window, Mr. Bones looked in and saw Millie's face tighten. She closed her eyes, rolled her head to the side, and then reached out her hand. A smile slowly appeared on her face then her body went limp. He stood there watching her arm slowly fall to the side of the bed as she breathed her last breath. Mr. Bones reached up and placed his gloves on the window. She was gone, and her gesture was saying goodbye to him. *She must have known I was standing out here the whole time,* he thought.

He felt a sudden rush of anger well up inside. He turned his head and looked over at the man sitting in the black car. He knew the man was one of those people he always had to run from. This time, he wasn't going to run. This time he was going to face him and then he'd face the two inside. He took one last look back at Millie. If he were capable of crying, he would be crying now. "Goodbye, my love. I will never forget you Millie." With that, he turned, slipped through the bushes staying within the shadows, and then headed toward the back parking lot. When he reached the area, just behind the black car, he looked out to ensure he was alone. There was no one. He stepped out, approached the back of the car, and crept up the side. The man's window was open. Mr. Bones quickly reached inside and grabbed Jack's shoulder.

The sudden attack took Jack by surprise. From the strength of the grip, Jack knew he was in serious trouble. As the grip became tighter, his eyes watered and he cried out in pain. His mind then slipped into neutral when the man calmly demanded with clinched teeth, "Get out of the car."

Jack moaned reaching up grasping the handle. He slowly opened the door. Mr. Bones released his grip, allowing him to stand up. When he did, Mr. Bones grabbed the back of his neck. Jack knees buckled from the pain.

"Your gun, take it out slowly and toss it inside the car." Jack reached down, slipped his gun out of its holster and tossed it on the seat. "What do you want... my wallet? Here, take it." he moaned.

"Who are you?"

"I'm Agent Straw, FBI," he moaned between his teeth. "Would you like to see my badge?"

"FBI, what is that?"

Jack's eyes rolled to the back of his head. *The guy is playing with me.* "It's the Federal Bureau of Investigations."

"Are you with the two inside?"

"Yes, sort of."

"Reach inside the car and grab the keys," Mr. Bones ordered, shoving Jack's head down inside the open door. Mr. Bones yanked him up when Jack had the keys in his hands. He spun him around and pushed him toward the back of the car. "Open the trunk!"

Jack's hand came up shaking. He missed the key hole twice, found the hole, stuck it in, and turned the key. The trunk opened.

"Get inside!"

"What?"

Mr. Bones tightened his grip. Jack's knees buckled. "Your right leg was broken before."

"How do you know?"

"Did it hurt?"

"It hurt like hell," Jack gasped, still wondering how he knew.

"If you don't get in that trunk, I'm going to crush every bone in your body - one at a time, and then I'm going to pick you up and toss you in."

Jack took hold of the trunk and fell inside. "What are you going to do?" he asked, looking up at the hooded man.

Mr. Bones looked down at him and slowly closed the trunk. He quickly checked the parking lot. He was still alone. He lifted his arm in the air, rolled his fingers into a fist and drove it down into the trunk. His fist went through the metal and just missed Jack's face. Jack screamed, and then everything went quiet. Jack lay there for a moment looking out through the hole.

Mr. Bones leaned over the trunk. "Don't make a sound - not even a whisper until the sun comes up or I'll open this trunk and snap you in two! Do you understand?"

"Yes. I understand. I won't say a word."

Everything went quiet for a second. Then suddenly, Jack felt the front of the car lifting off the ground, as Mr. Bones lifted up the front bumper. His body slid to the back of the trunk, and then he felt the car drop violently. He lay there listening. Nothing -dead quiet. He looked out through the hole in the trunk feeling his whole body trembling.

After Mr. Bones let go of the bumper he walked toward the brown car in front of it. When he reached the back passenger door, he looked back at Jack's car and smiled. *One down and two to go*, he thought, reaching for the handle. He gave it a violent yank. The door opened. He got into the back seat and shut the door. Looking toward the back entrance to the nursing home his eyes became like flames and then his body collapse down onto the floor.

David and William walked down the dimly lit corridor and then stopped when Pam rounded the corner.

"Evening, gentlemen," she whispered. "How'd it go? Did you like Millie's story?"

David cocked his head and smiled. What could he say? His head was still spinning, and William needed a doctor. All he wanted to do was get the hell out of there. "I must admit she has quite a story."

"You're telling me. She's an awesome story teller. She should have written a book about her life. I think my favorite story, besides the story of Mr. Bones is her story about how she sat and watched Babe Ruth point his bat and smack the ball out of the park. Did she tell you that she was a Yankee fan?"

"Babe Ruth, did you say?" William asked.

"Yes. She knew all the players from that time. Did you know that Babe Ruth was the highest paid player back then? Millie said that he earned one hundred thousand dollars just to hit a ball. Hell, the players today would cry in their beer if that's all they made. So, did she tell you about Mr. Bones?"

"You mean Samuel Remington?" David remarked.

"Samuel Remington?" she replied, wrinkling her brow.

"She said that was Mr. Bones' real name. She said that he was a great frontiersman who lived in the woods," David said, watching Pam's facial expression go from being amused to total confusion.

Pam stepped back, puzzled. She looked at the two of them. They both looked as confused as a one-dollar bill sitting inside a jar full of pennies. "The story she told me, Samuel Remington wasn't Mr. Bones. Look, I was just about to make myself a cup of coffee. If you two have some time, I'll tell you the story she told me.

David and William looked at one another.

"I'll fix you both a cup, and we can sit in the lounge."

David turned and looked at her.

"I think you might want to hear what she told me." Pam said, raising her brow.

"OK," William replied. "I hope it's good."

"It's better than good. It still gives me the creeps every time I walk in there and look down at that welcome mat next to her window."

David felt the nape of his neck go cold. He tossed a glance at William. They could read each other's thoughts without saying a word. *I wonder if ghosts wipe their feet when they enter a room*? David thought.

"Which way to the lounge?" William asked.

"Follow me." she replied, turning and walking down the corridor. When she walked into the lounge, she poured them each a cup of coffee and sat down. David and William sat down at the table opposite her. The three sat for a moment enjoying their coffee, and then Pam set her cup down. "You know, I was hoping she'd tell you the same story she told me. However, I'm a bit confused as to why she told you that Samuel Remington was Mr. Bones."

"Maybe she told us another story because we're cops." William calmly replied.

"Why would that matter?"

"Because we're hunting a relative of someone who lived there," David said.

She was surprised to hear that. All she knew was what she heard from Kim. They wanted to speak to someone who had lived in Ironbark at the turn of the century.

"So tell me, Pam, if Samuel Remington wasn't Mr. Bones, then who was Mr. Remington?"

"Samuel Remington was a doctor from New York. He met Millie's father, Doctor Thomson during medical school. Once a year, he would ride up and visit Doc Thomson and his family. Millie said he just loved the country life style, and I guess he loved to fish as well."

William glanced over at David. Their assumptions were correct; Millie was hiding the real identity of Mr. Bones, but why?

"So, he was a doctor, and he loved to fish," David asked. "I suppose he loved children too."

Pam smiled. "Yes he did. The way Millie talked about him; he was someone truly special to her. She said Mr. Remington would spend time with her up in her bedroom drawing the birds."

David nodded and smiled. She had mentioned that to them. "OK, Pam, why don't you tell us the story she told you."

Pam looked across at the two men sitting there in their crisp suits. They may have been real nice men, but to her, they were all business. What she told them in the next half hour was hair-raising, to say the least. It was something you'd remember from a childhood nightmare.

"One night, when I went in to check on Millie - before we lowered the corridor lights, I found her up and staring out the window. When I walked in, I said hello and asked her if everything was OK. She just stood there staring out the window with her back to me.

I walked up behind her, put my arm around her shoulder, and looked outside to see what she was looking at. It was a beautiful night. The moon was up, and there was a slight breeze blowing through the trees. That was all I could see. Then she turned her head and looked at me. She may have been looking right at me, but I could see in the depth of her eyes that she was a million miles away. Have you ever seen that look before?"

They both nodded.

"Before I talk to you about Mr. Bones, I'd like to tell you what happened to Millie after Jimmy was murdered. She may have told you that she was depressed, but I think it was more than that. Her father, even though he was a doctor, could not have properly diagnosed Millie back then. After listening to her story, I suspect she had Post Traumatic Stress Syndrome, which as you know is a severe case of depression. All she wanted to do was stay in her room. She hardly went out or spoke to anyone after that. Her biggest wish was for Jimmy to come back, and she thought that if she wished and prayed hard enough, he would.

I never thought children could honestly love each other as adults do. However, the way she spoke about Jimmy - to me, it sounded so unreal. It sounded like Millie was talking about her husband, and not just a childhood friend. That may sound funny, but I think she had an adult love for him. Not in a sexual way, but emotionally - it was a very adult relationship that she and Jimmy had.

"After Mary Baker's abduction, Millie said that strange things began happening around her house. At first, she thought her parents were rearranging things in her bedroom once she fell asleep."

"Like what?" William asked.

"She said that it all started when she woke up one day and saw her doll, Miss Maple, sitting on her small writing desk facing the window. She thought it was odd because she had taken her to bed that night. She always slept with her dolls. She thought her mother, or her father had come in, taking the doll from her bed and setting it by the window. As the days went by, she noticed other items in her bedroom moved while she slept. One morning she woke up and noticed a drawing on her table. It was a beautiful drawing of two birds. This alarmed her because neither one of her parents could draw. Her father used to come up and sit with her as she drew the birds that flew up on the big limb outside her window, but he never could draw as well as she did. The birds in the drawing were perfect. They looked so real. Have you ever seen drawings of birds where the feathers look real enough to touch?" They both nodded.

"Then one night as she slept holding Miss Maples and Raggedy Ann, she thought she heard her name being called. When she opened her eyes, she saw a figure standing in the doorway. At first, she thought it was her dad because he was wearing her father's hooded coat, pants and boots. When she sat up to take a better look, the man slowly turned and closed her door. In the morning, she thought it was probably just a dream."

William felt tiny prickles run down his neck when she mentioned the hood. He slowly turned to see David's expression. Their eyes stayed fixed for a split second. William then sighed and looked back at Pam.

"Now, what I'm about to tell you may sound silly, but I truly believe every word Millie told me that night," Pam said, and then paused reaching down and taking another sip of her coffee. She set the cup down and continued. "Millie and Jimmy use to play in her father's office in the back room of the house. Her dad had a real male skeleton that hung in the corner. They use to take him apart, scatter the bones all over the floor, and then try to put him back together again. The game was; they had to pick up a bone, name which bone it was, and then place it on the floor. When the skeleton was put back together, they would hang him up again. Millie said that they got really good at it. After awhile, they both could recite all the names of the bones.

"Here's something I thought was amusing. Millie told me that every time they started playing the game, Jimmy would grab the head, set it on the floor, and yell out, "head." Millie said she laughed every time he did that," Pam said and then paused, looking across at them. They both nodded and smiled. She sat back, gave a slight sigh, knowing that once they heard what she was about to say, they would probably both get up and leave. *Or,* she thought, *they would call an ambulance and cart me off to the funny farm.* "I guess I'll start the story this way. The skeleton's name was Mr. Bones." After she said it, she just sat there and waited.

David leaned back shocked. William thought his heart had stopped. The two just sat there like wooden statues - hoping she would say, "got-cha", but she didn't.

"Mr. Bones?" David said, finding his tongue.

"Uh-huh. That's just the beginning," she replied, sitting back. "The rest of her story may just give you nightmares," she continued.

David looked over at William - with that half-hearted smiled glued to his face.

"Are you two ready?" she asked, taking them out of their thoughts.

"Yes, please go on," David replied.

"Millie told me that one afternoon while she was in her father's office sitting in his big chair she heard a voice whisper her name. She said it scared her, and she jumped out of the chair and started running for the door. When she reached the doorway, she heard the voice again. It said, "*Millie, don't leave.*" She quickly turned around and stood there. She looked about the room and saw no one. Then her eyes landed on Mr. Bones hanging there in the corner. In that moment - her whole life changed. The skeleton's head slowly turned and looked at her. She said that it scared her half to death and she ran down the hall screaming. Her mother came running from the kitchen and caught her in the hallway."

"What is it Millie?" she said, panicking and holding her.

Millie clung to her mother pointing back toward her father's office.

"What honey? What is it?"

Millie turned her head and looked at Mr. Bones hanging there. His head was down. *Did I just see what I thought I saw?* Her little mind unraveled. She looked up into her mother's eyes. Her mom looked scared, frightened and worried all at the same time.

Before she could tell her, she thought of all the strange things that were happening inside her bedroom. Her dolls being moved, the drawing on her desk, the man she saw standing in her doorway. *And now,* she thought, *I just saw the skeleton move.* While clinging to her mother's dress she felt this strange feeling wash over her, and she instantly thought of Jimmy.

"Honey, are you going to answer me?"

Millie came up out of her thoughts and looked up at her. "It was a spider," she lied.

"A spider?! You were screaming because of a little spider? Where did you see it? I'll go take care of the little bugger," her mother replied, letting her go and walking toward the office.

"No, I think I stepped on it when I ran out of the room. It just startled me; that's all."

"Are you sure?" she replied, turning around.

"Yes."

"Alright then. I have to go out and feed the horses. I want you to stay put."

"Yes, mom. I'm sorry I screamed."

Her mother smiled and rubbed her head. Millie watched her walk down the hallway toward the kitchen and out the back door. She slowly turned and looked inside her father's office. She wanted to walk back in, but her feet stayed glue to the floor.

"Jimmy, is that you?" she whispered, staring at the skeleton. Mr. Bones just hung there.

"Please, Jimmy. If that's you, please don't scare me. I've missed you so very much."

Mr. Bones lifted his head, turned, and looked at her. Millie clasped her little hands to her mouth. "Oh my God!" she gasped, clutching her hands to her face. "Is that you, Jimmy?"

"Millie," the skeleton replied.

"It IS you! What are you doing inside Mr. Bones?" she asked, walking toward the doorway. She stood there looking at him. Mr. Bones wiggled his spine, unhooked himself from the metal prop, and stood up. Millie shook her head in disbelief. She could not wrap her mind around what she was seeing. Yes, she prayed that he'd come back, but she never thought her prayers would be answered. *But why is he inside Mr. Bones?* she thought.

"I heard you calling my name after those bad men took me. I do not know where I was. It was so dark and lonely. All I wanted was to be with you again," he said.

She stood there looking up at Mr. Bones. "You moved my dolls?"

He nodded.

"You drew that picture of the birds?"

He nodded again.

"It was you who was standing in the door with my father's clothes on?"

"Yep, that was me. I didn't know how to tell you that I was back."

"But, why?" she asked.

Jimmy shook his head. "I didn't want to scare you. I knew that Mr. Bones never scared you, so I thought I would use him. If I had come into your bedroom without being inside Mr. Bones, I would have scared you for sure. This way I can be with you, like a real person. I'm sorry if I scared you, Millie," he said, reaching out his hand.

Millie looked at it. She reached out, took hold of the skeletal fingers and looked up at him. Tears formed in the corner of her eyes. They slowly rolled down her cheeks.

"Now, Millie, don't cry. I'm here now, and I'll never leave you again."

Millie wiped her tears and stepped back. "OK, I'm ready," she said, letting go of his hand and stepping back. "Come out of him; I want to see you for real."

As she stood there watching, a small glowing figure stepped out of Mr. Bones. It was Jimmy. He looked like an angel. She noticed that the color of his eyes had changed. They were sapphire blue; sparkling like diamonds. They were the most beautiful things she'd ever seen! "Wow, Jimmy, you're beautiful."

Jimmy smiled raising his brow. "So, you're happy to see me again?"

"Yes, but." she started to say looking at him standing there in front of Mr. Bones. She was amazed that the skeleton was standing there all on its own. Just looking at him made her cry all the more. She was happy but shocked. She wiped her tears and thought of what to do next. They could not go out and play like they used to. They could not sit in her room and draw birds. How were they going to be together with him this way now? "Jimmy?"

"Yes, Millie."

She stood there thinking about what they were going to do and then she had an idea! *He could use my father's clothes and stay inside Mr. Bones!* "My father's clothes, they fit you when you're inside Mr. Bones, right?"

Jimmy smiled.

"Well, you'll have to wear them from now on if we go out together. You can't be seen like this."

Jimmy looked down at himself and shook his head. "I don't think so," he replied, turning and stepping back inside Mr. Bones. Millie looked up at him and smiled. "Now, before my mother comes back, you get back in that corner."

Jimmy nodded, and then asked, "What about gloves?"

Millie looked down at his hands and smiled.

"You're right. I'll put a pair of gloves inside my father's coat."

Just then, they heard the back door open.

"Hurry, get back in the corner!" Millie whispered, running out of the room.

In the nights that followed, Millie and Jimmy spent hours in her room as her parents slept. Then the day after Jill Farmer's abduction, she told Jimmy what was happening. Jimmy got up and stood looking out the window. "Is there anything you can do?" she asked, looking up at him.

"Their names are Boone and Darrell," he said, staring out the window

"You know them?" she asked, standing up and walking over. *He had to know them. They were the bad men that killed him*, she thought.

When Jimmy said their names and remembered what they had done to him, he became angry. "Yes, I know them. They're pure evil."

"Indian Joe, Blackfoot, Chief Running Bear, and a bunch of other men are hunting them down," she replied.

"What about the sheriff?" he asked, turning his head.

"Yes, he is too. Some of the white men think the Indians are killing all the children. Can you help?"

"Yes, I can help. I can hear the children cry when someone is hurting them," he replied.

Millie looked up at him. "Please come out of Mr. Bones for me."

The skeleton turned around to face her. She watched Mr. Bones' body begin to glow again. It sparkled like a million fireflies as Jimmy stepped out and stood there. Millie shook her head in disbelief. They smiled at each other.

"Do you hear the spirit of the owl and the great white eagle like Indian Joe does?" she asked.

He wasn't sure if he could or not. He only knew of the light and the darkness; a place people travel to - right after death. In that thought, he reached out and touched her face. She felt this sudden coldness with his touch. "I was standing in front of a giant expansion of light. Behind me was a pit of darkness that had no bottom. I believe if you fell in there would be no way to escape. That's when I heard your cries. Indian Joe is a wise man. His heart is pure, and his ears are keen. I think that's why he can hear the spirit world."

Millie stood there confused. Her little mind could not comprehend a word he was saying. *Where did he go after he was murdered? Was it the spirit world Indian Joe always talks about?* She stepped out of her thoughts looking at him. His eyes were mesmerizing like dazzling blue gems. It was if she could see into the future looking into the depth of them. "Will you catch 'em?"

He leaned over and kissed her on the cheek. His lips felt like the morning mist floating across the lake. She wished she could touch him, hold him, and kiss him back. She smiled when he stepped back and looked at her.

"I'll catch 'em. They'll never harm another child again," he replied, turning around and stepping back inside Mr. Bones. Mr. Bones came to life and stood erect. "I have to go now. I'll be back before the sun comes up. Leave the back door open for me," he said, walking toward her door.

"OK. But, Jimmy, please don't hurt Indian Joe or Blackfoot. I know those two will find them first. You know that, don't you?"

"They have nothing to fear from me. It's Boone and Darrell who'll see the darkness," he replied, walking out.

Millie walked to her bedroom door and watched Jimmy take the stairs down. *He seems so different now,* she thought, turning and walking over to her bed.

Chapter 20

Jimmy walked to the back door, slipped on her father's boots, winter jacket, gloves, and then stepped out into the cool night air. He looked up at the star filled sky thinking of Boone and Darrell. His anger began boiling like molten lava! He was no longer that little boy who wanted to play and explore. That little boy was gone. He would become Mr. Bones. His only mission now would be to hunt down those who hurt children.

He walked past the barn looking into the forest and wondered if Indian Joe and Blackfoot were hot on their trail. He knew Millie was right - those two would catch Boone and Darrell first. They had the hunting skills of wolves and the keen nose of a bear. He suspected they'd kill them and bring back their scalps. However, he had other plans for them. They would pay the price for their wickedness, and he was going to make sure of that. As he stood there in thought, he heard something on the wind. It sounded like a child crying off in the distance. *Those bastards,* he thought. *They've struck again!* This time, right on the outskirts of town. He took off through the forest toward the Pinto River. When he came upon the river, he stood there listening. There, just up ahead on the other side of the river, he heard the muffled cries again.

He ran fifty yards down the east side of the river toward the farms. He stopped and listened. The sound of the breeze blowing through the trees, crickets chirping, and the rushing current of the Pinto River hummed in his ears. Just on the other side of the river, he heard a twig snap. He cocked his head, looked across and then looked down at the water. The current was running fast. He quickly looked up into the canopy of the trees with the limbs hanging over the river. He jumped and caught a low hanging branch and pulled himself up. He walked the branch to the trunk of the tree and stood there listening. He could hear the sounds of someone walking through the forest on the other side. He quickly walked along the branch that was hanging over the water. From there, he jumped across onto another tree limb, made his way to the trunk, and jumped down to the ground.

He looked down searching the ground. His eyes changed from blue to glowing red flames when he spotted bootprints in the wet mud. He bent down and noticed the deep imprint; the person was carrying something. He stood up and followed the print into the forest. Then suddenly he stopped when he saw another set of bootprints. "It's Boone and Darrell," he hissed, looking down and outward to where the prints led.

Up ahead, about three hundred yards from the river's edge, Boone and Darrell stopped. Little Mary Baker was pounding on Boone's back as he was carrying her over his shoulder.

"You little shit!" Boone scolded, grabbing her by the neck. He pulled her around and swung her forward so he could set her on the ground. Her neck snapped. Her little body went limp in his arms.

"My God, Boone, what 'cha do that fur? I'm not rapin' a dead girl."

"Christ, I didn't mean to. She wouldn't stop pounding on me. But, don't worry, she'll stay warm long enough for us to take turns with her. Now, let's keep moving," he replied, lifting her back up over his shoulder. He started walking again.

"Wait," Darrell said.

"What?" he replied, turning and looking at him.

"Did you hear that?"

"Did I hear what?"

"Shh…. Listen."

Boone stood there, and then he heard it. It sounded like someone was coming. He looked at Darrell with fear. *It can't be*, he thought. There was no way someone could have spotted them.

"Someone's following. What if it's natives? You know what they'll do if they catch us," Darrell whispered. That thought sent ripples up Boone's neck. *They'd more than kill us - they'd skin us alive.* He looked into Darrell's eyes. Terror was all he saw.

"If they catch us, Darrell - it will be a long time dying. We got to get the hell out of here, fast!" he whispered, turning and rushing off.

"Boone."

"What now," he asked, turning back around.

"We have to get rid of her. If they catch us with her..." his voice trailed off

Boone panicked, lifting the little girl off his shoulder. He frantically looked around for a place to hide her. There was none. He quickly carried her over next to a tree and leaned her body up against it. "Darrell, you head back to town. I'll meet you in the Sheppard Mountains," he quickly said, standing up.

"Head into town? Are you crazy? Those red skins will kill me fur shur!" he replied, looking back toward the river.

"Hurry, we don't have much time. Just stay still every once in awhile. Remember, they can't see us in the dark. Use the cover of the trees and get back to the Pinto. From there, make your way back into town. I'll head toward the Forgotten Land and try and lose them there."

With that, Boone took off into the woods heading south toward the Sheppard Mountains. Darrell stood there for a second. He was scared, so scared that he urinated on himself. He took off to the north toward Lake Ontario. From there, he'd circle back, cross the Pinto River, and head back toward Ironbark.

Mr. Bones crept silently through the foliage, following the tracks. A hundred yards in he stopped when he saw Mary Baker lying there against a tree. He walked up to her and knelt down. She was dead. Her neck had been broken. He stood up, looked around, and then looked back down at her.

He did not know what to do. If he carried her back now, he'd lose his chance of catching them. *She was dead,* he thought, *there's nothing I can do for her now.* He quickly turned and started searching the ground for their tracks. One set of prints headed south - the other headed north. *Why did they split up?* he thought, looking south and then north. *They must have heard me.* He bent down, looked at both sets of prints. He decided to follow the one heading south.

The tracks led him straight to the Forgotten Land. He stopped at the edge of the forest and looked out over the rough terrain. He had never been there as a boy. It was off limits. He knelt down underneath a stand of trees and listened to the wind. He could hear the fast moving current of the Pinto River off in the distance.
He turned and looked at the Sheppard Mountains on the other side of the Forgotten Land. "That's where they're hiding out," he whispered. "I am sure of it." There were only two ways in, and both were risky; cross the Forgotten Land, or wade into the Pinto River and follow it through the mountains.

That thought gave him a vision. They were using the waterways to get around. That's why they built the shanty deep in the woods not far from the Willow Creek. After they murdered me, they used Willow Creek to escape to the Pinto, from the Pinto - they headed upstream along the Forgotten Land and into the Sheppard Mountains.
Mr. Bones stood there until the wee hours of the morning pondering his next move. Daylight was coming, and he had to get back. He thought about Mary. He wanted to take her home. There was no way now for that to happen. He had to get back himself before Millie's parents woke up.

Dawn broke with the sound of screaming in the little town of Ironbark. Cory and Ruth Baker's little girl was missing. Cory rode like the wind toward the sheriff's office. He rushed through the crowd, up the wooden steps, and knocked on the sheriff's door. Ben walked over and opened it. Cory stepped in looking as mean and angry as a bear with its leg in a trap. Before Cory started screaming about his little girl, the door suddenly opened. It was Chief Running Bear, Indian Joe and Blackfoot.

"Can you hear that outside?" Chief Running Bear asked, looking at the men sitting there with Cory.

"Yeah, I hear it. We all hear it. It sounds like a pack of wolves," Ben replied.

Chief Running Bear walked over and looked down at Cory.

"You think we took your little girl?"

Cory shook his head.

Chief Running Bear nodded toward the door. "They think we did," he remarked.

Cory looked at up Chief Running Bear. He slowly glanced over at Indian Joe and Blackfoot standing there. All he wanted was his little girl back.

"I'll tell 'em I know it wasn't you. Just find my little girl before I lose my wife, too. She's half-crazed already."

"Deputy, get over to the Chamber's, tell them to go see Ruth. Blackfoot, I want you to go fetch Doc Thomson," Ben ordered.

The men nodded and walked out. Ben walked over to Cory, sat down, and put his hand on his shoulder. "I think its best you go home, too. We'll take it from here. Indian Joe will go with you and start tracking," he said, looking up at Indian Joe.

"Where was she taken from?" Indian Joe asked Cory.

"She was asleep. The bastards took her from her own bed! How in God's name could I have allowed that to happen? How am I going to live another day if anything happens to her?"

"You didn't allow anyone to take her." Ben replied. "You were asleep."

Indian Joe waited for Cory to stand up. Cory looked at him, opened the door, and walked out with Indian Joe right behind him. The crowd stepped back seeing Cory standing there with Indian Joe. Cory saw the guns in each of their hands. Before Cory could speak, Chief Running Bear walked up behind him and placed his hand on his shoulder. Cory moved aside. Chief Running Bear stepped out and looked over the crowd.

"How long are we going to stand here and allow these redskins to hide behind the Sheriff's badge?" one man yelled. "You know they did it!"

Indian Joe looked at Chief Running Bear. He never over stepped the Chief, but this time he had had enough. He stepped out in front. All eyes were glued on him. He stared back into their faces raising his hands. When the yelling stopped, Indian Joe spoke.

"The spirit of the owl has told me that they are not Indians who have taken your children. They are white men doing things to make it look like we did it."

The people were shocked and pressed Indian Joe for more information. Indian Joe folded his arms and spoke again.

"The mighty spirit has seen them. They run like a pack."

"How can we believe you? Your visions have led to nothing. We've lost three already," someone yelled out.

"Yeah," the crowd erupted in unison.
Indian Joe waved his hand. The crowd went silent. "Oh hear me Great Spirit of the wind and sky – tell 'em I'm coming," he shouted. After he spoke, he placed his hand on Cory's shoulder and started down the steps. Cory followed. As they waded through the crowd, the crowd moved aside. Cory and Indian Joe mounted their horses and took off down the road.

That morning, as the news of Mary Baker was inflaming the town, the Thomson's were getting ready for breakfast. Millie was as happy as a honeybee in a patch of wild flowers. She bounded out of bed with Miss Maples and Raggedy Ann and ran to the stairs humming a tune. Her father smiled as she strolled into the kitchen and sat down at the table.

"What has you so happy this morning?" he asked.

She rolled her eyes thinking of Jimmy. "It looks like a beautiful day outside," she replied, glancing over at the back door. There by the door were her father's boots. Jimmy was home. She gleefully smiled.

"It sure is wonderful," her father replied, glancing up at Mary. She smiled.

"I haven't seen the sun in days. I would like to go out to the barn and play with Katie and her chicks - if that's alright."

"That's fine Millie, you can come out with me to feed the horses as well," he replied, taking his napkin and setting on his lap.

Just as they were finishing breakfast, they heard a horse out back. Doc Thomson stood up, wiped his mouth and headed for the door. "It's Blackfoot. He's alone."

"Oh. I wonder what brings him out here so early?" Mary asked, standing up. Doc turned, looked at her, and then glanced over at Millie. She was still eating her breakfast. Mary saw the look in her husband's eyes. Her face went ash white. *Could another child be missing?* she thought, walking toward the door. They booth stepped out, closed the door and stood there.

Blackfoot dismounted and hitched his horse to the rail.

"Good Morning," Doc greeted him, walking down the steps with Mary.

Blackfoot turned around and looked at them. The look in Blackfoot's eyes wasn't good.

"Oh, dear Lord, don't tell me there's another child missing," Mary asked, grabbing her husband's hand.

He nodded looking around. "Where's Millie?"

"Inside," Doc replied.

232

"I'm afraid so. It's Mary Baker this time. Cory came in this morning and reported it to Ben."

"How?" Mary gasped.

"She was taken from her bed last night."

"Oh my God!" she gasped, clutching her face in her hands.

Blackfoot looked at Doc. "Ben wants you to come to town. Daniel was ordered to fetch the Chamber's so they could be with Ruth."

Mary looked over at the Chamber's house next door. It looked quiet.

"Give me a minute, I'll get my medical bag," Doc said, turning and walking back to the house.

Blackfoot and Mary watched him leave then settled their eyes on one another. "From now on, you watch your little girl like a hawk."

Mary's mind splintered. She could not imagine losing Millie. "She'll be by my side like honey on a bee until these devils are caught!"

"Good," Blackfoot replied, nodding.

"Where's Indian Joe?" she asked.

"He went to the Baker's place. He'll try and pick up the tracks from there."

"Are you going to meet up with him?"

"No. I'm taking the rest of the men back to Marshall Lake. We'll be watching the shanty out there."

She nodded. Doc walked back out and headed for the barn. Millie came to the door and stood there. Mary looked up at her. Millie's expression said it all. Her smile was gone, she wasn't humming anymore, and she knew Millie's day was going to turn into a nightmare when she heard the news.

"Where are you going, Pa?" Millie asked.

"They need me in town. You stay with your mother," he replied over his shoulder.

After they rode off, her mother brought Millie back inside. She sat her down in the parlor and told her the news. It struck Millie like a whip. She started to cry.

"Oh, Millie, I just don't know what to say."

Millie held her mother tight thinking of Jimmy. She knew who took Mary, but what could she say? *I've got to tell him, but how?* she thought, with her mother sitting there. She let go of her mother, wiped her tears and asked, "What are we going to do?"

Mary closed her eyes. Then she realized with Doc gone, they were alone! She started to panic. *We should have gone with them!* She looked down at Millie and then over to the door.

"We need to lock up the house. Don't you leave my side for one minute, you hear me?"

"I won't."

Mary got up, took Millie's hand and then went around locking the doors and all the windows. She then ushered Millie to her husband's office, opened the closet and took out the shotgun. She pushed the lever near the hammer and the double barrels opened. It gun wasn't loaded. She reached up, grabbed the box of shells and slipped two rounds inside the chambers.

As her mother was loading the gun - Millie glanced over at Mr. Bones. His head was up. *He knows what happened,* she thought. He must have heard everything. She looked at her mother. Her mother wasn't paying any attention. Millie closed her eyes and thought hard, *Oh Jimmy, Jimmy, Jimmy - what are we going to do?*

With shotgun in hand, Mary took Millie by the hand and led her out of the room. Millie didn't have time to look back. When they left the room, Mr. Bones turned his head toward the door. Yes, he knew. He wanted to tell Millie, but never got the chance. All he could do now was to wait for an opportunity to leave. Time was running out. He had to find a way into those mountains before another child went missing.

Pam paused, sitting up. She reached over and took a sip of her now cold coffee. When she looked at Detective Bradshaw, something washed over her. "You know, I feel kind of stupid telling you this story," she said.

"I'm sure you do," David replied. "I haven't heard a good ghost story since I was a kid."

"It's more than that. Millie also mentioned that one of the men who came from New York to assist Sheriff Coleman had the last name of Bradshaw."

David smiled nodding his head. "That was my grandfather."

Pam nodded. *A child would have caught that*, she thought. "I see," she replied. "So why are you two here talking to Millie? I mean, you don't think there's a connection, do you? What happened in Ironbark happened a long time ago."

David looked at William. William rolled his eyes. Millie's story was so far out there he didn't know what to say. "I'm sure you're well aware of the children being abducted and murdered here in New York," David asked.

"Yes, everyone knows," she sharply replied. "It's absolutely disgusting that we have animals like that in our midst. I'm just glad you caught him before another child was murdered," she continued looking into his eyes. *They're looking for someone else. That's why they're here.* That thought spun her around. *The two cases are the same.* She closed her eyes. *Millie's imaginary friend, and that stupid welcoming mat in front of her window - this can't be happening.*

"You seem to be a million miles away." William spoke up.

"I am. You two seem to out there as well, or you wouldn't be sitting here."

"What do you mean?"

"Because, what happened in up in Ironbark is now happening here. And that begs another question. Now that the murderer is dead, are you two chasing someone else?"

"You should have been a cop," William replied.

"You don't think…" her voice trailed off.

"No. We don't think we're chasing a ghost if that's what you're thinking." William replied.

"Yes, that's what I was thinking. What about Millie and her imaginary friend, and that welcome mat sitting next to her window. I mean, it must have given you the creeps to see it sitting there. And if that isn't enough to split your mind in two – seeing you both here now *is* actually freaking me out!"

"I guess you would be, after telling us this story."

"Well, I am not through yet. Is there anything else you'd like to tell me before I continue?"

David studied her gaze. It was time to find out who Millie was hiding and why.
"Let me start with this. Do you honestly believe Millie's story?"

Pam felt the weight of that question. She figured they'd laugh. Then she got an idea. She could turn the tables and talk about Samuel Remington. "I just told you what I think," she said. "Now, let me put a bee in your bonnet. You two just walked away believing her story about Samuel Remington. I mean really, do you honestly think a man could jump a six foot, embankment and then take off like a deer?"

William glanced over at David as his mind drifted back to Corporal Carter seeing the man jump an eight-foot fence. *No human could do that either*, he thought. In all his days as a cop he never thought he'd run up against a case where a ghost is the primary suspect. Sure, they came across crazy people throughout their day - every city had them. This, however, was totally different. Millie was not a drug addict or a drunk; her mind was intact.

"You two look like you agree with me," Pam spoke up.

"You have a point," David replied. "I'll tell you this much, Pam. We're here because the two cases are very similar."

"I already suspected that. How similar are they?"

"It's all right here," William replied, holding up the old report.

She looked at the file. "Is the story I just told you in there?"

"No. But some of it matches," William replied.

"Oh, I'm sure it does, or you two wouldn't be here right now. So, how much can you tell me?"

"Well, the person we're chasing seems to have the same power."

"Like Mr. Bones?" she questioned.

They both smiled. She smiled back. "Do you think Millie's crazy?" she asked.

"No. She's not crazy," David replied.

"Alright then, I'm listening."

"Well, the two bootprints match. Besides that, the person we're chasing jumped an eight-foot security fence."

Pam nodded. *This is becoming a nightmare,* she thought.

"Look, maybe you should finish your story," David said.

"Where do you want me to begin?"

"Let's start were Teddy Cotton was brought back," David replied.

"You know he was the last to be taken?"

"Yes."

Pam sat back looking down at her cup. "Would you like another cup of coffee before I begin?"

"Sure," they both replied.

After she returned, she took a sip of her coffee and sat back down. David and William did the same.

"Well," she started. "Millie told me that Teddy was still alive when Mr. Bones carried him back to town."

"Excuse me?" William replied startled. Pam looked at him then glanced over at David. "I guess that's not in your report, but he was. The reason I believe it to be true is that if Mr. Bones had found him dead, he would have left him and gone after Boone and Darrell - just like he did with Mary Baker. However, when he discovered that Teddy was still alive, he bundled him up and headed back to town. That's when the Yammers' saw him."

David sat there listening. He could not believe how much she knew. *Millie must have told her every little detail of what happened,* he thought.

"So you're telling us that Teddy was still alive when the Yammers' found him?" William asked.

"That's what Mr. Bones - or actually Jimmy told her. So... Teddy must have died while he was carrying him, or he died soon after he set him down on Hollow Trail."

While David was listening to her, he thought about Indian Joe's statement about him discovering three sets of prints on the other side of the river when he found Mary Baker's body. Millie said it that the third bootprint was actually Samuel Remington prints that Indian Joe had discovered. He sighed now, believing that it was in fact Mr. Bones. *This is insane,* he thought. "Alright, Pam, let's hear the rest of the story from where you left off," he requested, stepping out of his thoughts.

Pam took a sip of her coffee and set it down.

Chapter 21

Pam closed her eyes, drifting back to the night when she sat with Millie. She remembered Millie saying that after the Yammers' brought Teddy back that night, the whole town went stark raving mad. The following morning there were more guns on the street and enough rope to hang every man and woman from Ironbark to Rochester, New York. Detective Roger Bradshaw, David's grandfather and his partner, Detective Jim Dole, told Sheriff Coleman to ease off and allow the town to split up into teams and search for the killers or someone was going to get hurt. She remembered Millie saying that it was like releasing the dogs from hell on the perpetrators. Ben agreed and split everyone up into teams.

Before Jimmy left that night, Millie slipped out of bed and crept downstairs to talk with him. When she entered her father's office and closed the door, she saw Mr. Bones standing by the window looking out. "Jimmy," she whispered, closing the door behind her.

He turned around. She walked over and took his hand. "Have you heard the news?"

"Yes. I was the one who found Teddy. They hurt him real bad, but he was still alive."

She wanted to cry. "He's dead, Jimmy. My father won't tell me what they did to him. The whole town is going to explode. The Yammers' said that they thought my father had done it because of the clothing the person was wearing. They were right about the clothing. You must be careful out there."

Mr. Bones nodded.

Millie turned and stepped back. She quickly turned around and looked up at him. "I wish I could tell the Sheriff the truth about who they are."

"You can't," he replied, turning and looking out the window. His anger began to boil. Teddy was dead.

"Jimmy," she whispered, taking his arm. He turned his head and looked down at her. She stepped back when she saw his eyes. They were like flames of fire.

"Don't do that. You're scaring me," she gasped.

"I don't want to be Jimmy anymore."

"What? What are you talking about? You come out of him right now, you hear me?"

Mr. Bones' eyes went dark; his arms fell to his sides as Jimmy stepped out and stood there before her. Millie gazed upon him as if she was seeing at an angel. He glowed like the moon. His eyes were a sparkling light blue. She did not know what to say so she started by saying his name. "Jimmy."

"Yes?" he replied, looking into her eyes. He could see she had a million questions and wanted answers. She reached up, touched his face, or at least - tried too and smiled. "Please, don't scare me like that again."

"I'm sorry. I didn't mean to."

"I know you didn't mean to. You startled me, that's all," she replied, lowering her hand from his glowing face.

"Millie?"

"Yes?"

"I can't help them, only Mr. Bones can."

She looked at him knowing what he meant. She glanced up at Mr. Bones standing there behind him.

"You want me to catch them, don't you?"

She looked down. "You know I do."

"Then I must become Mr. Bones."

She slowly nodded. She too wanted the pain and suffering to stop. "Just remember, everyone will be out there. I heard that Indian Joe and Blackfoot are going to the Sheppard Mountains. That's where they think those two are hiding. You just be careful, alright?"

"I will," he replied, seeing tears welling up in her eyes. He leaned over and kissed her cheek, turned around, and slipped back inside Mr. Bones. She watched Mr. Bones straighten up, turn his head, and look down at her. "I will always be Jimmy to you, but from here on out - I am Mr. Bones," he said, turning and looking back out the window. He honed his thoughts on Boone and Darrell. He wanted to crush them both into dust. *If I do that, the rest of the evil out there would fear me forever,* he thought. "I have to go now," he said, turning his head. "You go back to bed, and I'll try and be back before sunrise," he continued.

She touched his hand, squeezed his fingers, and then turned for the door. Before she walked out, she looked back to see him looking at her. She smiled and walked out. As she crept down the hallway, she knew he was changing, and she wondered if he would always be Jimmy to her.

After she left, Mr. Bones walked to the door and listened. The house was dead silent. He crept through the hallway to the back door. There, he put on Doc Thomson's clothing and boots and then left. Walking down the steps, he thought of Indian Joe and Blackfoot. He knew he'd have to stay one step ahead of them if he was going to catch Boone and Darrell first. He looked up into the moonless sky and then back at the house. *I must be back before sunrise,* he thought. He wondered if Millie's parents would even notice that the skeleton was gone. He dropped that thought and took off toward the Pinto River.

When he got to the river, he stood there for a moment just listening to the current. He walked along the edge until he came to the large tree he had climbed to cross over the river. This time he looked across and then walked straight into the river. The current was fast - the river was deep, but nothing was going to stop him. After wading out - he quickly covered the distance to where he discovered Mary Baker lying against the tree.

His deep hollow sockets turned into flames of red looking down. The fire that burned inside him was pure anger seeping out of every joint of his skeletal body. Jill Farmer, Mary Baker, and Teddy Cotton flashed before him. They were only children; young, innocent children who had their entire lives in front of them. If that wasn't enough to make you wretch, the manner in which they were murdered was unimaginable.

As he stepped away from the tree, he noticed a fresh track alongside his old one. He knew that it was Indian Joe. He followed them along the trail leading toward the Forgotten Land. Through the thick foliage and hilly terrain, he walked silently through the darkness. When he came upon the stand of tall trees where he had stood before, he realized Indian Joe's tracks were no longer visible. He imagined that Indian Joe made it this far and then doubled back to gather Mary's lifeless body and to take her back into town.

That same night, as Mr. Bones crossed the Forgotten Land, Indian Joe and Blackfoot rode out by horse and dismounted at the Willow Creek Bridge. It was there that the two waterways came together; Willow Creek and the Pinto River. Blackfoot told Indian Joe that he was going to try to take his horse across the river and find a way through the Forgotten Land. Indian Joe nodded. He prodded his horse over the bridge and headed toward the Pinto River. Blackfoot followed him. Before the two of them split up at the bank of the river, they'd agreed to one thing; if either caught up with them - they were to slit their throats and bring their bodies back to the bridge and wait. Indian Joe headed down the Pinto River - Blackfoot crossed the river and headed west through the Forgotten Land.

As the two made their way into the unknown - they did not realize that Mr. Bones had already crossed the Forgotten Land and was now heading through a small passage inside the mountain range. It was not long after navigating through the rough mountainous terrain that Mr. Bones found a bluff overlooking the back forest on the other side of the Sheppard Mountains. He stood there looking down at the small glow from a fire pit that sat in front of a cabin, a cabin well hidden. *Very cleaver,* he thought, *right at the base of the mountain - hidden deep within the forest.*

His eyes scanned the landscape around the cabin, looking for a trail. *There, right along the base of the mountain.* The trail looked as if it led along the eastern base heading toward the Pinto River. Mr. Bones nodded, thinking of a plan. He would take them in the wee hours of the morning when the fog still held its grip on the forest. He looked up into the night sky. *If I start down the mountain now I just might catch them still sleeping.*

After Indian Joe waded down the river approximately a half a mile, he spotted a small rocky inlet. He exited the river with his horse. There, he tethered it, bent down and started searching for tracks. He was not surprised to find some. He looked up into the deep dark forest. He could slightly see a small path leading in. *I got you now,* he thought, standing up. He looked back at his horse and then thought of Blackfoot. He wondered if Blackfoot had found a way through Forgotten Land. *Even if he did make it across he'll be no help to me now. I am on my own with this one.* That thought made him pause. *Should I take the chance going in alone?* He looked into the forest not knowing how far in he would have to travel. He decided to wait until morning when he could see farther up the trail.

It was pre dawn when Mr. Bones finally found his way down from out of the mountains. He picked up the trail leading to the cabin, but he wasn't sure how far off it was when he spotted it high up on the bluff. The air around him felt like a blanket of mist. He could hardly see the trees and foliage up a head in the thick fog. He set out down the path, almost invisible himself. Creeping from tree to tree, staying well hidden within the foliage, he traveled around the base of the mountain toward the cabin.

When he came upon a clearing up ahead, he stopped and knelt down within a stand of thick pine trees. There, camouflaged by the trees, he spotted the cabin. The next thing he saw was a man walking out and heading over to a woodpile. With ax in hand, the man started chopping up some wood. He recognized the murdering bastard right away. It was Darrell.

Mr. Bones slowly stood up. His eyes turned into flames. Before taking a step forward, he noticed a long dead branch on the ground. He lifted his foot and stepped on it. The branch snapped. He looked up seeing Darrell quickly turn and face him. Darrell's face went slack; his eyes filled with fear - seeing a figure standing in the shadows of the trees - wearing a heavy hooded coat, long dark pants, gloves and snow boots. He stood straight up with axe in hand. "Mister, you sure have a lot of guts coming here," he said, turning his head toward the open door. "Boone get out here – we've got company!"

Boone looked toward the open door. *What company? Maybe it's a bear, or wolves, or...* his thoughts trailed off. *What if it's someone?* He started to panic walking toward the door. When he got there, he planted his eyes on Darrell staring down the path. He stepped further out and looked. His heart leaped inside his throat seeing a man standing twenty-five feet away within the low branches of the trees.

He slowly walked out and stood alongside Darrell. This was trouble, and he knew it. He turned his head and looked at Darrell holding the axe.

"Whatcha think Boone?" Darrell whispered from the side of his mouth. "He hasn't said a word. Got no manners, I reckon."

Boone took two steps forward. "Who are you and how did you find us?"

Mr. Bones cocked his head to the left and then to the right but said nothing.

Darrell looked at Boone. Their eyes locked. They both knew that it was going to take a killing to get rid of this. "Are you just going to stand there and not answer?" Darrell spat.

Mr. Bones said nothing. He stepped out of the trees and stood on the path.

"We're going to cut you up real good mister if you don't start using that tongue of yours," Darrell warned.

Mr. Bones cocked his and then took three steps forward. *I'll be doing all the cutting today,* he thought. *Nice and slow- until the two of you are dead.* Yes, he was going to take his time, just as they did to him. He saw Boone's eyes slightly twitch while shifting his weight. *He's going to try to run back inside and grab a gun.* Mr. Bones quickly shifted his eyes on Darrell. His knees were shaking; slowly bringing up the axe. *That will be your first mistake,* he thought.

"Well, are you going to say something, or maybe…" Darrell's voice trailed off, glancing over at Boone. Boone's eyes said he was going to run back inside. Darrell smiled. *He's going to try and get the rifle.*

"Now!" he yelled to Boone, lifting the axe and throwing it at the man. He could hit anything at that distance, but his mind splintered when he watched the man grabbed the axe right out of mid-air, and throw it straight back at him. He ducked just in time. The axe embedded itself into the cabin right behind his head.

Boone heard the loud thud. He spun on his heels and made a dash for the door. Mr. Bones cut the distance between he and Darrell so fast that Darrell didn't have a chance to turn around and grab the axe. His eyes went wide seeing the man rushing toward him. Darrell quickly pulled out his knife and sliced at him. Mr. Bones grabbed his arm and snapped it like a twig!

Darrell screamed, releasing his grip on the knife. Mr. Bones grabbed it and then slammed it into his right thigh. Darrell bent over screaming in pain. Mr. Bones jerked him up and then slammed his fist into his head. Darrell went flying back hitting the cabin. Darkness filled his brain as his body slumped to the ground.

Mr. Bones looked down at him and wished he could spit! He turned, walked inside, and saw Boone shoving bullets into his rifle. Boone looked up in fear. He quickly tried to raise the rifle and fire. Mr. Bones grabbed one of the wooden chairs and threw it at him. The chair hit Boone so hard that it lifted him off the ground, sending him flying into the corner. His rifle fell to the floor. Mr. Bones grabbed the wooden table, walked over and threw it on top of Boone. He heard Boone moan in pain from underneath.

With both unable to move, Mr. Bones looked around the one room shack. He spotted several coiled up ropes, two meat hooks, two bear traps, and on the counter he saw a box of four-inch 'L' shaped nails that resembled railroad spikes. He remembered now - they called them cabin shanks. He grabbed the ropes, meat hooks, and bear traps and walked outside. He tossed it all on the ground. He went back in, grabbed the box of cabin shanks and walked over to the open door.

He looked down a Darrell lying there, out cold. He pulled the axe out of the wood, bent down and poured the box of cabin shanks onto the ground. He picked one up and then reached over and grabbed Darrell's arm. Darrell moaned; he was regaining consciousness. Mr. Bones lifted Darrell's hand against the doorframe, placed a shank in the center of his palm, and then slammed the flat, butt end of the axe down on the shank head. The shank ripped through his palm and sank deep into the wood. The pain shattered Darrell's senses. His scream could be heard a mile away. He desperately tried to pull his hand free from the wooden frame.

Mr. Bones looked at him, walked back inside, grabbed Boone from underneath the table and yanked him to his feet. He manhandled him toward the door. When he reached the entrance, he lifted Boone off his feet and threw him out onto the ground. Boone landed hard some ten feet away. He slowly rolled over onto his back. His head felt like a turned over beehive - from the buzzing in his ears.

"Now, Boone," Mr. Bones finally said. "You're not a big man at all, are you?" he continued, walking over to the pile of gear he had tossed out earlier. He picked up one of the ropes and walked over to him.

Boone turned his head and spit dirt out of his mouth. "What do you want?"

"I came for you and Darrell," he replied, reaching down and pulling Boone's boots off.

He grabbed his feet and tied them together. He then walked up and pulled Boone's arms back so hard that one snapped! Boone screamed out in pain! "Ah… Come now. That didn't hurt, Boone. Whatcha screaming for?" Mr. Bones said, rolling him over. He tied his hands together behind his back and secured the rope through his belt.

Mr. Bones stood up and slowly walked over to the meat hooks on the ground. He picked them up and walked back in front of Boone. As he looked down at him, he lifted one hand high into the air and came down hard, sending one meat hook into his upper right shoulder. The meat hook sank deep between his shoulder blade and collarbone. The air in Boone's lungs rushed out. A blinding white light exploded inside his head. Mr. Bones took a step sideways, raised his other hand and drove the other meat hook into his left shoulder!

Boone screamed gasping for air. His whole world was spinning out of control. The pain set his brain on fire! "Darrell," he choked.

Darrell was still floating between the light and darkness. His vision was blurred. When he tried to move, the pain from his broken arm and the knife sunk deep into his thigh shattered his thoughts of getting up. He slowly turned his head to see his hand nailed to the doorframe. It was over for him, and he knew it. All he could do now was to watch in horror at what was about to happen.

Mr. Bones walked over, picked up the other rope and walked back to Boone. He took one end of the rope and slipped it through the eyelets of both meat hooks. He doubled the rope to ensure it was secure. He then stood up and fastened a loop at the other end. Looking up into the tree overhead, he tossed the rope over a branch. He yanked on the rope pulled it down. Boone moaned, feeling the meat hooks dig deeper into his back while being lifted off the ground toward the branch overhead.

"What are you doing?!" Darrell yelled.

Mr. Bones held the rope as Boone swung back and forth through the air. It was like hoisting a rag doll, he felt so light. "I'm going to do to him just what you did to me," Mr. Bones replied, turning his head toward Darrell.

"We haven't done anything to you! We never saw you in all our born days, mister!"

"Oh, really? Don't you know who I am?"

"No. Why don't you take off that hood so we can see you?!" Darrell shouted.

Mr. Bones cocked his head. That was going to happen, but not just yet - at least. *They'll see me alright*, he thought. *Right before they die.* He turned his attention back on Boone swinging in the wind. He slowly hoisted him higher until he was head level with him. He walked over, tied the rope around a tree trunk and walked back up to Boone. There was swelling around Boone's eyes; his tongue was hanging outside of his mouth -as if gasping for air. "Boone, you remember me, don't cha?" he asked, pushing his body back and forth. The meat hooks dug into him swinging in the air.

Boone tried to speak. It was no more than a moan.

"Stop it – you're going to kill him!" Darrell yelled again.

Mr. Bones let Darrell speak as he kept his attention on Boone. "Does that hurt, Boone? I hope so because pain is good for you. I remember you saying that a little pain turns boys into men. Don't you remember saying that to me while you and Darrell took turns hurting my backside?"

Boone's mind splintered. He remembered saying that to a boy, but not to this man standing there in front of him. *How would he know that?* he thought.

Mr. Bones waited for an answer. When he got none - he pushed Boone again. Boone moaned. "Now, you just hang there awhile, Boone. I want to show you what happens to men who hurt innocent children," he continued, turning toward Darrell. Over his shoulder, he kept taunting Boone, "Now, don't close your eyes, Boone. If I see them closed, I'll go inside, grab that carving knife, and come back out and cut your eyelids off - so you can't close them at all!"

Boone tried to swallow thinking of that. He wasn't going to close his eyes - not even to blink. His heart sunk knowing that it was Darrell's turn. *What was this mad man going to do to him?* he thought, helplessly hanging there.

As Mr. Bones approached Darrell, Darrell kicked at him, and began yelling, "Get away from me — you crazy bastard!"

Mr. Bones reached down to grab his free hand. Darrell tried to push him away. Mr. Bones caught it and then crushed his hand slowly. Every bone turned into dust. Darrell screamed out in pain. Mr. Bones knelt down, picked up a cabin shank and the axe. Darrell's arm lay there limp. He picked up his hand and pressed it against the other doorframe.

"No, no - please," Darrell begged.

Mr. Bones said nothing - placing the shank in his palm and driving it into the wood with the axe. Darrell violently shook while screaming. His eyes rolled to the back of his head.

Mr. Bones looked at him. "Now, Darrell, you sound as if that hurt. You sure weren't screaming like that when Boone hung me up on a meat hook. You sat there laughing, as I recall.

So, why aren't you laughing now? Come on - let me hear you laugh."

"I don't know what you're talking about!" he gasped. "We never hurt you! We've never seen you before!"

"Yes, you know who I am. You and Boone raped me, hung me up and then slit me open like a deer," he replied, standing and walking over to the coil of rope. He walked back, took one end, measured it off and ripped it in two as if it were a string. Darrell's eyes grew wide. *No one can do that to a rope without a knife*, he thought. Terror filled his eyes as Mr. Bones ripped off his boots and tie his feet together.

"What are you doing?! Haven't you had enough?!" Darrell screamed.

"No, not yet," he replied, picking up another cabin shank. Darrell began kicking at him - trying hard to fight the man off. Mr. Bones grabbed his legs and knelt down on them

He then placed the shank against one of his heels and drove it in deep! Darrell's whole body violently shook feeling the sharp metal rip into him. Mr. Bones smiled, turned his head and looked over at Boone. "You better keep them eyes open," he said, picking up another shank and driving that one into Darrell's other heel. Darrell was losing it. He was slipping into the abyss of darkness. "I don't think you'll be doing much running now, Darrell. Not with them cabin shanks in your heels," Mr. Bones said, getting up and grabbing the rest of the rope.

He walked back, tied a figure eight around Darrell's feet, and then stood up. He looked up into the tree for a limb to toss it over. When he did, he left the rope just dangling there. He then picked up one of the bear traps and placed it underneath the limb. With his gloved hands, he pried it open and locked the latching spring back. He stood there a moment allowing Darrell to think of what was going to happen next. "Now do you remember me?" he asked.

"No!"

"You don't remember sitting out back of that shanty next to Marshall Lake laughing while Boone drove that meat hook into my spine?"

Darrell tried to think through the pain. They raped a little boy and then hung him up. He remembered laughing watching Boone slice the kid open. *How does he know all this*? he thought.

"Very soon, Darrell, you'll know who I am," Mr. Bones said, reaching out and taking hold of his left wrist and yanking it off the doorframe. The shank head ripped right through his palm. Mr. Bones quickly pulled the right hand off and then pushed Darrell over onto his stomach.

Darrell tried to get up, but the pain was too great. Mr. Bones took a small piece of rope, pulled what was left of his hands back and tied them together. He stood up, walked over to the rope hanging in the air and pulled on it; lifting Darrell into the air by his feet. Darrell swung back and forth for a moment and then his body stopped right over the bear trap. He looked down at the menacing thing with its large metal teeth sticking up along the circular rim. He saw enough bears trapped to know the pain it could cause. He knew what was about to happen and there was nothing he could do.

Mr. Bones stood there looking at him upside down. "My name, you want to know my name?" he asked.

Darrell cocked his head to the side and looked into the hood. Mr. Bones cocked his head so he could see him. Darrell's eyes grew wide with terror! "My name is Jamie, Jamie Chamber. The boy Boone gutted like a fish. You see what you've done to me, what you turned me into?"

Before Darrell could open his mouth to scream, Mr. Bones lowered him inside the bear trap until his head hit the circular dish at the center, causing the trap to violently snap shut! The trap shut with such a force that the metal teeth drove into his torso, breaking ribs, and crushing his lungs. Darrell's body heaved, and then went limp. Blood began oozing out of his mouth. His eyes rolled back and never returned.

After Mr. Bones hoisted him back into the air and tied the rope off, he pulled the knife out of Darrell's thigh. With that done, he turned and faced Boone. Boone hung there barely alive. His eyes filled with fear seeing the blurry figure walking over to the other bear trap. *Poor Darrell,* he thought, wading over what he just witnessed. Mr. Bones picked up the trap and walked over to Boone. Boone knew he was next. He did not want to die this way. Mr. Bones set the trap underneath him, pulled the trap open and set the spring.

He then stood up and looked at Boone. "I'm surprised you're not laughing. I can still hear you and Darrell laughing. I'm sure you both laughed too when you raped and murdered my friends; Jill Farmer, Mary Baker, and Teddy Cotton!"

Boone couldn't speak. He was drifting in and out from the agonizing pain. He knew that this man, whoever he was, knew everything. How he knew, was beyond him.

"You don't remember me either, do you?"

Boone shook his head, focusing on the man.

"Maybe this will help you to remember," he said, turning and walking over to the tree, he had tied the rope to. He slowly lowered Boone's feet and legs inside the bear trap until his heels hit the dish at the center. The trap slammed shut! Boone's body shook. The metal teeth sank into his legs breaking them both. His head rolled back from the force.

Mr. Bones hoisted him up to head level again. After he tied the rope off, he walked over and faced him. "Are you a man yet, Boone? Don't you remember saying that to me in the woods?"

Boone's eyes rolled forward. He looked at the hooded man standing there with Darrell's bowie knife. He watched him reach out and place it against his cheek. The blade felt cold and wet. He didn't realize it, but it was Darrell's blood.

"Do you remember this?" he asked, running the sharp edge along his cheek.

Boone said nothing. His tongue was down his throat.

"Don't you remember, Boone? You used this same knife on me. You gutted me and then sat there and laughed," he continued, pushing the sharp point against his nose. "You know, Boone, I'm not going to gut you like you gutted me. No... You see, I remember when Millie and I would go down to the dock and fish. We loved going fishing, but she never liked gutting them. She hated to harm anything. Her father told us that the best way to kill a fish quickly without too much pain was to pierce its brain with a knife. That's what I am going to do to you."

Boone tried to open his swollen eyes. Mr. Bones put his hand up and waved a finger in front of his face. "Would you like to know my name before I kill you? It's Jamie, Jamie Chamber. The little blonde boy you abducted from Casper's Hill."

Boone drifted back to when he took the boy, but could not understand why this man was saying that he was Jamie Chamber. He couldn't be that boy! That boy was dead! Before he could answer, the man said, "Would you like to see what you turned me into, Boone?" Boone had no answer. His mind was too numb to think.

With that, Mr. Bones pulled back his hood exposing his face. Terror ripped into Boone's eyes! He opened his mouth to try and scream, but it was too late. Mr. Bones quickly drew the knife down to his side and then in a flash - he drove it up underneath Boone's jaw! The blade drove through his lower jaw - through his mouth, and stopped deep inside his skull; piercing his brain. Boone's body went limp. He hung there swinging like a rag doll.

Mr. Bones let go of the knife, stepped back, and pushed Boone's body. It swung there in the morning sunlight. He turned around and looked at Darrell. His skin was already turning purple. Then suddenly from behind him, he heard something! He quickly spun around and placed his ear to the wind. Someone was coming! He panicked looking for a place to hide. He glanced up at the tall trees before the clearing. He quickly ran, jumped up, and caught a branch. He pulled himself up and stood there. *Climb higher,* he thought, reaching up and taking hold of the next limb. When he was forty feet up in the tree, he took hold of the trunk and waited.

Chapter 22

Mr. Bones froze when he saw Indian Joe fifty yards away walking alongside his horse. He was slowly moving forward searching the ground. *How did he get his horse across the Forgotten Land?* he thought, looking at the horse. Its underbelly was soaking wet. *You are a clever, my friend. You came down the Pinto River.*

As Indian Joe approached, Mr. Bones steadied himself against the trunk of the tree. He knew if he made one sound, Indian Joe would hear him. Then suddenly, Indian Joe stopped just before the clearing. The look in his eyes was complete terror. Mr. Bones slowly turned his head and looked down at Boone and Darrell hang there. He knew they looked ghastly - he must have looked ghastly himself - when they found him too.

Indian Joe tethered his horse on a bush and stood there looking around. Mr. Bones knew what he was doing - he was looking for the one who did it. Walking in slowly, Indian Joe scoured the ground for tracks. He knelt down putting his fingers inside a bootprint. He stood up slowly, pulled out his bowie knife and focused his attention on the cabin door.

When Indian Joe got there, he stepped inside. There was no one there. When he walked back out, he looked up at Boone and Darrell. Mr. Bones could see him sigh as he walked to the center of the clearing. He then sat down facing the door. He took off his deerskin pouch from around his neck and opened it. He reached inside his buckskin jacket and pulled out a pouch with power. He sprinkled some on his head and then ran his finger down each side of his cheeks.

Mr. Bones was intrigued. *What was he doing?* he thought, *calling out to the spirits?*

With that thought still echoing inside his head, Indian Joe began chanting in his native tongue. Mr. Bones looked up into the morning sky. Daylight was approaching. *I have to get back, but how?* He knew Indian Joe would sit there all day among the dead trying desperately to save his own soul from the spirits that did this horrendous act.

As Mr. Bones watched and listened to Indian Joe chanting, he knew he wouldn't be able to escape undetected. With that, he thought of a plan. He would have to confront Indian Joe. It would be his only way out. He stepped away from the trunk and then dropped down through the tree catching a low-lying branch. He hung there for a moment and then dropped to the ground right behind Indian Joe! The sound of his boots hitting the ground made Indian stop chanting. He sat there as still as a rabbit knowing what was behind him. It was the spirit of death.

Mr. Bones stood there looking down at the back of Indian Joe's head. He knew Indian Joe wasn't going to make a move or speak. "Were you calling the spirits to find me?"

Indian Joe turned his head slightly to the right. He wasn't going to turn around. He didn't want to look back. "No. I knew you were still here. I'm praying to the spirits to protect me."

Mr. Bones nodded. "Where's Blackfoot?"

Indian Joe looked up into the sky, and then back at the cabin door. He knew he wasn't talking to a living soul. He could hear the spirits whispering. He knew it was the dark one standing behind him. "We split up at the river's edge. He headed west into the Forgotten Land to try and find a way through the mountains."

"What about the others, are they coming as well?"

"No. They're searching the area around Marshall Lake."

Mr. Bones let the silence stand between them for a moment. He needed to get back to Millie. As he stood there thinking about his next move, he looked up at Boone and

Darrell. *If Indian Joe could get his horse in, then he could take these two back.* "Indian Joe," he said, and then paused.

Indian Joe turned his head again. Mr. Bones could see and feel his fear.

"Here's what you're going to do. You're going to go back and bring more horses in. Then you're going to cut these men down and leave them just as they are. Do not remove one thing from their bodies. You'll burn this place to the ground, take them back to town, and hang them up just as they are, in the big oak tree down by the dock. You'll inform Sheriff Coleman to make up two signs and tie them around the bodies. I want the signs to read: '*Warning - This is what happens to those who hurt children*'. I want them to remain hanging from that tree for one week. If I do not see them in two days, you and Sheriff Coleman will take their place. But you'll be in worse conditions, you understand?"

Indian Joe glanced up at the two men hanging there. He thought of the children. These two rightly deserved what they got. His stomach tightened thinking what could be worse. He didn't want to dwell on it. He had never witnessed a man dying like that. He knew the dark one standing behind him would keep his word. "I'll do all that you say," he replied, looking at the ground. After he said that, there was silence between them. Mr. Bones then gave him his last warning.

"You're a wise man Indian Joe. Do not try to find me. Tell the town to go about their business. It's all over."

"I can't track you for you are not of this world. No one can track the wind that blows through the trees. I hear the spirit of the great owl. He tells me that you are the one who stands between the light and the darkness. You are the one who walks with children."

Indian Joe paused and waited for a reply. There was none. Mr. Bones was already gone. Indian Joe never heard him leave. He closed his eyes and began chanting once again.

After Pam said that, she stopped talking and just stared out into space, as if she was still there within Millie's story. David and William allowed her the time to come back to the world, as they too were trying desperately to digest it. David's many years on the force, investigating so many strange cases, had him biting his nails on this one.

William, however, sat there thinking about Indians Joe's words to Mr. Bones. *No one can track the wind that blows through the trees. You are the one that stands between the light and the darkness - the one who walks with children. That's why he hunted Kevin Downer down,* he thought. It sent chills down his spine and he knew now that Kevin got off easy. If the man had more time, he knew Kevin would have looked much, much worse than he did. He looked over at David and could see he was chewing on Pam's story.

Pam stepped back into the world and looked across at the detectives. They looked like they were in a minefield of thoughts. She thought she'd add some more explosives to the field. "You know," she said, bringing them back to the living. "What really had me scared after I sat with her the entire night and listened to her story, is when she pointed over to her window and said that Jimmy still comes often and visits with her. She said something like this - "I always tell him to wipe his feet when he comes through the window. His boots are always dirty."

David caught a lump in his throat. William just sat back. "So that's why she has the welcome mat by the window and not at the door?"

"Yes. The entire nursing staff knows about it and we just go along with Millie. It's kind of freaky if you ask me, especially after hearing her story," she replied, looking at David. She saw something in his eyes. She looked at William - he had the look too. "You two don't believe any of this, do you?"

David sat back crossing his legs. It was the only way to remain calm. "Well, Pam. I really must say no. I am sure you can understand."

She looked at William. He simply smiled with a nod. "So you're telling me that she made it all up? What about the welcome mat?"

"No - her story is the story. It's all sitting here in my lap," David replied, picking up the report. You just cleared one thing up."

"What's that?"

"Samuel Remington."

"I see, so you don't think Jimmy came back from the dead?"

"I never believed in ghosts," he replied, standing up. "But I also never heard a story like that either."

Pam stood up along with William.

"I'm glad we came. I wouldn't mind coming back and talking to Millie again. I'm sure if we talked long enough we could start punching holes in her story and maybe, just maybe, she'd tell us the truth," David said, handing her his cup.

William handed his cup over and smiled again. He just wanted to get outside where the air was fresh so he could think.

"She might like that. I'm sure she enjoyed your company," Pam replied, walking them to the corridor.

"Thanks for your time and the coffee, we'll see ourselves out," David said, walking down the corridor.

"You're welcome, gentlemen. Have a nice night."

They both put up a hand and waved. When they got outside, William stopped and looked at him. "So?" he said.

David turned. "I know what you're going to say so why not just say it."

"OK, we both know the ending in this old report."

"True - and so does Millie."

William cocked his head. "Yes, she knows. She knows the truth, and that's where our answer lies. We know that it wasn't Samuel Remington who told Indian Joe to take them back. So why did he? Why did Indian Joe, being a spiritual man, bring them back and hang them in that oak tree, if he wasn't scared of something out there?"

David pondered that. Before he could answer, William added more fuel to the fire.

"The way I see it, David is don't you think that if Indian Joe had found them and Mr. Bones was not in the equation, that he would have cut them down, dragged them inside the cabin, and burned it to the ground? Isn't that the way his people protected themselves from evil spirits?"

David let that question wash over him. He wasn't wise in the ways of Indian culture, however he'd read enough to know that they did that in some parts of the country. He spun his thoughts in another direction. It was Millie's comment before he left her room. *'You don't want to catch what you're chasing.'* That line stunned him, even more so when he raised his head and looked her into her eyes. It sent shivers up his spine. He looked at William. "I think there's only one way to make sure."

"And what would that be?"

"Let's check the ground next to Millie's window."

It didn't take a rocket scientist to figure that one out. If the bootprint were there, they'd both end up in hospital on meds. They quickly headed over toward Millie's window.

When they got to the bushes, David reached out and grabbed William's arm. William turned and looked at him. "We have to be quiet. I don't want to disturb her," he whispered.

William nodded, slipping in between the bushes. "Do you have your penlight?" he asked.

David pulled it out and handed it to him. William bent down and shone the light on the ground in front of

Millie's window. There, before his eyes, was the bootprint! It looked fresh too.

"Do you see anything?" David whispered.

William stood up, looked him dead in the eyes. He slowly handed him the penlight and nodded for him to look. David skirted around William and bent down. His mouth fell open. He quickly stood up and looked at William - who looked three shades whiter than a hospital sheet.

"Give me that file," David asked.

William handed it to him. David took the file and pulled out the photo. He turned, knelt down and placed the photo next to the print on the ground. It matched to a tee! His knees suddenly went weak. "Holy shit!" he whispered.

"It matches, doesn't it?"

David stood up and handed him the photo. As he did, his mind started to unravel. He quickly looked up into the tree overhead. William stepped back and looked up too. He knew what David was thinking.

"Put the light on that branch," William said.

David pointed the light up.

"There!" William gasped.

David's eyes went wide seeing the bark stripped off. It looked like someone had been using the branch to drop to the ground. He shut the light off and looked at William.

"Let's get the hell out of here," he whispered.

William nodded. They turned and rushed past the picnic area. When they hurried over to their car, they noticed Agent Straw's car parked right behind them. Jack was nowhere in sight.

"Where's knucklehead?" William asked, opening the door and getting in.

"I don't know - maybe he went inside. Let's get out of here."

William put the key in the ignition, started the engine and slowly rolled out. At the parking lot's exit, he asked, "Which way?"

"Go right. Let's drive the freeway for awhile."

"Roger," William replied, turning right when the traffic was clear.

When he drove to the I-275 entrance ramp, he quickly asked, "North or South?"

"South, there's less traffic heading out of town."

William nodded. He drove across the overpass and took the southbound ramp. Neither said a word for a while as William drove down the highway. David just sat there, feeling his whole world slipping over the edge. He knew from his experience that there was a thin line between sane and insane and it would only take a dose of fear to send you over that line. He was now walking that line; like a tightrope artist.

William looked over at him staring out blindly out the window. He looked a million miles away - *like way over the rainbow*. He too felt fear gripping his throat. He swallowed and then opened his mouth to say something - anything to bring them both back from the abyss of darkness. Then suddenly - Mr. Bones sat up in the back seat.

William saw him before he could speak. David, however, was oblivious to what was happening as he was staring blindly out the window. Mr. Bones quickly reached over and grabbed David's neck. He then took hold of William's shoulder. Both men gasped for air. It was so quick that neither man had time to think.

David felt paralyzed sitting there from the man's grip. His eyes began to water from the pain. William almost lost control of the wheel as Mr. Bones squeezed shoulder. "Keep driving and don't turn around!" Mr. Bones ordered.

William dropped his right hand off the steering wheel. He wanted to speak but nothing came out.

"Your guns, gentlemen - remove them slowly and hand them back to me," he said, loosening his grip.

They slowly reached down, unfastened their seat belts, took out their weapons and lifted them in the air toward the back. Neither man dared drawing on the person. They both knew they would be dead before pulling the trigger.

Mr. Bones let go of William and took both their guns. He tossed them on the seat next to him and then released David. William looked up into the rearview mirror to see him sitting back in the darkness. David and William wanted to look at each other, but fear kept them looking forward.

Mr. Bones sat there looking at them. He could have killed them both for making Millie relive it all again! *Samuel Remington*, he thought. *Millie almost pulled it off. However,* he thought, looking at the back of their heads, *these two will not let it go until they discover the truth.* He could see it in the tall detective's eyes before he left the room.

"Where are you taking us?" William asked, taking him out of his thoughts.

He looked at the back of the man's head. He leaned up in his seat. He could have easily crushed his skull. "Just drive, I'll tell you when to pull over."

As David sat there, his mind began playing Millie's last words to him, *'you don't want to catch what you're chasing.'* He looked out his side window and caught the reflection of the man sitting in the back seat. He could only see a dark figure wearing a hood over his head and then he thought of the gloved hand he felt on the back of his neck. His thoughts began to race backward. Corporal Carter's description of the person he saw on the railroad track slid to the front of his mind.

Carter said that the person was wearing black on black and his clothing just hung on him; as if they were on a hanger. His mind then raced forward to the story Millie told Pam. Why did she tell Pam the real story? Pam could have called the police. *No,* he thought. *Millie knew Pam would probably just accept it as a "story."* She lied to us because we're the police and we're hot on the trail for the one she was protecting.

David's mind began to race in a thousand directions – from one thought to the next, he was trying to connect the dots. He knew from the man's grip that he had the strength of ten men. Killing Kevin Downer was like killing a puppy – so were Boone and Darrell. All died swinging from a rope. That thought made his stomach go tight. The man in the back seat was not a man; he wasn't even human – he was Mr. Bones.

Without turning his head, he rolled his eyes toward William. Even in the dark, he could see that William was trying desperately to think a way out of this mess. He wondered if William had come to the same conclusion, that the man in the back was in fact Mr. Bones.

As they drove out of the city, the south and northbound lanes began separating with an island in between them. Up ahead, the highway went from four lanes into two. The city was now disappearing behind them. Suburbs took over the view. William continued down the highway until the suburbs were gone and the open meadows took over. The car's interior was dark except for the lights on the dashboard. *If he wanted to kill us,* David thought, *he could have them pull over somewhere along this stretch of highway, shoot them both, take the car and escape.*

Before he stepped out of those thoughts, Mr. Bones sat up. "Pull over and park in the grass."

William looked into the rearview mirror. He saw no cars. They were alone. He put his foot on the brake, rolled over to the side of the highway and came to a full stop just past a stand of tall trees.

"I want you both to get out on the passenger side and stand there."

They did what he said. Once they had exited the car, they stood there in the dark watching the man get out. He walked toward the front of the car. He was tall, very thin and walked with a purpose in his stride. Once he rounded the front end, he stopped near the bumper and turned to face them. David looked at the man's hands. He noticed that he didn't have a weapon; he didn't need one. He had the power of an elephant and could crush them both with his bare hands. All he wanted to do was to nudge William, get his attention, and see if he was all there.

William looked at him, and then quickly turned his attention back on the dark figure standing before them. By the short glance, David knew that William was just hanging on to his own sanity. His eyes looked like needles, sharp with fear.

Mr. Bones took a step forward. He reached up and pointed at William. "Get on your knees with your face in the dirt. If you dare look up - you'll be swallowing your own teeth."

William's knees buckled in fear. He fell to the ground knowing that they were both going to die. His last thoughts were not thoughts one would have before your eyes rolled back for the very last time. He only saw the images of Boone, Darrell, and Kevin Downer hanging from trees; brutally murdered by this man. He prayed that it would be a quick. Hopefully - just a crushing blow to the back of his head.

Mr. Bones looked over at David. He took another step forward. In that split second, he got a glimpse of the man's face or lack of a face at all. David froze.

"What did Millie whisper to you?"

The ride down the highway was enough to send a man over the edge, but now, as the man spoke, David was losing it for sure. It took him half a second to loosen his tongue from the roof of his mouth.

"She said, trust me, you don't want to catch what you're chasing." David replied, realizing this creature was standing outside Millie's window the whole time. In that terrorizing moment - he thought of Jack. *Is he dead?* He quickly dropped his thoughts when Mr. Bones pulled back his hood. Sure terror struck his heart looking into Mr. Bones' deep dark sockets and then taking in his rotted teeth. He felt himself slipping into the abyss insanity.

"You like what you see?" Mr. Bones asked, cocking his head.

David opened his mouth but nothing came out except dribble, "I… I…"

Mr. Bones leaned into him. His eyes appeared like flames within his sockets. They bore right through David. "Where did you get those photos? You answer me now, or you'll end up on a cold slab like Downer, but in much worse condition."

In worse condition, David panicked. "My grandfather was Detective Bradshaw. He assisted Sheriff Ben Coleman on that horrific murder case up in Ironbark."

Mr. Bones looked into David's eyes. He could tell the detective was telling the truth for he remembered that name. It was Ben and Deputy Harding, along with two other men from New York. They came to Doc Thomson's home to question the Doc. He did remember that one introduced himself as Detective Bradshaw. He stepped out of his thoughts looking at David. "Give me that file!"

David stood there - his shoes felt glued to the ground. "Go on," Mr. Bones said, nodding toward the car. David turned, opened door, reached inside and pulled out the report. He turned and handed it to him. Mr. Bones opened it, took out the photo of his bootprint and looked at it. He then slid the photo back into the file and looked at David.

David stood there watching him pull off one of his gloves, take the file within his skeletal fingers, and then lift it up into the air. Mr. Bones stared at the file. His eyes became like a magnifying glass. The file started to smoke and then caught fire. David watched the thing ignite in his hand; turning to ash and floating away on the wind. Mr. Bones never flinched as the flames engulfed his skeletal fingers. After it was gone, Mr. Bones looked down at William. "Stand up!" he ordered.

William tried to stand on his wobbly knees. He almost swallowed his tongue when he finally stood up and looked at Mr. Bones. The back of his neck went cold. Mr. Bones took a second to look them over. "Millie's gone," he finally said.

They stared at him confused. His words hit them like an arrow through the heart.

"I'm sorry," David replied, not knowing what else to say.

"I'm more than sorry. She was the only person I ever loved."

The air became cool, and with it, both David and William breathed a sigh of relief. He wasn't going to kill them; realizing that Mr. Bones was more human than the lowlife scum they dealt with everyday on the street.

"Jimmy?" William asked.

Mr. Bones turned his head and looked at him. His eyes changed from flames of red to sapphire blue. He stood back, and without warning, from underneath his clothing a million blue lights, like fireflies, started to stream out from everywhere. The lights came together to forming a small child standing in front of Mr. Bones. Mr. Bones' head tilted down, his body went limp standing behind the ghostly, small figure.

David and William took a step back as their minds tried to take it all in. There before them, was a beautiful blonde boy - whose eyes were as blue as the ocean peering into their souls. "Only Millie called me Jimmy," he said, looking up at them "Mr. Bones," he continued, turning his head, looking back. David and William looked up to see the skeleton lift up his head.

"You see, I don't have to be in him for him to respond. We are now one. I am the light – he is the darkness, and together we have a bond."

David slowly glanced over at William. William shook his head in disbelief. He looked down at the ghostly child standing in front of him. "How, how can this be possible?" he asked.

"There is a place between the light and the darkness where one can hear the voices of the living. It was there that I heard Millie calling to me. She was the one who called me back."

They both stood there in awe, as if they were seeing an angel. David could only think of one thing to say to him. "How many?" he asked.

Jimmy looked up at him cocking his head. He knew what he was asking. "I lost count a long time ago. The world is full of evil, which cripples and murders the innocent. Mr. Bones is the defender of the children. He protects the small and defenseless. Together, we destroy evil in whatever form it takes."

After he spoke, the wind suddenly picked up. William flipped up his collar and slipped his hands inside his jacket. From behind, they heard the sound of a vehicle. They both turned to see the headlights of a long haul truck coming toward them. They looked back at Jimmy. He was gone. They looked up at Mr. Bones. His blue sapphire eyes appeared. Mr. Bones looked at them and then slowly glanced up at the truck coming down the highway. They knew what was about to happen.

"With Downer now dead, this case is over," David said.

Mr. Bones looked at him, nodded and then reached out his hand. David went first, and then William stepped up and took his hand. As Mr. Bones held his hand, he said, "The one in the parking lot. He's inside the trunk of his car. Now, I must be going."

With that, Mr. Bones turned and started running down the highway, as the long haul truck was just about to pass. David and William stood there watching him run along the side the truck. He quickly jumped up onto the bumper and took hold of the double door handles at the rear.

While safely hanging on, he turned and looked back. He waved and then turned around, grabbing the lock and chain around the double doors and snapping it off. He opened the doors, stepped inside, and then closed the doors.

David sat back on the hood of the vehicle running his fingers through his hair. William walked up and sat alongside him. Neither man said a word as they watched the truck head down the highway. David sighed looking over at him.

"It's a nice night, isn't it," William said, pulling his collar up. David smiled. "That it is," he replied, thinking - *what better way to hold on to your sanity than by just letting go.*

He looked up into the star filled sky. "Did you notice the sign on the side of the truck?" he asked still gazing up at the stars.

"Yeah, it said, Sun Saddle Boots, Sioux City, Kansas."

"You think he'll make it that far?" he asked.

William took his eyes off the stars and looked at him. "I'm not sure where he'll end up, but I know one thing."

"What's that?"

"Where ever he goes, he'll be looking after the children."

David nodded looking at him.

Mr. Bones stood there in the darkness. His eyes began to glow a brilliant, sapphire blue. He cocked his head seeing small boxes stacked on top of one another. He walked over, picked one up, and looked at the picture on the box. It was a picture of cowboy boots. He opened the box, pulled one out and turned it over. On the bottom of the boot was the size - nine and a half. He put the boot back inside the box and then started searching for a box with his size. He eyes sparkled seeing a box with a pair of size eleven inside.

He took the box, walked over to the doors and sat down. He took them out, pulled off his boots and slipped on the new pair. They fit. He stood, opened the doors, and tossed his old snow boots out the door along with the box. After shutting the doors, he turned and spotted a place to sit down.

Sitting there against the side of the trailer, he noticed a small hole in the metal. He reached up, placed his finger in the hole, and pulled down. The metal split - giving him a large hole to look out. He leaned back in thought - *I have no idea where I am going, or where this truck is heading.* He let that thought slip away and thought of Millie. She was all he had and now she was gone. It made him sad. He only wished that wherever the truck was heading - it would lead him to the children. They were all that mattered - all he cared for now.

Come Monday morning, Mr. Bloom, Donny Brook high school's science teacher, walked into his class. He sat down and began preparing for the day's lesson on the solar system. He pulled out his planet charts and looked them over before his students started to arrive. When everyone was finally in his or her seat, he stood up. "Good morning. Did everyone have a good weekend?"

They all said yes, and then Mark Zimmer raised his hand.

"Yes, Mark?"

"Where's Mr. Nobody?" he asked, pointing toward the corner of the room.

Mr. Bloom turned and looked behind him where Mr. Nobody stood. *That's funny*, he thought. *Who took the skeleton? Maybe one of the other teachers came in this morning and borrowed him as a teacher's aide.* He smiled with that thought, *a skeleton being a teacher's aide.* He made a mental note to ask the faculty during lunchtime. He turned and looked back at Mark.

"I don't know, Mark, maybe he went fishing."

Everyone laughed.

In the end, none of the faculty at Donny Brook high school knew where Mr. Nobody was and they never found him either. Afterward, it became a game of sorts, as students and teachers started telling stories. Everyone had ideas as to where he may have gone. The stories seemed to grow after Mr. Bloom gave that crack about Mr. Nobody going fishing.

The Thriller Continues

ABOUT THE AUTHOR

Jeffrey Thomas Wright, born in the
State of Michigan. Father of
Three great children - Jeff,
Justin and Jaci.

Served in the U.S. Navy as a
Chief Mater At Arms, during
Peace time and war.

Personal quote:
The harder I work - the easier
hard work becomes.

Made in the USA
Charleston, SC
03 May 2013